The Last Duty

Also in this series

The Last Duty

Isidore Okpewho

Longman

Longman Group Limited
Longman House,
Burnt Mill, Harlow, Essex

© Isidore Okpewho 1976

All rights reserved. No part of this
publication may be reproduced, stored
in a retrieval system, or transmitted
in any form or by any means, electronic,
mechanical, photocopying, recording, or
otherwise, without the prior permission
of the Copyright owner.

First published 1976
First published in Drumbeat 1981

ISBN 0 582 78535 9

Printed in Hong Kong by
Wing Tai Cheung Printing Co. Ltd.

For my mother and my father

But from the deeps of your blood with no
pain, in the just human time
we shall be born again

SALVATORE QUASIMODO

This story is *all* fiction

Part one

Breath burns more sulphurate
And blood calcifies into boulders
For brother to hurl against brother

JOHN PEPPER CLARK

Ali

'Ali! Ali! Ali!' shouts the surging crowd as my Austin Minimoke tries to wind its way through the people.

'Ali! Ali! Ali!'

The soldiers try to beat them back, but it is hard for us to check their overwhelming gesture of approval and goodwill. Just yesterday, late in the evening, a number of rebel planes had visited this town on a bombing mission. But we quickly put an end to that mission by shooting down one of the planes; the others turned back at once and headed back whence they had come. And now, as I drive round this morning to check if any damage has been done to any part of the town, I am greeted with deafening applause from a grateful population.

For a soldier this is an hour of triumph. The war is still on and every moment is pregnant with danger. But I must confess I feel great joy this moment, as all over the town the entire population raise their fists in solidarity, jumping and shouting and showing in every way how much they welcome our presence and our efforts.

'Ali! Ali! Ali!'

When I took over command of this post as Brigade Major about two years ago, I was quite aware of the tremendous task ahead of me. At the start I was certain that I could not be too sure of the support of everybody. This is a tribal border town between the Igabo and the rebel Simba. It was quite clear to me that we had to be very careful how we conducted our military duty here. When the federal army liberated this town from the rebels just over three years ago, many Simba people had to flee the town for fear of losing their lives. Time had long ago forged a tie between the two tribes, but I was sure that tempers here would be delicate. I have therefore all along tried to maintain an atmosphere of calm, understanding, and mutual respect—for how should I know what the people are feeling?

Right now I think I have made a good military point before the people of this town. But perhaps now more than ever I feel the weight of my responsibility as the commander of the XV Brigade of the federal army here. I am not merely charged with defending this post against rebel attempts to recapture it and indeed pushing forward the federal line, but I am equally concerned about the safety of civilian lives and the protection of the civil rights of everybody here, no matter what tribe he belongs to.

As the Minimoke leaves the crowd and makes its way back to barracks, I can hear the last faint sounds of my name dying fitfully out.

Toje

Every town must have a few people whose names lend respect to the community. They should be the town's foremost citizens, men of some distinction. It isn't that these are the first men to be called to arms when a fight ensues between their town and another—no, that's a thing of the past. There are occasions when credits or endowments are to be bestowed on towns, when what a town gets depends on who its foremost citizens are, so that when the name of such and such a place comes up, it is generally asked, 'Who is there?' A town is worth nothing if it has no names on whom its very credit hangs. I am one of those very few names that mean anything here in Urukpe. Everybody knows that—or should.

When the federal troops liberated this town over three years ago, the first thing that the commander wanted to know was who the elders were. Of course my name could not have been left out after that of the *Otota* of Urukpe, our big chief. When the present commander took over about two years ago, he did the same thing. They were both certain that the success of their commands here depended on their being accepted by people like me without whom this town would be nothing. I am a big man, and there is no question about it even if I have to say so over and over. I have made my mark in the rubber business in this town and in this state. This town has people like me to thank for whatever notice it has achieved today, and if any army commander here knows what's good for him and for his army, he had better get well attached to me. Recognition must be given where it's due, and that goes without any question.

If therefore anything happens to people like me that might detract from the position in which we are held, no sacrifice should be too great from anybody in this town to ensure that we keep our place, that we maintain our position. Every citizen has to pay, and even the army commander has to recognise that he should do something to ensure that the very foundation on which his success here rests is not undermined. Great names are rare, and must not be wasted.

That is why I have not hesitated to recommend a citizen here for detention on charges of collaboration with the rebels, and then suborned another citizen to draw up the details of the indictment. For I felt that Mukoro Oshevire stood in my way. And that again is why I have not hesitated to seek carnal pleasure with his forlorn wife now that I feel my manhood flawed, my potency questioned. For it seems only in the nature of things that everything possible should be done in the interests of a reassertion of my manhood as well as pride of place, if this town should continue to keep that treasure of notice which has been won for it by men like me. And what town is there that can survive if it becomes known that one of its most pre-eminent citizens has no claims to manhood?

I believe very much that once in a while, when expediency dictates, we have got to put aside all silly notions of justice and recognise the right of might. And I am a big man here.

Odibo

I know I am nothing. I know I have nothing. But why does he keep making me feel so bad?

'You gave her the parcel of clothes?' Toje asks.

'Yes, I did,' I reply.

The way he looks at me it seems he does not believe that I did. *He never seems to trust me.*

'Are you quite sure?'

'I swear to God,' I say. 'Her son was there, and if—'

'All right! All right!' he shouts at me. 'I haven't asked you to give any witness. All I wanted to know was whether you gave her the parcel of clothes. There's no need to swear over that.'

He looks away now, out through the door. He seems angry. Then he rises from his seat, and begins to pace the floor. *I wonder what he will tell me next.*

'Did she say for certain that she was coming?'

'Well, she . . . she—'

'Speak out, will you! Stop stuttering like the fool you are,' he shouts impatiently.

'Yes, she said she was coming. When I told her you asked her to come she said she was coming.'

'Right away?'

'She said she would be getting ready in a while. That was all she said.'

'You mean to tell me she doesn't realise that when I ask her to come she should do it right away, or are you so stupid that you cannot even convey the urgency of my request?'

I say nothing. All I can do is keep quiet and look at the floor. For how do I know what to say that will not offend him?

'Look,' he says. 'How did you go about the errand? You didn't just let her—'

He stops talking. Then he begins to look outside through the door. *I wonder what he has in mind now.* He moves closer to the door. Pushing his hat a bit backwards, he begins to look more keenly. There is a soldier walking with a swagger in the direction of the house of Oshevire's wife. Toje holds the doorpost, and keeps his eyes on the soldier. He only takes his eyes off when he is sure that the soldier is going somewhere else. Then he turns round to face me again.

'Did you merely leave the parcel with her and say, "Toje says you should meet him at my place"—was that all you did?'

'Well, I waited for a while—'

'You waited for a while!' he bawls. 'Besides, have I not told you that when you call the woman, you should wait behind and keep her son company?'

'You did,' I answer him.

'Well, why are you here?'

'I'm sorry!' I tell him. He seems very angry and can do anything to me, probably strike me.

'Look here, Odibo,' he says. 'Do you not realise that the woman is in trouble?'

'I do.'

'You do? And don't you see that I am trying to help her?'

'I do.'

'No, I don't think you do,' he says. 'Because I think you are too dumb to realise that. You are just a dumb mass of body ambling about without any sense in your head. So stupid that even though you realise that a woman is afraid for herself and her child you do not see that if she has to go anywhere for any reason somebody should be there to keep her son company if only to reassure the mother.'

'I'm sorry,' I repeat.

But he doesn't seem to accept my apology. He keeps looking at me, and I begin to look on the ground to avoid his eyes.

7

'Look here, you fool,' he says. 'As soon as that woman steps in here I want you to run to her house as fast as your useless mass will allow you and stay with her son until she goes back again to the house. Do you understand that?'

'I do.'

'You had better. I want to see less of your worthless body.'

Then he keeps quiet. I am used to his fretting. But I do not know why he should continue to do this to me. Several times he has told me openly that my crippled hand has affected my brain, and that my body is useless. Well, I suppose he is right. I have little to say about the matter. But I only wish he would stop making me feel so unhappy. After all, it isn't my fault that I came into the world crippled in one arm.

Now he turns round at once to me, and pulls his seat close, to where I am standing.

'But tell me,' he says, 'how was she? How . . . how did you see her? I mean, what did you see about her?'

I look briefly at him. Because I am not quite sure what he means by the question, nor what kind of reply he expects from me. I clear my throat somewhat before I attempt a reply. *God alone knows what he means.*

'Come on,' he urges me impatiently. 'Tell me what you saw about the woman.'

'She was sitting there with her son,' I say. 'They were cracking melon seeds. She . . . she was sitting on a low bench—'

'What was she wearing?' he cuts in. 'What did she have on her body?'

He seems all over me with curiosity.

'She had on just a wrapper around her waist and a brassiere around her breasts.'

I stop and look at him, wondering if the reply is satisfactory.

'Come on,' he says. 'Tell me how she looked in those things.'

I think he would like me to give a delightful picture.

'The brassiere was a bit loose,' I continue. 'So loose that on a closer look you could see the tops of the breasts and also the points where the nipples pushed the cloth out, jutting out rather invitingly. And the cloth round her waist was so loose also that you could see the ridge of her hips as they swelled out above the edges of the cloth. And every time she made a movement the roundness of her hips seemed to be further emphasised. And the rest of her body was bare and very smooth.'

I stop talking. Because I notice that while I speak his mouth hangs open more in wonder than in delighted curiosity.

'You . . . you mean you saw all this?' he says, menacingly now. 'You actually saw all this?'

'But—'

'Shut up, you dumb fool!' he shouts at me.

'But you asked me—'

'Asked you to do what? I merely told you to take a parcel of clothes to the woman and ask her to meet me here at your place. And you stood there to stare at her breasts and her hips.'

'I was not staring—'

'Then how did you manage to notice all those featur   if you weren't staring?'

'You asked me to tell you what I saw.'

'Yes, but it never crossed my mind that you would have your eyes all over the woman. Or did I tell you to do that too?'

'Forgive me,' I plead.

He sighs and shakes his head.

'Odibo.'

I look up at him in response.

'Let me make things quite clear to you. And I want you to listen to me very carefully. When I ask you to go to the woman's place for any purpose, do just what I ask you and nothing whatsoever beyond that. Do you get that?'

'I do,' I say.

'If I ask you to take anything to her, take it there and come back without engaging in anything that isn't supposed to be part of your mission. Do you hear me?'

'I do.'

'Or do you imagine there's anything you should be doing in her house other than what I ask you to do?'

'No.'

'Then I want you to remember that. Because if you ever conceive that you can do what you like I shall have no regrets about taking your job and your allowances away from you and giving them to someone else who would gladly listen to my word. You can then go and fend for yourself—and God help your one hand!'

He gets up at once and starts pacing the floor again, up to the door and back, many times. His face looks very heavy.

'Forgive me,' I tell him.

But he does not answer me. I don't know what I can do. I really don't know what I can say that will put me on the safe side of his temper.

Aku

I see my little boy fumbling with the shirt that Toje has bought for him, and all I can do is shake my head. He can never know what thoughts are now ravaging my mind as I look at him. But I am glad. The sorrows I have known since they took his father away are too much even for my one life. It would be a plight too sad to contemplate if those sorrows were visited on him too.

'Mama,' he says.

'Yes, my son,' I answer him.

'How do I put on this shirt?'

'The way you normally put on a shirt. Just make sure the buttons come out in front and that the pockets are not turned inside out.'

He keeps on at the shirt. He is overjoyed, and I leave him there in his mood and go in to get ready to meet Toje. . . .

However hard I try, I can never keep my mind from dwelling on these sorrows. For what else can it feed on, imprisoned as I am for so long in a solitude that seems to have no end? When the federal troops liberated this town over three years ago, and all the members of my tribe ran away because it seemed the only sensible thing to do at the time, I was sure that I was doing the right thing by staying behind. *Oh how I trembled in the bush clutching my year-old son in my arms!* I was sticking with my man because I couldn't conceive of any kind of existence other than with him. Of course, after a short while the glamour of my decision dulled in my eyes, when I discovered that I was going to have to face the harsh realities of that decision. But then it was enough that my man was around, and I thought that if anything happened to me at the time it was all right for me so long as he was by my side. Now three years after they took him away into detention I do not feel so secure any more and, sad as I am to admit it, I am beginning to question the wisdom of that original decision to stay. But do I have any choice?

'Mama,' my boy calls from the parlour.

'Yes, my son.'

'I have finished putting on the shorts too.'

'That's all right. Hold on awhile. I'll be coming to examine you very soon. Have you cleaned off the sand in your hair?'

He makes no reply. Guilt urges silence.

'Quickly now,' I say. 'Go and clean it off.'

'Yes, Mama.'

I put the finishing touches to my own dressing. As I look in the mirror my thoughts rush back at me. The mirror returns me a not-so-attractive image. I begin to wonder how much longer I can go on in this state of affairs—myself and my child. For about one year now this town has been subjected to constant attacks by the Simbian forces, by air and by land. Once in a while an air raid visits us, and bodies are counted. For the next few days there is a great scare all over this town. I can hardly walk on the streets, can hardly even venture to the market to buy food for my child and me, because hostile eyes assail me from all sides and all but tear the heart out of me.

Where can I run, what can I do? If it weren't for the goodness of the federal army commander here, who has warned that nobody should take the law into his own hands, where would I be today? If I can no longer go to the market to buy foodstuffs for my child and myself, then how can we survive? *And one day someone asked me if I was buying up food to send to my people! My people? My people?* Very few people in this town ever want to visit my stall and buy things from me. The only ones that seem to come over to me are the soldiers. How long can I survive in this town if I stay isolated from the entire community except for a few soldiers who happen to stray to my stall?

And now I see a new danger, a new kind of danger. For several months now Toje has shown us kindness. He has continued to buy clothes, food and other necessities for us, and to give me money from time to time. I feel very certain that but for his subvention my child and I would collapse under the weight of our rejection by the community. But here lies the danger. It seems I am having to pay a price for the assistance that he is rendering—and what a price he seems to ask! I can see it all quite clearly. I am not a child, and I cannot deceive myself. I know what Toje wants of me. I can see it in his eyes each time he talks to me. I know. I am not a child. My husband is the first and only man ever to have known my body—I can swear to this. I know what it is all about. I can tell what's at the back of a man's mind as he scans a woman's body with his eyes. I can read Toje's eyes, and I can feel the message of his breath as he stands close to me. What's more, he has often talked to me in language that can make a woman go crazy. He has not laid a finger on me yet—I do not know what holds him—but his eyes and his breath have told me more than I would ever want to know. And if it weren't that I have been determined never to do anything that would bring shame upon my husband, though he is far away, I would long ago have succumbed to Toje's unspoken demands and thrown the door open to him without restraint.

Yet I must go to him now, for what choice have I? Until he actually lays his hand on me and convinces me that he harbours immodest motives behind his gesture of kindness, I am prepared to play this whole pretence out and believe that he has nothing but good intentions towards me. . . .

I open the door slowly, and go into the parlour. Oghenovo is standing right before me, proud in his new clothes, looking prim and well-adorned. He grins joyfully at me, his innocent eyes gleaming with a satisfaction that courts approval. I grin back at him, but the smile quickly fades from my face. For a brief moment we regard each other with a silent question in our eyes, with him pleading, *Mother, won't you tell me how beautiful I look?* and me thinking, *Poor child, what do you know?* For every time a gift like this comes from Toje I have told him that it was sent by his father who is away on a journey to Iddu!

He lowers his eyes and scans himself, starting from his feet. He seems convinced that the disappearance of the smile from my face has to do with the dirt on his feet. But when he looks up again at me, I smile once more, unwilling now to ruin his happiness. On a sudden impulse he rushes at me and buries his head in my bosom. I hold his head for a brief moment, rubbing it somewhat, and using the opportunity to hold back the tears that try to spring to my eyes. When finally he disengages himself from my bosom my face is ready with a fresh smile.

'Turn your back and let me look at the other side of you,' I tell him.

He complies quickly. I turn him round and preen him to better order, and he submits himself gladly to my plying hand. I let him gloat a little more over his new acquisition.

'All right now,' I tell him eventually. 'You can take off the clothes. I want to go somewhere.'

On hearing that, he looks up at me, and I can see that the joy has gone from his eyes.

'Where are you going, Mama?' he asks.

'I am going out. I will be back soon,' and I nudge him towards the room to take off his clothes.

'Mama, can I come with you?'

'No,' I say firmly, for now the time is hard upon me. 'There will be no need for you to come. Now hurry and take off those clothes.'

He moves sullenly towards the room. No sooner does he get there than I hear the sound of gunshots from somewhere not far away! At once I rush into the room and, following the civil defence instructions, Oghenovo and I dive quickly under the bed and lie flat on our bellies. But then I remember that the doors and windows are still open. I rush out from under the bed to shut them all.

By this time the gunshots have stopped, but I can hear the frenzied movement of vehicles outside. Having shut all the doors and windows I quickly rejoin my son under the bed. The frenzy outside continues and I press my son closer to me. We lie in this position for a while, until I am sure that the danger has subsided. Then slowly I crawl out from under the bed and move to one of the windows from where I can take a look. Holding the metal sills, I peep through a crack to see what might be happening outside.

There is nobody coming towards our house, thank God. But I can see a number of armed soldiers running about. Some of them are converging in formation on a house some distance away from our own—I think it is Fegaje Omomaro's house. Suddenly a jeep speeds by in wild fury and draws up ahead of the house to shed yet more armed soldiers. An unarmed officer with a red cap on his head begins to issue frantic orders. With their guns at the ready, all the armed soldiers move into the surrounded house. In no time at all, two of them have dragged another soldier from the house, holding him on either arm, and are now pushing him towards the waiting jeep. A few other soldiers follow, and hop into the vehicle after them. The jeep comes alive, and in one sudden thrust jolts off and is blotted out of view. The red-capped leader of the group is still inside the house with a few more of the armed soldiers. . . .

Everything seems under control. But I am staying on at the window to see this whole thing through. My heart is beating fast, and my sweating fingers are labouring for a hold on the window sills. How can I tell what this new event means for me and my child?

Oghenovo

in the afternoon when my mother was sleeping, i sneaked away from the house and went to see onome and i showed him the clothes that my father had sent to me from where he travelled, and he asked me who bought the clothes and i told him that it was my father who had travelled away to iddu, and he said it was a lie, that my father did not buy me any clothes, because he was in prison, and that the soldiers had put him into prison because he stole something that belonged to them, and i told him he was lying, because it was my father who bought me the clothes, and that my mother told me so, that my father would soon be coming back from where he had travelled, and he said it was a lie, that my father was a thief, and we fought and fought and i beat him and poured sand into his eyes and he cried and cried and i ran away. . . .

and then i came home, and my mother asked me where i had gone, and i told her that i went to show onome my clothes, and that onome said my father was a thief and did not buy me any clothes, because he was a prisoner and the soldiers had put him into the prison because, because, because he had stolen something that belonged to them, and my mother said you foolish boy why did you go away from this house without my permission, and she beat me, and she beat me, and i cried and cried and cried, and when i had finished crying she said if onome calls your father a thief can't you call his father a thief too, and she said your father did not steal anything, she said your father is a good man and will soon return from where he went *i am going to tell onome that my father is a good man*

Ali

A man must do what he has to do. It may hurt a few people, but right and expediency must always be the determining factors in his decisions.

The military execution of this morning was the first the town had ever witnessed. Of course, that's not saying that such a grim picture of death was unknown to these parts. No. Criminals had long been hanged by the neck according to the law. Murder was not unfamiliar. Indeed, crime gangs had taken the law into their own hands and committed disloyal members to the hanging-tree. But never before—not even in the remembered history of this country and certainly not since the war began—had so much spectacle attended an occasion when, for the sake of a private quarrel, a soldier had to be posted before controlled volleys of gunfire.

What happened about two weeks ago here was a mere private love dispute. But it brought with it an atmosphere of tension and insecurity, feelings that I have been trying to keep under control ever since I took command of this post.

For the past year this town has become used to occasional air and guerrilla raids by the rebels, who are still to be cleared completely from around this section of the state. At the start of the war, civil defence instructions were issued all over the country. Thus people now know what to do any time a raid occurs and is countered by a resounding barrage of shots from federal guns. People take cover everywhere—in a bunker, under a tree, at the foot of a wall, under a bed, anywhere they can find any form of shelter. For a few days after a raid an automatic embargo falls on free movement. But people are now used to all this and can even tell the difference in sound between federal and rebel guns. Yet the mere sound of gun-fire signals some kind of danger. That was why, when two weeks ago a lone federal gun rattled its fury, people hardly stopped to think what side the gun belonged to, and the whole town took to panic on the wild report that 'the enemy' was around. Fear. Plain ancient fear. For even after it became known that the gun incident was the result of a petty love dispute, people kept very much indoors for some time, convinced that any kind of shooting even at a time like this was a terrible thing—a bad sign—particularly when it took helpless life along with it.

It was a plain little case, and it took the military tribunal less than a week to deliver its findings—no different from what the people of this town had come to discover for themselves—and to give its verdict. And such was the fearless unrepentance of the killer that he told his story to the tribunal with all the cold-blooded vividness at his disposal, recounting every detail with frenetic gusto, as though happy to be given the chance to delight his audience.

Briefly, a private and his sergeant had fallen in love with the same girl. Or rather, the private had a girl, and the sergeant was trying to take her away from him. Something like that. The private found his welfare frustrated by the sergeant's superior advances. Smarting silently under the frustration, he continued to suppress his anger until he could take it no more. He knew about every single visit the sergeant paid this girl. So on that terrible day, when he was certain the Landrover was on its way, he picked up his loaded S.M.G. and set out for the girl's place in slow but determined steps.

When he arrived, the vehicle was there all right. His pace didn't change. He cocked his gun, and with one violent kick of the leg he flung the door open. After a quick look around he made for the bedroom. And there, just awake from her slumber, the girl was lying in plain, shameless nudity on the bed, with the sergeant's camouflage shirt and belt slung over a nearby chair. She screamed, sat up quickly and tried to cover herself. But the soldier's gun was at the ready, and she knew it. She called his name and begged to explain. One look of contempt down her lewd figure told him what had happened, told him he had to put an end to it all. Anger now knew no verbal language, except one muttered curse, 'Harlot!' He screwed his mouth, clenched his teeth, pulled the trigger and— *tat-tat-tat-tat-tat!* The girl writhed for a few seconds, and slumped between the blood-soaked sheets.

Just then the sergeant rushed in from the latrine, supporting his unbuttoned trousers with his hands.

'What!' he bellowed, and stood stock-still, his mouth hanging open from the exclamation.

The private pointed the gun at the sergeant's stomach, and set it at automatic.

'Sule! Why did you do this?' asked the sergeant, wide-eyed with fear and wonder.

But the look of savage intent was still on the soldier's eyes and screwed mouth. He didn't say a word.

'Give me that gun!' shouted the sergeant, his right arm out-stretched. 'I command you to surrender your gun at once!'

The private shook his head, slowly but determinedly, eyes wild but alert, and just as slowly and determinedly tightened his finger on the trigger. He was breathing faster now, and spots of sweat were beginning to assemble on his brow.

'Surrender your gun, I say!'

Eyes and gun were kept trained at the sergeant. Now the latter started moving slowly towards the private, his hand still outstretched and his eyes fixed on the other's. The private moved backwards,

17

with corresponding steps, his gun still pointed at the sergeant's belly.

'Surrender your gun!'

With one quick dash the sergeant grabbed the barrel of the gun and pushed it aside, away from his stomach. Just then the private pulled the trigger, and the S.M.G. went off into endless spurting as each man struggled to control it. But the sergeant was handicapped by his loose trousers, and the private had the edge on indignation and youth. The berserk gunfire ripped far and wide, until the private directed a furious knee-kick at the sergeant's testicles. The sergeant yelled wildly, and his hold on the gun-barrel slackened. At once the private manoeuvred the rattling gun towards the other's face, and made a ghastly mess of it. The sergeant flung his arms apart in dying agony, and crashed to the floor. The private quickly uncocked the gun, and dropped it on the ground. Standing over his victim, he was panting with heat and excitement. But he was neither sorry nor afraid. He had confronted death too often, face to face, to be scared by just one more picture of it on this creature. Besides, he knew that for him peace of mind lay only in getting rid of the sergeant; he had borne the provocation much too long, and there is a limit on a man's patience. So, in the midst of his breathless agitation, he allowed his anger just one more curse—'Bastard!'—kicked off the arm that now lay twisted and moribund over his boot, and wiped the sweat from his brow. Without the least hurry—because he knew all too well what would be coming to him—he picked up his gun and got ready to give himself up. For the prolonged action had given the Military Police sufficient time to pick up the alarm, round up the scene, and arrest the unresisting killer.

However, by the morning of the execution the people of this town had regained sufficient peace of mind to come and witness the event. Sufficient, I say—because even though a murderer was being brought to book, the very fact of a gun action that claimed defenceless civilian life was enough to throw the entire population into a long period of apprehension of the threat to individual civilian life. Keeping this town against rebel pressure has been for me a very tough job. But I have made it my business to see that a friendly relationship exists between my soldiers and the civilian population here in Urukpe. It's not that nothing ever happens. There is the occasional exchange of words in the market between the little girl who is afraid or unwilling to sell and the uniformed man who has little time to waste. And there is the not infrequent mêlée between the braggart soldier and the lorry driver who is determined that he isn't running his transport for charity and nobody is going to force him to do anything against the dictates of his economy and his manhood. Such things happen once in a while. But I stand resolved that discipline and a good atmosphere should prevail here in the interests not only of peace and unity but indeed of the war effort, at least as far as it pertains to my command.

Anybody with the least bit of awareness can see very clearly what the political atmosphere, and consequently the strategic risk, is in this town. Urukpe is one of these 'border' towns, comprised of people of the Igabo tribe (who are in the majority, since it is an Igabo town) and the Kweke clan of the secessionist tribe. Over three years ago, the town welcomed the federal troops which had liberated it from rebel occupation, and the people here demonstrated their loyalty and solidarity by assisting the federal army in eliminating rebel snipers, stragglers and even certain elements among the citizens who were considered pro-secessionist in their sympathies. But that was three years ago. How can I tell now—particularly since I took command here a whole year after that liberation—how can I tell now what time may have done to that momentary show of solidarity? Who knows how many hearts now yearn for the return of an association which time and tradition have forged between the tribes?

The last commander here, Major Akuya Bello, was relieved of his command on account of booze and plain lack of discipline. He failed to take account of the delicate politics of a place like this and the risks to the federal war effort here. For this reason, ever since I took command about two years ago, I have been determined that everything should be done to avoid upsetting that delicate balance and thus jeopardising the strategy of the federal war machine in this sector. Besides, it is clear to me that, if this country really means what it says in its slogan, 'To keep Zonda one is a task that must be done!', we are all committed to translating that slogan into concrete terms so far as it concerns not only our success on the field against the rebel forces, but indeed the rights and liberties of every single citizen of this country—man, woman or child, soldier or civilian— no matter where they come from or what marks they wear on their faces. *Allah*, I don't care what it costs me!

Two years ago, at a party given by the big chief of this town, the *Otota*, and members of the town council (over which he presided during the civilian regime) to welcome me as the new commander, I made it quite clear to the people what the federal intentions were. I also stressed that, if ever the occasion arose, these intentions would be enforced against any personal animosities or prejudices. A pity if anyone felt hurt as a result. On a couple of occasions since then, I have had cause to warn the civilian population here sternly against unwarranted provocation of soldiers—just for the same reason as I have not hesitated to invoke the appropriate military discipline against any soldier who tries to take advantage of his position or mechanical might. I am prepared to respect the traditional order of things here and to let people carry on as freely as they are accustomed to, although, of course, certain limitations have to be observed in view of the prevailing emergency declared by the Head of State at the beginning of this crisis. Naturally I am well aware that individual citizens of this town may have their own private conceptions and interpretations of the federal concern as I have pointed it out, but I will *not* let it be violated. And it was my personal request to the federal Chief of Staff that this public military execution—the first to be carried out in this country —should take place in this town. I wanted it to serve not only as instant deterrent to undisciplined soldiers who thought they could do anything they liked with their guns, but also as a general warning against any unwholesome meddling with helpless civilian women.

The execution took place at the town square. It should have been recognised as an occasion of moment and accorded the full military attendance that it deserved. But neither the Chief of Staff nor the Military Governor of this state, the Black Gold State, was there. For one thing, the civil war is still on, and though we have succeeded in pushing the rebels back several miles beyond this town, we are still within vulnerable range. Guerrilla attacks have been visited on us, and now that the rebels have acquired increased air power from Europe we are the target of occasional air raids—like the one that occurred just recently. Our supreme headquarters were therefore unwilling to commit any of our top officials to the risk that such a crowded affair involved. For another thing, the Chief of Staff was content to regard the execution as an affair belonging purely to the XV Brigade and to leave it to my officers and me to ensure that discipline was enforced in our post.

Thus the military attendance at the execution this morning was limited to my brigade. But the *Otota* himself, Chief Onagwolor Ovuede, was there. Since the war came to Urukpe he has been forced to curtail his civic functions and leave the scene to the soldiers, because he cannot pretend to provide his subjects with the protection that the present circumstances demand. But he was there with members of his council (those of them who have survived the military experience). I believe they came because they felt they *had* to answer the invitation to attend. My friend Chief Toje was there also, being a member of the council. Of the general population, many stayed at home because they were afraid of anything that had to do with the gun. But a large number attended nevertheless, prompted either by the irresistible itch of curiosity to witness an event that might happen only once in their lifetime, or perhaps by the desire to see justice done.

The firing spot was located a good distance away from the crowd. Ten rows of sand-filled sacks, each row four deep, provided a bulwark against possible bullets straying beyond their target. And right in front of this bulwark was a pole to which the soldier was to be tied.

Just before the execution took place I made a very short speech. I reminded all gathered there that the nation was still at war, and that the state of emergency proclaimed by the Head of State and Commander-in-Chief of the Armed Forces still prevailed, demanding of *every* citizen utmost vigilance and discipline. But I emphasised that, in spite of this, the laws of the country still remained, and that *every* citizen—soldier or civilian—was still bound by these laws. Individual rights and liberties were to be respected, and nobody had any right to take the law into his own hands, far less to take the life of a fellow human being. I repeated previous warnings against any form of confrontation between soldiers and civilians, and I stressed that I would not hesitate to deal ruthlessly with any acts of indiscipline whatsoever, whether they came from soldiers or civilians. I ended with a special warning against molestation of the female population, since they were naturally weak and stood the risk of being exploited by unscrupulous persons in a situation of tension and fear such as the present circumstances inspired. Having said that much, I took my seat. There was calm everywhere.

The condemned soldier was unrepentant as ever, indeed defiant. I was later told that he had bluntly refused to be taken to the execution ground unless he was chauffeured in a Mercedes Benz. He therefore had to be carried by force and thrown into the Landrover. When he got to the execution ground, he refused to stand up on his feet, and the officer who was detailed to conduct the firing ordered that he be tied at once to the pole. The officer read out the charges against him and the condemnation. All the soldier did was laugh throughout the reading. Not a laugh really—a dry, mirthless cackle, like a squawk in a graveyard at midnight. When he was asked if he had any last words to say before the execution, he demanded a cigarette. I let them grant his wish. The crowd was very silent. Halfway through his smoking he loudly demanded a bottle of White Horse. Nobody laughed. This time his request was ignored. The officer ordered his head bound with the black cloth. And it was at this point that the grimness of his fate finally dawned on the soldier. As the cloth came near him he shook his head violently. But the firm grip of duty was upon him, and he was fast to the pole. He took his last look at the world, and his head was wrapped securely in the hood. A firing squad of six took up their positions in a line ten yards away facing him. The officer gave his orders. The guns were trained on the soldier. And in no time at all conducted volleys of fire put an end to the killer's life.

The effect on the civilian gathering was no less than shock. Old men rose from their seats and shook their heads at this addition of yet one more incident to their catalogue of woes. *Allah*, what faces they wore! Women and children cried at the horror. Mothers clutched their babies fast to their bodies as they ran quickly to their homes. And as grimfaced soldiers untied their executed comrade from the stake, a patrol of vultures hovered darkly beneath the pale canopy of the midday sky.

In the car as I was being driven home, I sat pondering the unglamorous grandeur of justice and bounden duty. *Wallahi!*

Toje

I think—I am certain—I can only put it down to my thoughts. If I stop thinking about it maybe at least I won't feel as bad as I do now. And yet, how can I stop thinking? How shall it be told, how reported, that I cannot lie with a woman? Common fowls and dogs and goats do it in the streets, before the very eyes of the gazing world, and I cannot even enjoy the customary subconscious ritual of an early morning erection, which is the privilege of even the tiniest infant! What use is this flab of flesh, if it cannot perform the function without which a man is not worth the classification?

But I believe I think too much. Besides, I haven't even tried, and I think I have to try even if only to prove to myself that I am worth the power I *know* I wield.

Still, a man must seek to know what is the root of a misfortune that taxes his mind as deeply as it flaws his body. I can never know now whether it should be traced to my wife or to that reckless adventure with the slut at Iddu. For one thing, it looks absurd for a man, and a man of my stature and importance at that, to go scouring a big city in search of a prostitute only to lay a finger on her and swear it was from her I got the disease. That would be a stupid effort, a worthless one at least. For isn't it a hazard of the trade? And what man would stand up and swear to himself he didn't know what dangers he faced as he sought that costly fling? Besides, it was all done in the night. And since, as they say, these fellows change their stations ever so often, where would I begin a search for a face I saw many months ago and could never be certain

23

to recognise today even if she stood before me and called my name?

I hear too that, since these creatures know the risks of the trade, they take good care of themselves, so that one stands less chance of being infected by them than by ordinary women who, because their lives are ruled by the routine of living, would never suspect that anything could come into them.

I had long thought about this, had long exercised my mind on the matter. And, God, look what it has cost me. It was what brought me to have that confrontation with my wife, because I thought that a man has a right to clear his mind of anything that bothers him. After all, this is my house, I built this home, I *own* it, I married a wife and got these children and, if I cannot exercise my right of question as much as of positive control, who else is there to be called to account when any crisis comes to this house? And this was a crisis, still is. Otherwise, how can a man reconcile himself to that title when it seems very clear to him that he no longer possesses, has completely lost—strange as it may sound to a normal mind— that power which gives the title its very definition?

So I called my wife to me and decided it was time we gave the whole affair a talking-over. And I was very cautious about it, God knows it and I can swear to the honesty of my statement. I was very careful. I didn't want to make it sound as though I was *accusing* her of defiling me, of ruining my manhood. She knows I wasn't, and she dare not now challenge my intent at the time. I called her to me as a man would call his wife, his companion—I gave her that concession—so as to clear a problem that confronted the household. So she came and sat down before me, not suspecting in the least what it was I had called her for but coming up to me nevertheless as a wife should when she hears her man say come here. I put the matter before her, as politely and as cautiously as a man should who stood in my position. Why, I didn't say too much. All it amounted to was, Woman, here's what's happened to me, do you think that it could by any chance have anything to do with you?

'What are you asking me?' she broke out, eyes gleaming as though she would split my head in two and spill my brains that very minute. 'Toje, what are you saying?'

'Be calm, woman, no need to shout about it. It's only between you and me. All I ask is, could it by any accident be—'

'Accident?' she was up on her feet, glowering down on me now —*me!*—like an oversized serpent. 'Accident? What kind of accident?'

'I said keep cool!'

'And I said what kind of accident? Twenty-five years and ten children—seven healthy sons and three healthy daughters, and you come to accuse me of—'

'All right. All right.'

Haw! I had to get the situation under control. I had to dismiss her and end the confrontation, otherwise who could tell what might have happened? Whatever the situation was, whatever it was that brought a man to stoop low enough to ask his wife over for a *discussion* when he could well have made up his mind and taken his decision and done whatever his mind told him to do, I just couldn't sit there and let her run her mouth and pour her petulance standing over me as though she owned the house. I couldn't bear it. I was too big for that. I *am* too big for that sort of thing—I, Chief Toje Onovwakpo, a man well respected among my circle and all over Urukpe and indeed this whole part of the country, a rubber magnate of great account who has contributed in no small way to all the rubber on which our Black Gold State is today comfortably cushioned. Why, I could still have been doing much more if this war didn't come up and put a risk to the business, because we can't tell what manner of danger lurks in the plantations. I say, I could have torn that woman's frame right down the middle and by God nobody would have questioned it because I set up this home and I *own* it and it is up to me to take all the decisions and do all the shouting there is to do.

But that was it. I let her go. And today I still can't tell who put the disease in me. I am not even sure whether it was a mistake on my part to have let that animal leave my presence—whether I shouldn't have pressed for an explanation and settled my mind at least on that score and saved myself a good deal of the mental torment. But at least I did save myself further exasperation, for only God knows what I could have done then when a vile-mouthed woman so brazenly challenged my authority.

However, I think it is enough for me that I have had just one night of failure with her. That one fearful night, when I mounted my own wife only to find that my manhood had deserted me. And can I now go back to her and seek to re-enact the disgrace? I think this self-respect, small though it may be if I let myself think it so—I think this self-respect needs to be preserved for whatever it is worth.

That is one thing I have always told myself. Always let a woman understand that you have the upper hand, even when it hangs low beneath your waist. You let a woman recognise that she has any point of advantage over you and you will forever regret that you ever took her on. *Shuo!* I am still Toje Onovwokpo. I can still re-call what a scourge I was in my younger days. I can still remember how the sweet lusty damsels fluttered round me; how, when the time came for me to marry, the only problem was to decide who it would be. And can that power all have gone so suddenly? All right. If the physical appeal is no longer there, if I have now failed to attract with my looks because there is a wrinkle here and a greyness there and the pace has slackened somewhat, at least I have got some good money. And, damn it, if that is not enough appeal I do not know what else is. The rubber business no longer thrives, it is true. The machines have lain dormant for a while now, yes, and the able-bodied young men who tapped the trees have either fled before the advancing federal troops or have answered the call to arms. But, thanks to my speed and my enterprise, I have been able to secure this contract to supply the troops in this sector with food. Nobody can deny that a sizable income comes to me, and I can boast that if today a count was ordered I would have the whole town and even the wretched chief prostrating before me. If that is not enough power and appeal, what is? What else would bring all this respect that the whole town showers on me? What else would bring a self-righteous but misguided major like Ali to cower before me and treat me as though I was more important to him than his self-proclaimed federal concern? What else would cause a beautiful woman like Aku to stop pining for her imprisoned husband, leave her only child at home and make haste to meet me at the hut of my dumb and imbecile nephew?

Yes. This is power. This is happiness. Happiness is finding that a whole population still looks up to you when a mighty thing like war has brought them low. It is also knowing that you still have the power to beckon on a woman and she comes running to you happily because she can hardly resist you, knowing that you have the one thing which can decide whether or not she and her child can live.

That's money. And I am determined that this money will bring back to me everything that I appear to have temporarily lost. My wife will yet have occasion to fall on her knees and lower her head before me and curse the day that she made me shiver on my seat and wonder whether indeed I was master of what I know I set up with the sweat of my brow and the strength of my groin. And, between now and the time that any misguided sense of justice would bring the authorities at Iddu to set Mukoro Oshevire free of the chains they have thrown around him, I am determined to use his wife to prove to myself that I still possess that power which I *know* lies within me. I am still Toje Onovwakpo. . . .

But be that as it may. Day has broken fully now. My window is closed, but I can see spikes of dawn-light penetrating the cracks all round it. I have no wish to get out of bed yet because I want to get my mind clear on something. I am not quite certain what this boy Ali has on his mind. It seems to me that he is intent on bringing the entire town under his will. It is not enough for him that his soldiers fear him and the rebels dread his defences, and even that the common people here admire him. I do not grudge him his federal concern. I am all for him when he pulls his men's ears with the point of a bayonet or if he decides to wake them up every morning with a hand grenade or commit the occasional lecher among them to gunfire. But it does worry me when a misguided little monkey, just because he wears a uniform and carries a gun, gets up on his stilts to prescribe a code of morals for an entire population that was there long before he ever dreamed he would smell these borders. *Haw!* He kept saying 'soldiers and civilians', 'soldiers and civilians alike', as though the two went together. I do not know—I do not really care—how the rest of the town takes his bluff. The old chief is too scared and in any case too lame-brained to stand up and tell this opinionated scoundrel that he can *never* enjoy the goodwill of the people unless he recognises their freedom of

association between one another, whatever sanction he thinks fit
to impose upon these incontinent swine whom he commands.
I say, I don't care what the rest of the people think of the speech
he made yesterday. I am determined to safeguard my mission. I
know how to get him round. . . .

There is a good deal of noise in my household, mostly from
around the kitchen. My wife has sense enough these days not to
wake me before I am inclined to get out of the room. The children
have gone to school, and the rest of the family are about their
duties. The morning is getting old, and though my window is shut
I can still see those spikes of light through the cracks and slits around
it.

I am waiting for the newspaper boy. The fool hardly comes in
early enough these days. It's not his fault. Ever since the war
came to this town, notice and respect have shifted from where they
belong. Nowadays, when the newspaper van comes into the town
and dumps the bales at their office the vendors rush off to the military barracks first. They don't remember us any more. I wonder
what they think. I wonder if they know that those fellows have
much less education or awareness than people like me. I wonder if
they realise that when opinion on matters of moment have to be
sought it is to people like me that the governor—even the Head of
State—have to turn. Yet they have forgotten us, and the honour
now belongs to the soldiers. They have forgotten all so soon that
this town owes whatever notice it has to people like me, and if the
war had not come to it people like me would still be sitting over its
destiny.

There are very few people like me here. And of the few I am
without question the most outstanding. They have forgotten that
too. They have forgotten how I made it to the top. How I had
hardly overgrown toddling before I started following my father to
the farm, and the old man had trouble chasing me off to school.
And when the rubber trees in our enormous plantation came of age
and my father was too old to keep count of his property I took
control of the business and guided it to its present proportions. How
I have made an enormous success of it. How the government—
whatever kind we have had—hardly thinks or talks rubber but that

it joins my name with it. They have forgotten all this so soon, and now they go crawling up to *strangers* who haven't even got enough education to feel any kind of awareness except the smell of the enemy.

Sometimes I stop to ask myself, is it the fear of the times, or is it a sign of my loss of respect? How many people can have known what's happening to me? Can my wife have opened her mouth? I hardly think so. Of course, you can never trust women in these things. Twenty-five years and ten children, she is quick to remind me! But weakness rules their minds as powerfully as it does their hearts, and it takes just one little knock like what has come upon me to make nonsense of all those twenty-five years. Yet, better to let the matter lie than to give her another opportunity to make me question my stature. Because I don't know what in the present state of things I may be driven to do. Still. . . .

The boy finally announces his arrival. I get out of bed, and rub my eyes clean of yesterday. I wish I could do that to my mind also, but there it is. . . . I come out of the room, and everybody greets me, passersby too, paying me the respects that are due to a man of my position. God, the day is old—my watch says ten o'clock. But who says I must wake before ten? The scoundrel has gone, but one of my maidservants hands me the paper that he had deposited. My easy chair is spread out for me. I take out my glasses, and I sit down to browse the news of the day with that perception which not many of us in this town can boast.

I first direct my attention to the front-page comment, for very likely it will deal with this tribunal at Iddu which has been set up to determine the atrocities perpetrated by the rebels in this state and the activities of people who in one way or another collaborated with them. I have never really trusted these newspaper people. Too often they pretend to know more than they do and presume to pass judgment on matters which are far beyond their scope—let alone right—of judgment. A few weeks ago they were raving against what they called the hoarding activities of food contractors and the effect they thought these activities had on prices of foodstuffs in the open market. Now, how much do they know? Why don't they seek *our* opinion first? For after all, even if that were true, could they not consider that it was also within our power to send those prices tumbling down? Only last week they were urging the federal government to agree to meet the rebels *anywhere* if those people showed any genuine willingness for negotiations. Negotiations! What kind of negotiations? If any man is stubborn enough to commit his head to an act of rebellion, why can't he be man enough to last it out? Foolish talk, that's what I call it all. I think this war should take its full course. I think these bastards should be left to receive a good pounding, so that next time they hear any talk of secession they should run at ten miles a stride and not even wait to pick up their pants. Look what they have done to my rubber business. Why, I could almost single-handedly have supported the budget of this state, but for this costly diversion. Now I am left with a hardly comparable source of income, at least in terms of prestige. For I am reduced—me, Toje Onovwakpo—I am reduced to procuring food-stuffs and submitting them to the conceited inspection of this band of rascals. And these fools want to let the rebels get away with it at the conference table, where they are certain to make every effort to win by force of intellect. I don't blame these boys. They are sure of their daily keep, earned from a wicked distortion of facts and a mis-guided presumption at judgment. Little do they know the hazards involved in a change of business.

But that is not my main worry. This trial at Iddu, in which Mukoro Oshevire is involved. . . . Here it is. LET HONESTY PREVAIL AT TRIBUNAL. *The misfortune that has befallen our dear nation demands of each and every one of . . . It seems clear that certain individuals are using the opportunity presented by the tribunal to settle old scores and to practise new vices which are in no way related to this struggle which the government has been forced to engage in for the unity of our country. Whatever may have been the . . . It therefore be-hoves the honourable members of the tribunal to discountenance any false and unsubstantiated. . . . Equally undesirable is the high-handed attitude of . . . The mandate of the tribunal is therefore clear. No useful purpose will be served by keeping in detention citizens of this country, whatever their tribes of origin, who are merely the victims of vindictive and un-patriotic informers and who . . . The governor's words serve as a timely warning. . . .*

So this is what these rascals are up to? So this is their new trick? They now want to see the detained men released. They want to see them set free of their chains. They would like to see Mukoro Oshevire strut out of prison and make his way into this town before he is due, make a fool of me and my sworn desire. Just because of a small, innocent statement that the governor made two days ago. I remember what he said, I still have the newspaper around. What he said didn't amount to much: that the tribunal should apply more discreet and more expedient screening standards, so as to quicken the course of justice, whatever this may mean in the eyes of those to whom it has been entrusted. So—now these fellows want them all released? Against the wishes of good citizens who helped the same authorities identify the same crimes that are now on trial? Against the wishes of honourable men like me who were bold enough to stand up and point out the traitors in our midst who spared no pains to aid the rebels? All right—so I did not come out in the open. I made a secret report to Major Akuya Bello, went over secretly to tell him what the whole town knew Oshevire did, merely because I did not want this to be an open scandal involving my name. But the Major saw with me. He rightly reckoned that a man of my stature would not stand up to make a frivolous charge against another citizen. He saw with me and took the report to the authorities at Iddu, and thereafter Oshevire was bundled off there and thrown into detention. That was only as it should be. For what business did he have rescuing a damned rebel, just because his wife happens to speak the rebel language? Of course the charge does not say that he rescued the rebel from a mob—*I* have seen to that—but it all amounts to the same thing. Rescuing a damned rebel and collaborating with the rebel occupation, what difference is there?

So these news hacks want to see him released? I think this is a dangerous trend and has to be checked. Luckily Major Akuya Bello is a member of that tribunal, and if he has any sense in him he should not give the authorities reason to doubt the integrity of his report. Otherwise his military honour and record are in danger. But that is hardly my concern. If he is fool enough to bungle the assignment he should have himself to blame for whatever happens to him. All that concerns me is that Mukoro Oshevire stays in detention. Long enough for this war to take its full course. Long enough for full normalcy to return, and I can in safer circumstances establish a commercial lead in the rubber business too comfortable to be threatened by him.

Long enough for me to be able to use his wife to prove that I still possess that power which I am sure lies within me. By now, I believe, she knows what I want. I believe she understands that I am not investing in nothing, and that she has no reason to expect a man who is her husband's commercial rival to every now and then send her and her child clothes and keep. She knows that the whole town is against her and wants her removed. And I am one of the town, only an honourable and outstanding citizen of it, appointed by my position of importance to determine who stays free and who stays chained and indeed the welfare of the entire population—man, woman and child. I am still Chief Toje Onovwakpo. . . .

I get up from the easy chair and retire inside. The maid has sense enough to fold the chair and lay it where it should be. I have no time to take my bath or have my meal. The business calls for despatch. I must go to that boy Ali and probe his mind, for who can tell what his mind is in these things, the way he acts and talks these days? My mission, my desire, must be protected. . . .

I wash my face and my mouth, collect the documents of my purchase of foodstuffs, throw my cloth around me, and make for the military barracks. I must see Ali, know his mind. The day can hardly wait, even for a man of my importance.

Oshevire

I still don't know what I am doing here. But I don't care. The important thing is to be able to stand up to the situation and bear it all like a man. To be able to prove to your enemies that the forces of truth and honesty are stronger than any burden they will unjustly have laid upon you. To be able to vindicate the cause of justice, and, even if they succeed in taking your life in the end, prove to them all too clearly that theirs was an idle victory, for your honesty towers tall and superior above everything, like a wild palm, tough and upright.

It all looks very funny to me, though I know they mean it in all seriousness. Tearing a man away from his family and wafting him so far away into detention. On what charge? They say I collaborated with the rebels. All right. I can hardly deny it. There's no use in denying it. Yes, I collaborated with the rebels. Obviously they know better than I do what it all means, and they can put my 'crime' in much better language than I am capable of thinking up. So the best thing is to agree with them, and not fight it, for they know better. If saving a life means collaborating with the rebels, then that indeed I did. If pointing the way of safety to a little boy, his breath nearly out of him from fleeing in helpless frenzy ahead of a wild mob that sought his life in a most unequal chase—I say, if showing the way of safety to a fellow human being means collaborating with the rebels, then of course I am guilty of that. And I am proud to be so guilty.

For what kind of answer could I have given to my God if I had turned down the boy's desperate plea for help? What sort of happiness could I have been living in now, knowing within myself that I deliberately and with my eyes wide open let that boy lose his life at the hands of a frenzied gang, when it lay within my power to avert the horror? My God, that boy could have been my own son! To this day I don't know him and couldn't even recognise his face if he stood to be identified among two other people. I don't recall ever setting eyes on him before that moment. But that wasn't the point. My immediate impulse was hardly to ask him, Son, whose child are you? The wild and frenzied plea in his eyes and the shredded loin rag proved all too clearly that he scarcely had a chance to beg mercy of his pursuers.

He was too young to deserve that fate. From what I saw at that brief meeting with a living death, he was hardly more than thirteen. And what could a thirteen-year-old child have done to deserve that deathly stampede? Of course I knew what was happening all over

33

the town. Similar hunts and pursuits had been visited upon many other Simbas who were unlucky enough to have stayed behind after their kin had run away in the wake of the federal victory. Some of them, poor creatures, had fallen into the hands of their pursuers, and only God knows what their fates were. Even their friends and relatives fell into like misfortune for the mere sake of the remotest connection. And though my wife, a Simba herself, was by now part of me and therefore, I thought, an authentic citizen of our town, she did not wait to be told that wild unreason ruled the town. She fled right into the bush near our house with our year-old son. My God, what panic I knew as I came home from the plantation to find that my wife and child were nowhere in sight! But then the federal government had made several broadcasts over the radio, appealing to the people to be calm and not take the law into their own hands, and threatening severe penalties on any acts of lawlessness and violence. Anyone would have thought that peace had returned to our town. How then could I have guessed that I would venture into my plantation only to be confronted by the kind of horror I had thought the federal assurances had banished? And who, in all sincerity, would have acted differently from me when he found himself face to face with an event that so frighteningly challenged him to demonstrate true human sympathy?

For the mob came wildly after the boy. Though he was the first that I saw, I had not the least doubt in my mind that he was in a most desperate plight. The way he threw himself down at my feet and made me feel that if he died I was to blame for it—I just never could have come to terms with such culpable cowardice if I had let the boy be robbed of his life in that irrational chase.

Now that chase seems to have caught up with me. Months passed, and then came the witch-hunting. And here I am today at the state capital of Iddu, detained on a charge of 'collaboration with the rebel occupation.' *Hm-hm-hm!* It looks funny to me. But God knows that this is not a laughing matter.

And I ask again, was it a crime that I responded to a perfectly justified human impulse, and to the equally humane appeal of the federal government, by saving a life that I saw stood in danger? Well, if they say so, they have to be right. But God help them. And help me too. Because even at the risk of losing my life and bereaving my wife and child, the thought alone of whose love and devotion keeps me alive today in this woeful place, I am going to keep on protesting the rightness of my action and denouncing the shamelessness of the charge.

I will go down fighting. Stand up and take it all like a man, I have said to myself. By that resolve I stand. . . .

The business for today is about to begin. Three of us have been singled out for today's proceedings. I think they have decided to hasten the affair. Devoting a day or a stretch of days to one man has cost them a good deal of time and patience. Because they have to have a good deal of patience for people like me, who just don't care a damn. If a man walks up to you and tells you you did something you are *sure* in God's name you didn't do, won't you tell him no for as many times as he makes his charge? '*You did it!*' 'No, *I didn't!*' '*Yes, you did!*' 'No, *I didn't!*' '*Yes!*' '*No!*' '*Yes!*' '*No!*' '*Yes!*' '*No!*'— even if it takes the whole of eternity. It's not out of disrespect for the law or established authority or anything. Nobody has ever laid a charge on me before. God knows I'm a law-abiding citizen. I have never taken anything that didn't belong to me. Never sought after another man's wife. And in my rubber business I have tried as much as possible—as God is my witness—to abide by the government's instructions and have made sure that I haven't adulterated my latex. Fair play, honesty, integrity—they have guided my life. At least I have *tried* my best. I can't say I'm perfect, but I've tried my best. That's why it goes too much against the grain for a man to point an unjust finger at me and all I do is grin and call him God's most honest son. No. He'll have to kill me to make me submit. It's not out of disrespect for the law or anybody. It's just that it's not *right*, it's not *fair*. No, they need a lot of patience for people like me. . . .

My fellow detainees and I have been brought here in a Black Maria. And here we are seated on a bench, stiffly guarded by two armed soldiers and a policeman, whom you couldn't ask for cigarettes. A lot of people are assembled today, as every day. We have become a kind of spectacle. I believe people would have actually paid to see us, if there was a price. Somehow it seems the authorities have decided there's no use in paying to see a collaborator—he's not worth much anyway.

Presently the chairman of the tribunal and the commissioners appear, and the entire assembly—all of us—rise in deference. They stride up to the platform and take their seats, six of them in all, including Major Bello. There is a lot of shuffling around. A lot of whispering across seats too. They smile and they frown. They gawk and they laugh. Then they exchange papers, and point things out to one another from them. They seem to be saying a lot, only God knows what. Not that I mind. *Stand up to it all like a man.* Nothing will move me from that resolve. I know they are all very big men, and I imagine they are all very honest, very intelligent and very respectable, men whose lives could not be bothered by country bumpkins like me. But here's their chance to prove it. Here's their chance to justify these chains that I have had on me for three years now. Their chance to tell the world why a poor country planter, not much better than the men he paid to tap his trees, was all of a sudden whisked from his family and dragged off into detention, charged with giving support to the rebels when all he did was save a poor life that could well have been his own. I believe that among all those papers lying on the desk before them they should be able to find all the clues. They should be able to find some kind of solution and an answer to the big question. Either they can justify this incarceration, being the intelligent men that they are, or else they will live up to their honesty and their integrity by seeing through the injustice and taking me back where they brought me from.

There is a lot of murmuring, from all sides. Up on the platform where the almighty panel sit, and in the gallery among the crowd that have come to watch us perform. I do not know what is in the minds of my fellows. On my left is a rather young man, I would say about twenty-five years of age. I am not really sure how they say he collaborated. I know he has been up for trial once or twice since the whole thing began, but I have not been able to gather much. He has not said anything that would give me a clue either. He is a rather impatient young man. I think he was at university and he has a lot of book knowledge up his head. The few occasions that he has had reason to talk about the matter, he has merely ranted a lot of slogans and big words that have not made any sense to me. Perhaps he is one of those impatient young educated men who always write about this or that in the newspapers. That's right. He did talk about newspaper articles and things of that sort. But he is too impatient to make any sense. My only worry for him is that he will get up there and start abusing everybody and so make things very bad for himself. Or he may just start reciting all those words and things he has been pouring on us in the prison, or even try to be too smart for the panel and thereby infuriate them into losing whatever sense of fair play and whatever patience they may have. Sometimes he gets very agitated when he talks, and that won't help him very much here.

The other man, on my right, is about my age—I would say about forty. He was a government official, and from what he told us he is charged with actually facilitating the occupation of our state by the rebels. He maintains a very studied peace about himself. Most of the time you see him staring straight ahead, hand on bushy cheek and eyes hardly blinking. He once told us in the prison he wasn't ever going to shave until the whole mess was over. And I think I believe him. He seems to me a man of deep conviction. Each time he sees a man shaving he merely goes by, as you would pass by a man urinating, doing a perfectly natural thing that, though you are not doing the same thing yourself, does not in the least constitute any distraction for you from your routine of thinking or living. I think he is a very intelligent man too—he has that in his bearing, always looking as if he is trying to work something out. He has none of the youthful charge of our impatient friend here, but I think he knows a great deal. And though I have never seen him in the box, I think he is the sort of man that would get up there and trade argument with argument, point with reasoned point. He will not be brash or even loud about it, but his impact will not be mistaken. The set look on his face seems to carry with it a stubborn resolve. Isn't it nice to have a fellow by your side, to know that, though you are not likely to share the same fate with him, you are joined with him in a fellowship of self-convinced will? No doubt he has a wife and family whom he has been forced to leave, and this binds us even more. He says his name is Obanye, and he is a Simba. I really can't say where our impatient friend comes from. If I remember rightly I think I heard him talk once about 'world-citizenship' or a 'community of men' or some such stuff. *Hm-hm-hm-hm-hm!*

The proceedings are now about to begin. Looking round me I can see the crowd has increased. I can also see the lawyer of our angry young friend walking hurriedly up the hall to a table immediately beneath the panel. As he walks past us he throws a greeting smile at us, and the young man by my side is all aglow with response. There is on his face a look of relief. Not the relief you feel when your saviour has arrived. I don't think the young man feels that way at all about his predicament—and he hardly sees it as a predicament. He is so angry that he has taken an offensive attitude in the matter, and for him it all boils down to his wanting to blow the brains out of that pack that sit on the platform. Although he has hired a lawyer to plead his case in a legal style, as far as he is concerned he has merely enlisted somebody else in his offensive, so as all the more effectively to overwhelm the panel—indeed, the government—by sheer force of numbers. I can almost feel his heart knocking, so eager is he to launch his attack.

His lawyer walks up to his table and bows to the panel, with an apologetic smile on his face. I think he is part of the reason the trial hasn't started yet. He takes his seat on the other side of the table, opposite the counsel to the tribunal, but on the left hand of the secretary to the tribunal, who sits at the head of the table. The lawyer exchanges smiles and greetings with them. Then he hurries through his papers.

It is hard to tell what lies at the back of the mind of the counsel to the tribunal. He wears a benevolent face, and I am sure that he is by nature a good man. But when he starts throwing his questions his manner changes, his face bristles, and his veins swell.

The secretary and counsel to the tribunal exchange papers and consult one another. There is so much fellowship between them that those of us on trial may well have reason to be sorry for ourselves.

But self-pity is unknown to me now. For self-pity can sometimes amount to an admission of guilt. And what have I done that I should feel guilty, what have I done to any man? They may commit me to perpetual incarceration—why, hang me by the neck or even set me before a volley of gunfire; but what will they have gained? I am prepared for it all.

'Ehem,' the chairman clears his throat, and everybody is set for the opening. 'Today is the seventy-sixth day of the sitting of this *Tribunal of Inquiry Into the Conduct of the Rebel Occupation of the Black Gold State*, and I declare the proceedings open.'

There is silence. Unbroken silence, underscored only by the soft shuffling of papers and of human feet, with here and there maybe a cautious cough and the swing of a window. Counsel to the tribunal rises from his seat.

'The first witness for today, in the person of Mr Samson Ajijala Etuwewe,' he calls. 'Samson Ajijala Etuwewe, will you please come out and take your seat in the witness box. Thank you.'

A bespectacled young man of about thirty walks down the public gallery towards the witness box. He is dressed in *agbada* and gathers this neatly about him as he walks.

'Come on,' urges counsel. 'Quick, take your seat.'

Suddenly our young friend stirs beside me, very impatiently, and jumps from the bench.

'Look at him!' he screams, pointing at the seated witness. 'Look—look at him! Is he not ashamed of himself?'

'Will you keep quiet there!' the chairman shouts back at him.

'*He* should be the one to keep his mouth shut, if he has—'

The soldier by his side brings a hand down upon our friend's shoulder, and pushes him down on the bench.

'I say he should be ashamed of himself,' shouts our friend again, springing up and bristling like a mad dog.

'Look,' says the chairman, 'if you don't behave yourself this morning I am going to take a most severe action against you. So behave yourself before—'

'Nonsense! All you do is sit up there and listen to this swine level all manner of lies against me. And you call it justice. What—'

The soldier is at him again, this time applying the butt of his gun on our man's shoulder to bring him down on the bench.

The chairman can pronounce his terror any time now, the way his brow is creased with fury and his lips are tensed and his eyes appear to be burning through the glaze of his spectacles.

The audience is calm. The lawyer is distressed, merely holding a hand to his brow and shaking his head in sad notice of his client's conduct.

'Mr Aboloje,' the chairman addresses the lawyer, 'I have a mind to commit your client to—'

'The sooner you did that the better!' Our young man is up again, straining to ward off the obtrusive butt of the soldier's gun. 'All you reactionary elements will be levelled by the revolution. I have no doubt in my mind that—'

The soldiers's gun is hard this time on him, practised and sure, and our friend collapses under the pain, holding his hand to his afflicted shoulder and wincing in torment. His lawyer is worried, and rises slowly on his seat to look at his man.

'That's all right now Mr Aboloje,' says the chairman. 'I think he'll be all right in a moment, and maybe this time he'll be sensible enough to—'

'You lie!' Our friend is up once again, undaunted and unbroken. 'The revolution will take its course, and woe betide all you retrogressive elements who cannot—'

The soldier cracks down on him again, subduing his victim once more with the same measure of trained heartlessness, and on the very same spot. This time the audience is touched by a sense of horror, and a wave of murmuring sweeps through the gallery. Our man is truly in pain, even his youth can hardly bear the burden any longer. His lawyer rises at once and looks at the chairman. *Oh God, oh God!*

'Your Honour,' he says, 'may I humbly request that my client be treated with a little more understanding. I think that if the good soldier by his side continues to apply the same method of subjugation my client will be left in such a physical state that he will not be able to aid this august tribunal in its enquiry.'

'That's all right, Mr Aboloje,' replies the chairman. 'Your request is noted. Could the guard please apply a little less vigour when calling witnesses to order. I think it is in the interests of an orderly execution of our—'

'Nonsense!' Our man blares again, defying his agony. 'Are you now trying to control the system that you established? Aren't you ashamed to be—'

'Will you please sit down!'

'I will not sit down!'

'Sit down, I say!' the chairman says, thumping the table now.

The young man makes to leap forward. The soldier, now at a loss what method to apply in pursuance of his duty, looks quickly now at the chairman, now at his prisoner, finally using his random judgment to pull the man down by the collar of his shirt.

'All right,' says the chairman, 'I think I have to put a stop to all this,' removing his spectacles in a flash and blinking a couple of times. 'Guards, take him back to the prison. Mr Aboloje, will you please see your client off to that van and caution him properly. I have no wish to re-open his case until such a time as I am satisfied that he is ready to cooperate with this tribunal. Thank you.'

The young man is led off to the Black Maria by the soldier and a policeman, both armed and wearing implacable faces, like ritual masks. They are holding the boy on either arm. His lawyer gathers his papers with the same distress you could see on his client's face, and follows.

A noisy murmur goes through the audience.

'Silence, everybody,' says the chairman. 'I would like to take this opportunity to deliver a few words of caution. We should all bear in mind that this is a tribunal, not a trial, and I hope the difference is understood. Nobody here is an accused—we only have witnesses among you. Nobody here is being accused under any charges, as in a regular court case. Whoever is called up here for questioning is only a witness being requested by the state, under the terms of reference of this tribunal, to help ascertain a few facts and to help clear the state's doubts in respect of the particular situation under consideration. Everyone here therefore must give his full coopera-tion to the tribunal, and I appeal to all witnesses to take particular note of this. We have a limited time within which to carry out all our investigations and wind up the enquiry. I think it is in everyone's interest that we observe the right sort of conduct so as not to pro-long this period unnecessarily. Any further behaviour of the kind that we have just witnessed will be viewed very seriously by this panel. I hope that is clear.'

He gazes briefly but concentratively at the hall. Then he puts his glasses back on, and sighs.

'All right,' he says. 'Counsel, call the next witness, please.'

Obanye and I look at each other, and smile. If he feels the same way as I do—and I feel certain that he does—then we have just looked at each other not out of any fatalistic thought about what is coming, but as a way of seeking reassurance from each other that we will live up to our manhood, whatever happens. Outside, the light of day is as clear as truth. All that gives me satisfaction, all I really care about, is that God sees through to my conscience. Need I then feel or act otherwise than in accordance with the dictates of a clear conscience and just manhood?

Ali

I cannot pretend to understand the actions and minds of people in general, much less those of a people I don't understand fully yet. It is hard for a military man, I am aware, with all his uniform and his martial gear, to be able to inspire confidence in a people used to a more peaceful life than that which prevails at the moment. But try as I may, I find it hard to guess what was at the back of the mind of an honourable man of this town like Chief Toje, when he confronted me here in my quarters two days ago with the kind of language I could hardly associate with a man of good intentions. It does baffle me.

It was about ten or eleven in the morning. I was getting ready to be driven to inspect the troops in their trenches and posts, and was just tying my boots on. Suddenly I heard a bicycle bell ringing. On looking through the window, I noticed Chief Toje riding towards my quarters. He was all done up, with his feathered hat and long beads, his white collarless long-sleeved shirt, embroidered check wrapper and brown leather shoes, and the stylish ivory walking stick hooked on to the bicycle handle-bar. He was rattling those bells although there were no soldiers in his way. He had gone past the barracks' check point. Since he is our food contractor, he comes here very often, and I had instructed the soldiers to waive the normal security checks in his case and let him through every time he came to the barracks. So he kept rattling those bicycle bells even after he had got through the check, and I began wondering whether he was trying to be extra cautious or was being over-zealous in announcing his presence. But he was here in full distinctive outfit. I was struck by the dignity of the man.

'Hello, Major,' he greeted as he alighted, giving me a big benevolent smile. 'Good morning.'

'*Ah!* Chief,' I responded, with due reverence on my face and person, hurrying up towards him in spite of my loose bootstrings, gripping his proffered right hand in both of mine. '*Migwo*, sir,' I genuflected, following the custom here.

'*Vren, doh,*' he replied, patting my head in a paternalistic gesture.

I showed him to a chair. He sat down, took off his hat and laid it and the walking stick on the ground beside him, still smiling with benevolence.

'You know, Major,' he said, 'every time I come into this barracks of yours, I get a deep feeling of satisfaction.'

'Chief,' I said, 'you know you are always welcome here.'

'No—let me finish,' he held up his hand. 'You don't know what I mean yet. Here you are, fighting a perfectly just war to knock sense into a pack of rascals, doing your utmost to fulfil a noble mission, and here I am doing the very best I can to see that you and your soldiers are well fed and in a state of perfect readiness for the mission. I cannot help feeling that some fellowship joins us together.' I nodded. 'You may say I am being paid for the job, but you cannot deny that it would not be carried out well if I did not put my will into it. Do you get what I am trying to say?'

'Of course, sir. I fully understand.'

'No—listen. I want you to understand me perfectly, for you may go away thinking, Ah, this troublesome old man! But let me tell you something. You weren't here when the federal troops liberated this town over three years ago. I was. It was *we* who brought them in, thanks to the resistance *we* organised in this town against those accursed rebels, which facilitated their rout. But that's another matter. Now, when the federal troops got in here, a few people said they were harassed and molested and all that. But nobody was molested, nobody was touched. These people were only being worried by their own evil conscience, and that's why some of them are where they are today, securely chained by the strong arm of our government. They were never molested—we were only helping the federal troops consolidate their hold on this town, and some of us tried to sort out the bad ones from our midst. That's how all that rumour got around that civilians were being brutalised and even killed. So, because of all this, there was general fear and restlessness throughout this town. It got so bad that hardly anybody was ready to cooperate with the federal troops any more. Can you imagine that? But a few of us leading citizens got up and said, No, this can't be. How can you call a man into your house and after he has entered refuse to let him sit down? It just didn't look right. So we bestirred ourselves. And that was why the food contract was scarcely announced before I submitted my tender. Major Bello, who was in charge then, did not underrate my goodwill. In no time I became food contractor to these forces—I hope I am not holding you from going anywhere? I see you are dressed to go out.'

'Well, not really, Chief,' I said. 'It's all right. I'm sure you have come to talk business with me. It's on your face.'

'Yes, indeed.'

His shirt had two pockets, and from one of them he took out the case for his glasses. There was a great air of knowledge and grandeur about him, as he wiped the glasses with an ear of his wrapper and slipped them carefully over his eyes. I was impressed. From the other pocket he fished out some documents and unfolded them. He cleared his throat.

'Sorry, Chief,' I interrupted. 'What about some whisky?'

'Fine. Fine,' he said. 'We might as well rinse our mouths while we talk!'

I gave orders to my batman, and he produced scotch and two glasses and poured the drinks for us. The Chief tossed the liquid into his mouth in a flash, and blinked hard.

'Good whisky,' he pronounced. 'Good whisky. What brand is this?' He was looking over his spectacles at me.

'Black and White,' I replied.

'Good whisky,' smacking his lips and nodding appreciatively. 'Ehem. Yes.'

He returned to his documents, and I took the opportunity to tie up my boots.

'Now, Chief,' I resumed. 'Is there any problem?' For I noticed some gravity in his looks as he pored over the papers.

'Yes,' he said, taking off his glasses. 'Just one little palaver. I don't want to bother you so often with these food matters, since as you know I should deal directly with the quartermaster. But I must say I don't enjoy the way he has been behaving towards me lately. I am not a small boy, you understand?'

'Very well, Chief, I understand.'

'Yes, but *he* doesn't. Now, I know how much trouble I take to get these yams and plantains and all the rest of the provisions.' The delivery was measured, as grave as his stare. 'But Alao doesn't. I know how bad the roads are, chewed up and broken by the military vehicles and the business of long fighting. You know that too. You also know that farming is no longer as regular as it used to be. There are very few farmers these days. Many of them have gone into the army. Many have run away into the rebel territory. And a large number of those left are afraid to go into the bush for fear of running into a rebel ambush or of stepping upon some deadly object. You were witness the other day to the body of the poor farmer brought in from the bush, mangled beyond all recognition after he stepped upon a hand-grenade. The only reason anybody goes into his farm today is that there is hardly any alternative to keeping body and soul together. Do you understand me?'

I nodded.

'Right. It's therefore a matter of grave surprise to me for the quartermaster to be so inconsiderate, even insolent, in his attitude towards me on account of what he considers the poor condition of the foodstuffs. Look,' he pointed to the documents spread before him, and I obliged by stooping. 'Can you see how he has cancelled the bills? Can you see that?' I nodded again. 'Look at this line. You see how he has cancelled out *Two thousand* and written down *One thousand five hundred?* His reason was that the yams were lean and lifeless and full of rotten stubs and bruises. Now, to begin with, this is not new yam season—new yam season is long past—so how can you expect to find any yams so sleek? Besides, what else happens to yams when you stack them by the hundreds into a lorry but that they get bruised? Or does Alao expect me to wrap every one of them up in cotton-wool or chicken-down just so that they don't get bruised?'

I smiled and shook my head in sympathy.

'Okay. Look again at this line.' Again I did. 'You see, he has done the same thing with plantains. You see—*One thousand seven hundred* for *Two thousand*. His reason? Some of them are ripe and some chipped and bruised. Look, Major. You know the situation,' he said, wiping his sweaty face with an ear of his enormous cloth. 'There are no less than about twelve to fifteen military check points between here and Iddu, and I am sure that is a great underestimate. I have followed one of these lorries that I hire for the transportation on two occasions, and I have sworn never to do so again. We were stopped by the soldiers at each check point and ordered to off-load the entire lorry for a search. Now, you can imagine how long it would take to off-load a whole lorryful of yams, and then load the yams on again, each time taking care to avoid getting the yams all "bruised and chipped", as Alao would like to call them. And that is not to mention the long hours of probing and questioning that the soldiers did at each point, sometimes even threatening to impound the whole load because the bill said *One thousand* and the lorry had one thousand and two yams, which made us in their eyes dishonest people because we had cheated our own selves out of two yams. But to cut a long story short, it took us no less than two days on each trip to reach this town from Iddu. Sometimes it would take my men more time, if by any chance the lorry broke down on the way. Now, Major, under such circumstances, would you not think there was a chance that a few plantains might start ripening—after all, we don't grab them as they are hacked off their branches. We buy them by the heap from our dealers. Do you understand me?'

'I do, Chief.'

'All right. So I said to Alao, suppose you let one or two soldiers ride with my men each time, so as to avoid these endless delays at the military check points? Or, better still, assign just two military trucks for the purpose. I am prepared to negotiate for a reduction on my charges. He said he couldn't, because all trucks were used for transporting troops and military stores, and he couldn't allot two whole trucks for use in hoarding yams and onions and such things. Now, how can any man hold me responsible for delays and results that are not my own making? And all I get is a loss, after all my labour—imagine cutting down all those figures almost by half. I consider that a cheek!'

'All right, Chief, I'll look into the matter,' I said, brushing my shirt sleeve so as to look at my watch.

'It's a cheek! And I don't expect to be treated in this way by a small boy like Sergeant Alao. Nobody in this town treats me in this way—nobody in this town would dare do so.'

'Okay, Chief, I'm sorry. I'll—'

'I am Chief Toje Onovwakpo, and if Alao doesn't know that he should ask round the whole town who I am. Not even the *Otota* would treat me in this fashion. It is a cheek!'

'I'm sorry, Chief. I promise you I'll look into the matter,' I said. 'I agree with you it's a bit difficult, this business of getting the food down here. I'll talk to him. And we'll also look into the question of military escort. I think something has to be done. After all it's the food that *we* will eat. I'm sorry.'

He hissed, and wiped his face again. He folded the documents and put them back in his pocket.

'Have some more whisky, Chief,' I offered. 'You have hardly touched the bottle!'

I filled both our glasses, and he lifted his and took a short draught. He was still wearing that nettled look in his eyes, which the whisky only helped to deepen. I drank a little myself, casting a brief glance over my glass at the man. I was a bit sorry for him, and I thought to myself, He certainly deserves more respect than this. This war isn't my doing any more or any less than it's his; but he obviously enjoys considerable respect in this town. And if I truly hope to keep a secure post, if I hope to maintain a secure rear while I push forward my front, then I owe it to myself to be realistic and secure the goodwill of men like this who can cut my heel if they have a mind to.

That was what came to my mind as I took that brief look at Chief Toje. I probably have a strong and reliable force. But there is no denying that martial success must be guided somewhat by a sense of danger. Only a foolish traveller starves his camel of water.

The Chief took another draught. Then he cleared his throat, and looked at me. All at once his face opened in a narrow-eyed beam, his stained teeth showing.

'Forget it, Major,' he said. 'I'm sorry anyway for bringing a problem to you this early in the day.'

'No, Chief, it's nothing—'

'No, no, no, no, no!' he held up his hand. 'I know you're only trying to be nice. Let's forget all about this, all right? We cannot allow Sergeant Alao to spoil our relationship. You can be sure that I have the greatest respect for you today.'

'Thank you, Chief.'

'Yes, I mean it. I am not joking. I have the greatest respect for a man who can put his foot down and order one of his soldiers shot before the eyes of a whole town, rather than let that soldier spoil the name of an entire army.'

'Well, Chief—'

'No, no, no! I mean it. You know, our people have a proverb which says, "A little ache can spoil a good head." Look, when I was a little romper my mother used to smear pepper over my anus if I fought anybody's child. The result was that any time a child of my age-group insulted me I always thought of pepper before answering him. That's what I call discipline.'

'Well, I thought—'

'You thought rightly, Major. And I admire that speech you made before the execution. It was marvellous.'

'Thank you, sir.'

'Yes.'

He was sitting like a judge, his legs spread, his trunk erect, his head tilted at an authoritative angle.

'I mean it. It was necessary to make it clear to everybody, be they soldier or civilian, that human beings should be respected and no-body should think he was above the law. I think you should really keep a close eye on this town. I don't need to remind you of your duty.'

'Thank you very much, Chief.'

By this time I was getting restless. It was too early in the day to indulge in pleasantries.

He cleared his throat again, and wiped his brow.

'Otherwise, you know,' he continued, 'people would tend to forget that the war was still on, and the emergency too. Besides, there's the need to reassure people of their safety, so long as they conduct themselves properly. And the weak have to be protected.'

'True, Chief.'

I was getting convinced that the whisky was beginning to make its impression on my honoured guest.

'Look, Major, I'm all for you, whatever you decide to do in this town. And you can be sure that when I support you, it's no ordinary support. You can ask them about me in this town,' he said, empha-sising the point with his eyes.

'I know, sir, I'm quite aware.'

'Good. Particularly what you said about the weak and defence-less.' He was eyeing me keenly now. 'You probably don't know it, but there's one such weak and defenceless person whom I'm helping to protect in this town.'

'Oh, really?' I asked.

He nodded. There was something uncanny in his gaze now.

'Three years ago, shortly after the federals took this town, one of our citizens was taken away into detention in Iddu for collaborating with the rebels.'

'Mr Oshevire?'

'That's right. You know about him?'

'Yes.'

'Good. Well, what do you think of him, Major?'

'Actually, sir, I never knew him. As you know, he had been taken away before I assumed this post. So I hardly know anything beyond what I have read in the papers, and of course the little bits of rumour about him that I picked up.'

He looked very closely at me.

'Look, Major,' he said softly, 'let no one fool you with any rumours. That's all they know how to do in this town.'

I nodded in agreement, maybe not so much in belief as merely to be agreeable. He was still gazing at me, and I was beginning to feel there were more words in that gaze than he wished to let fall from his mouth.

'Anyway,' he relaxed, 'he's the one I mean. You probably know too that his wife and child are in this town?'

'No. I mean, I didn't hear that much. But of course I would imagine that as a native of this town he must have relatives still here.'

'Well, not very many,' he shook his head. 'His parents have long since died. Of his relations there are few that he is on good terms with. Some he has angered by refusing to sympathise with them in a long-standing family feud—he is a very stubborn man. Others he has alienated by marrying a rebel.'

'Sir?' I didn't think I heard him properly.

'A rebel,' he leaned over to confirm, with that uncanny glint still in his eye. 'His wife is a Simba.'

'I see.'

I looked at my watch now.

'She's the one I was telling you about. She and her son are very lonely now. The whole town has ostracised them, some in genuine horror at the act for which the man is being detained, and others of course out of fear of being implicated for association. Even his friends have deserted him. And every time there is an air raid by the rebels or guerrilla action around here, she has been very afraid that some people might take it all out on her and her child. So she has kept very much inside their house for fear of being attacked. You can imagine what a plight she is in—unable to trade to make a living for herself and her child, unable even to go to the market to buy food. She once confessed to me that she was afraid they might poison the food they would sell her.'

'Really?'

'Oh, yes,' he was still glaring at me. 'Their town has not been liberated yet, or she would have gone.'

I was touched. *Allah*! I was touched.

'Well, I think I had better take her into protective custody then.'

'Oh no, no, no!' he objected, quite strongly. 'You shouldn't do a thing like that, Major. People would be afraid of you—they would think you were beginning to arrest people one by one for no just cause.'

'But this wouldn't be an arrest, sir.'

'I know. But they wouldn't understand. I know my own people. Besides, these are uneasy times, and the slightest military move is viewed by people with suspicion, even if it is done in their own interest. There's enough fear as it is now. Let's not make the situation any worse. I'm sure you understand.'

I nodded slowly. I thought there was sound sense in what the man said.

'Besides,' continued the Chief, 'as I already told you, I am doing the little I can to ease their suffering. Oshevire and I were in the rubber business, though each man to his own, and I thought I should aid a fellow in his troubles. So once in a while I send her clothes, food, money'—he was emphasising the quantity by gestures of face and hands—'and all sorts of things. I used to go there myself, but I have stopped doing that. You probably don't know what people are like in this town. Gossip, gossip, gossip, all the time. And seeing a big man like me pay frequent visits to a woman— ah! That's fit topic for weeks. And I've got a family of my own too. So these days I send my nephew to take her those things. And any time I think she needs words of comfort and reassurance I ask my nephew to tell her to meet me at his place. I think it's much better that way.'

Again I nodded.

'So you really have no need to worry about her, Major,' he said, 'She is being well taken care of.'

'Well,' I said, somewhat hesitant, 'if you say so, sir.' I was torn between duty and deference to a noble heart.

'That's right,' he emphasised, with that touch of authority.

The matter still exercised my mind, and for a brief moment I was lost in thought.

'Well, Major,' he said, picking up his hat and his walking stick.

'I am sorry to have taken up so much of your time this morning.'

'No, it's all right, sir. The day is still young.'

'Where was it you were going?'

'Inspecting the soldiers in their trenches, sir. Things are still rough, as you know.'

'Quite true. You have my sympathy—it's quite a job keeping the ground you have won and trying to push forward your line at the same time. But let me tell you something,' he looked up at me, ominously, putting the stick down again. 'You military people have as much danger of sabotage from within this very country as from the rebels.'

There was a glare of seriousness in the dull white of his eyes.

'I think you are right, Chief.'

'Did you read the papers this morning?'

'Yes.' I was a bit dubious. I wasn't sure what exactly he had in mind.

'Good. Did you read the editorial comment?'

'Oh—yes. You mean about the tribunal?'

'Exactly. Now, that is the kind of danger that I am talking about.'

He was fixing me with that kind of stare that wants you to say something, a leading stare. I merely responded to that with elusive glances, uncertain, barely indicative of rapport, but agreeable just the same.

'Yes, sir. These newspaper people are trouble-makers.'

'Oh, yes,' he said, full-heartedly. 'Tell me, Major. What have they got to do with that tribunal, if the truth should be told? Just because of a little statement the Military Governor made? They probably believe those people are being held in detention for no just cause. If you ask me, Major, sometimes I think that you soldiers are not exercising your power sufficiently in this country. Everybody thinks they can just say anything they like, and get away with it.'

'Well, sometimes it looks like that,' I said, looking steadily now at him. My smile was gradually fading away. 'Why?'

I thought I had to take that sort of stance.

'Look here, Major, listen.' This time he put down his hat. 'You were not here during the rebel occupation. I was. I can tell you everything that happened.' Again that measured gravity. 'I can tell you all that these traitors did, those of them who were in this town. They have their God to thank, most of them, that they ran away with the rebel troops at the approach of the federal forces. Otherwise a lot of blood would have been spilled in this town by angry people seeking just revenge. Look,' he moved closer to me, 'my wife was in the market one day selling her *garri*. One of these rebel supporters bought a large quantity, and refused to pay. And when my wife challenged him to pay, he called one of their soldiers, and the soldier promptly told my wife to shut up and consider herself lucky her life was being spared her. Now can you imagine a thing like that?'

I nodded faintly. I was still listening.

'And now these newspaper people want the detained men set free, just like that. What kind of justice is that?'

'Yes,' I said. 'I heard a lot of these things happened. I think it was terrible.'

'Terrible!' he spat. 'You mean abominable!'

That stare was still on me. But I was getting used to it by this time. He sat back, and shook his head at me.

'No, Major, you are too good. I don't think you can appreciate the seriousness of what these people did. Besides, you weren't here to witness it all.'

'No, sir. I think I quite understand what you are saying. As I said, I heard a lot about what they did when they were in occupation of this state. I am a soldier myself, and I know what soldiers are capable of.'

'Oh, yes. But their soldiers were horrible. *Horrible.*'

He kept watching me.

'And I can give you the name of every single man in this town who collaborated with them. I know them. Most of them ran away with their soldiers, when they smelt what was coming to them. Only a few unfortunate ones stayed behind.'

I kept nodding, and he kept staring.

'You see Oshevire—the one they are detaining at Iddu?'

'Yes.' I became interested.

'Well—hm,' he dismissed. 'I don't want to say anything. But do you know what he did?'

'What was it?'

'Major, I don't want to say anything. But he was one of the worst rebel supporters in this town. The way he was fraternising with those people, the numerous secret meetings he—Hm, look Major, I don't want to tell you anything.'

This time I was the one staring at him, and he the one avoiding my eyes. Indeed, he was a little uneasy, and you could see him rubbing his hands together endlessly, barely holding himself from saying what he wanted to say.

'Wonderful,' I said, half urging him to continue.

'You see that tribunal they are holding at Iddu?' I nodded. 'I hope they do the right sort of thing after it. And I think they should ask further questions, gather all the facts, and—well, I don't want to talk. But tell me, Major, are you not in any way helping them in their enquiries?'

'Eh, no sir,' I said, hesitantly. For I wasn't sure what he meant.

'You mean that if the tribunal asked you, in your position as commander of the forces in this town, indeed, as commander of this town—almost—if the tribunal asked you to furnish them with facts you wouldn't tell them anything?'

'Like what, sir?'

'Like, for instance, helping to furnish them with further information on how some of these people here collaborated with the rebel forces.'

'But, sir,' I chuckled, half-amused, 'I don't know anything.'

'Yes, but you could ask questions, and I'm sure you wouldn't find the whole town unwilling to cooperate with you.'

'But the tribunal wouldn't do that. That's not my job. I'm a soldier, and my mission here is to fight to protect my area of command. I have nothing to do with the tribunal. They know I'm just a soldier.'

He shook his head, and I thought I could read disappointment on his face.

'Still, I think the newspaper people are wrong,' he said. 'I don't think those people should be freed from detention before the entire truth of what they did is out.'

'I agree with you, sir,' I concurred. I felt called upon to do so, seeing him in that mood.

'Well, Major,' he said, picking up his hat and walking stick again, and rising. 'I won't keep you any further. The day is fast advancing, and we each have a lot of work to do.'

He picked up his glass and tossed in the last of the whisky.

'Thank you very much for calling, Chief,' I said as I rose after him. 'I hope we'll be seeing each other very soon.'

'Oh, yes. Very soon, Major. Very soon.'

He took his time stepping down, and out. I was following him at a respectful distance.

'I think I'll try to see you later in the day,' I said. 'Then we can spend some more time. Sorry I'm in a bit of a hurry this morning.'

'No, no, no! That's all right. See me when you are free later today. There's a lot to talk about these days.'

'Quite true, Chief.'

'Right. Goodbye, Major.'

'Goodbye, Chief.'

He pulled his bicycle to, and kicked up the stand. I stood aside to see him mount. He balanced the walking-stick along the pole, hooking it over the handle-bar. Then he raised his right leg over the bicycle. But the wrapper had got hooked to the carrier behind. He hissed and cursed, bringing the leg down again and pulling in the cloth. I thought I heard a word like 'dare', or something like that. I can't remember now. Well, he balanced the bicycle in a firmer grip, threw the leg over it again, got seated, and pushed off.

'Goodbye, Chief,' I called after him.

But he didn't say a word. He just waved and rode off, hunched over the bicycle in all the imposing style of a man who owned a good deal. Again that ceaseless rattling came from his bell, all down the open path and even past the check-point at the gate where the soldiers had respectfully pulled up the bamboo barrier to let him through. Allah, that man is something!

Well, I got back into the house. I sat down for a while to ponder the whole incident. It probably didn't amount to very much at the time. I was sure the Chief was an honourable man. If a man felt strongly about anything, then of course the need would arise some-time for him to let it out of his belly. And if the man was an honour-able man like Chief Toje, his honour and his grandeur would in no way be diminished for the fact that he let his passion overflow.

But somehow I could not fight the feeling that I was taking a chance. What if there was something in all this? I tried to think back systematically over all that took place that morning between the Chief and me. And that poor woman's plight haunted my mind. For how much goodwill could the Chief have felt towards her, if he felt so badly about her husband's role during the rebel occupation of this town and even welcomed his detention? Think how deeply he denounced the collaborators' role. Fair enough. Then think how readily he objected to my taking the woman into protective cus-tody, when if he really cared for her welfare he should have been sure that she could count on no better safeguard against the town's thirst for vengeance.

So I made up my mind. I was prepared to give the Chief due respect, but I was going to draw a line on that. Beyond that line lay my concern for the safety of Oshevire's wife and the federal will. Beyond it lay the consideration that the woman was free to live in this town like everybody else, and I wasn't going to let any-thing rob her of that right. If she died it was a terrible shame.

I called my batman. He came up briskly and saluted.

'At ease, Dombraye,' I said.

'Yes, sir,' he replied, relaxing.

'Listen, where does Corporal Akpoterabo come from?'

He raised his eyes to the ceiling in thought.

'Doesn't he come from this town?' I asked.

'I don't think so, sir,' he replied, hesitantly, shaking his head.

'Well, do you know any of our soldiers who comes from this town?'

'Yes, sir.'

'Who is that?'

'Private Okumagba, sir. Of "B" Company.'

'My own Company? Good. Call him here at once.'

'Yes, sir.' He saluted and was off.

Something had to be done at once. I owed that to my conscience.

Okumagba was introduced to me, and saluted, his face stern as the devil.

'You can leave us now, Dombraye.'

'Yes, sir!'

I turned to Okumagba.

'At ease.'

He relaxed.

'You come from this town, not so?'

'Yes, sir,' he replied, quickly and with a proud smile.

'Good,' I said, looking down and rubbing my nose a little. 'Do you know about this man called Oshevire—the one being detained at Iddu?'

At once his face contracted.

'Yes, sir,' he seemed to say through clenched teeth.

I trained my eyes on him.

'What do you know about him?'

He cleared his throat, and looked down.

'He was a rebel supporter, sir.'

'Was he?'

'Yes, sir.'

'How do you know?'

'Everybody in this town knows that, sir.' He shifted a bit from his position.

'Yes, I heard so. But how do they know?'

He swallowed once or twice, still shifting uneasily.

'The rebels were always in his house, sir, and . . . and . . . he was always with them. He was supporting them, sir. He was siding with them.'

'I see,' I said after a while.

I could see he was uncomfortable. I didn't wish to trouble him any further. He had a right to his prejudices, and he wasn't alone in his conviction.

'Ehm, do you know about his wife?'

'Yes, sir.'

'I hear she is very lonely. Do you think anybody will do anything to her in this town?'

He looked down. The contortion showed once again on his brow.

'I don't know, sir. I can't say, sir. Well, you can never tell. Maybe they will do something, maybe they won't. I can't say, sir. But she is a rebel, and . . . I can't say, sir.'

I sighed. The picture was all very clear to me. I had to do something determined.

'Okumagba.'

'Sir,' he stiffened up to attention.

'I am putting that woman in your care.'

'Sir?'

'I said I was putting Mrs Oshevire under your protection,' I said, raising my voice and my eyes to him.

'Yes, sir!'

He was like a cornered rabbit, frightened and uneasy.

'And you'd better make sure nothing happens to her.'

'Yes, sir.'

'Where does she live?'

'In their house, sir.'

'I know. Where is their house?'

'In the middle of the town, sir. Close to the town council hall.'

'How close?'

'About . . . about fifty yards, sir.'

'Can one see the house clearly from the town council—or are there any houses in between?'

'One can see clearly, sir.'

'Good. Listen to me.' He maintained stiff attention. 'Listen carefully, because this is going to be your detail from now on, until I decide to call it off. At six o'clock every morning you should pick up your gun—fully loaded—and station yourself by the council hall, in a position that gives you a good view of the woman's house. You will pretend to be guarding the council premises, and that is what you should say if anybody tries to question you. But from there you should watch the woman's house very carefully. Make sure she doesn't find out that you are keeping her under surveillance, or she might become frightened of a soldier's presence. But watch that house very closely. Do not disturb either her or her son. And do not molest anyone going to visit her. I hear nobody visits her, but once in a while you will see Chief Toje or his nephew. Do you know Chief Toje?'

'Yes, sir.'

'And his nephew?'

'I think I know who you mean, sir. He is a cripple, one-handed. He works for the Chief, sir.'

'What's his name?'

'Odibo, sir.'

'Good. Don't bother any of them. I think they are trying to help her. Do you understand all I have said?'

'Yes, sir.'

'Good. You should be there from six in the morning to twelve midnight. Arrangements will be made to get you your meal at the appropriate times. If you find anybody around after seven-thirty when the curfew begins, arrest that person at gun-point. But don't shoot, unless the person tries to resist arrest. And, as I said, don't let anyone know your exact mission. Now, is that clear?'

'Yes, sir!'

'Good. And remember this: whatever happens to that woman will happen to you. Is that clear?'

'Yes, sir!'

'You are dismissed.'

'Yes, sir!'

He saluted briskly, and marched off.

Well, that was it. I was sure I was doing the right thing—at least I was trying to do my best. You can't please everybody, but you can try to do your best. For Chief Toje I kept my respect, and still do. But that woman meant more than just the wife of a detained man. For me she was the measure of justice. Besides, I have enough trouble as it is already, and I don't want any more. Of course, my military duty here is paramount, and everything else is secondary. But I wasn't going to look idly on while people here— whatever their position in the community—used me to police their prejudices. If I didn't take the decision I did, I might find myself faced in the end with a situation in which everybody thought they could do whatever they liked, just because I was trying to ensure that life went on as normal here. *Allah*, no!

Odibo

What use is this awkward mass of a body, he said, if you cannot help yourself. And you have no mind. No sense. Nothing. All you have is a huge body. And that is no use to anyone. No use at all, not even to yourself. Utterly useless. . . .

I know I am not worth much. Or anything. I know I cannot help myself or anybody. I cannot think or do anything. But it is hardly my fault. I have only one good arm. And what can a man do with only one arm? They say I inherited it from one of my family long dead. I don't know. All I ever grew up to see was a stump where a left arm should be. And however it came about—my getting one arm instead of two like everybody else—is it impossible that the same fate that gave me one arm should have addled my brain?

I don't know. Perhaps I will never know. Perhaps I am not supposed to know. But I only wish that Toje would make less of it. I am quite satisfied going along with the lorry every now and then to Iddu to bring down the foodstuffs for the soldiers. I worked on his rubber plantation when things were peaceful. Before the war came, and we stopped doing the rubber. I was happy then, and satisfied. I didn't complain. And I am not complaining now. Now that I go with the trucks to Iddu for the soldiers' foodstuffs.

But things have changed. Ever since Toje became mixed up with Oshevire's wife. Calling me names in her very presence. Telling her I am no use, to my very hearing. Pointing to my crippled arm and saying what can I do with only one arm. That I am useless, and that without him I would be a dead man by now because I can't fend for myself. It is not fair, to try to disgrace me in the presence of somebody else, and a woman at that. I know I am not much use, but he should at least allow me a little pride. And give me a chance. For maybe someday I can try to do something to help myself, and stand on my two feet. And then I won't have to offend his sight any longer. And he won't need to bring shame upon me, most of all in the presence of a woman.

Now I am on my way, as usual, to call her. I hate to have to go. For every time I see her I think of what Toje always does to me in her presence. I don't know why he does so. And I don't feel happy every time I see her. Who knows, one day she too will tell me I am no use to her, no more use than to bring her food and clothes and summon her to a meeting with Toje in my house.

I don't like the whole business. I know I have no choice. I cannot protest against this strange service, for one word could rob me of all the favours that Toje sees fit to bestow upon me in his kindness: food, old clothes, even the very glory that I am in his service and under his control. But I know I don't like the whole business. Formerly, I would summon her from her house, and I would stay outside my place while Toje met with her and her son Oghenovo. Now she comes alone. For Toje says I should stay in her house and look after her son while she comes alone to meet him in my place. I don't like it. But what can I do?

Yet, if the truth should be told, what has he got to do with her—and alone with her in my place? I cannot now remember, but I do not think that Toje had much cause to pay frequent visits like this to Oshevire while he was a free man, before the soldiers came and took him away. And now he makes me take much food and clothing to her at her house. And asks me to tell her to come and meet him at my place. It is all very strange, this business with another man's wife in the secrecy of my wretched place, that can hardly provide any sort of comfort to decent people.

I don't like the whole thing. And I don't like the woman. I can't understand what it is that they are doing with each other. I suppose I am not meant to understand. But as long as that woman is around, I know I will continue to be an object of ridicule. And perhaps one day she too will laugh at me. Women are like that. And that is why all my life I have had nothing to do with any woman. It is bad enough with men. Women would only drive me to kill myself. . . .

Sometimes I dream mighty dreams. I dream I am a full man, complete with everything, including two strong and healthy arms.

Ruling over this whole town, and sitting comfortably on top of inexhaustible riches, and my house paved with gold. I wake up cursing God for burdening my sleep with such painful fancy. For I know I can never realise even the minutest portion of that wild fantasy. I don't have anything up my head. And something my late father said to me long, long ago keeps coming back to my mind any time it dares run away with itself: *God never leaves a job half done....*

The day is slowly drawing to a close. My only prayer is that they be quick with whatever it is I am about to invite the woman to my house for. And that curfew time come quickly on, so that I can be once again the occupant of my wretched hovel. I don't like this whole business. But what can I do?

Aku

I took it all for good intentions. What else would you call it, if a man came to you with food when hunger threatened your life and that of your child, brought clothes to you when you had neither the money nor the freedom to go out and shed yourself of your rags, traded good cheer with you to beguile the gloom of solitude and the burden of painful thoughts?

Yet, I know, I saw it coming. I cannot deceive myself about it now. I am still a young woman. My skin is firm, my breasts are still a handful, and only one child has passed through my womb. So I cannot now in all honesty say it would never come to the mind of any man to want me. But until Toje laid his hand on me, and breathed the hot breath of desire down my body, I was still willing to let doubt rule my mind and read nothing but good intentions in all he did for me.

I was at home with Oghenovo. He had suffered a wound from the wooden bar that he had set up in the yard for jumping, and the wound now became a little sore, on the shin. I had washed this sore and came in to rub palm-kernel grease over it. It was then that I noticed Odibo coming towards the house. He was wearing that grave and begrudged look that I have always known him with, stepping towards the house with his head facing downward and his legs taking slow and uncertain steps. He seemed to come against his will. If I didn't know him I would have said the screaming heat of the afternoon put that look on his face. But I didn't mind. If I am at their mercy, and I know I am, then I should be prepared to accept their moods. What difference would it make to the dog whether the food was hurled at him or served up in gleaming china?

'Nothing wrong, I hope?' I asked.

For even after he stepped into the house he still wasn't looking at me and didn't offer a greeting, his eyes scanning the floor nervously like a dog looking for fleas.

I still had Oghenovo's leg in my lap, with my greasy hand rested on it near the spot of the sore. Odibo shuffled about for a while (I was following him with my anxious eyes), then leaned against the wall with the shoulder of the whole arm, not the crippled one. He was looking out through the door, past me and my son, looking begrudged and hang-dog as ever. I sighed, then rubbed Oghenovo's sore leg a little more.

'What is the matter now?' I ventured, for I didn't like this kind of silence, with the man standing so menacingly behind me and my boy. 'Have you brought a message?'

'He says come.'

I looked at him.

'Now?'

He grunted in the affirmative.

I sighed, and finished the job on my son's leg. I heard the man ease off and sit on the floor.

'I suppose I will have to lock up the house and take Oghenovo along with me?' I asked.

'He says I should stay here with the boy.'

He still wasn't looking at me, or he was stealing furtive glances now and then—I could almost feel the pinch of his eyes. I was somewhat confused. The sun was departing now, slowly, but daylight was still very much in evidence and certainly it wasn't time for people to be having their evening meals. I had two choices before me, or three. If I wanted to respond to the urgency of Toje's call, I should have left right away and let Odibo feed my son when supper-time came. But I couldn't well leave what my son was going to put in his belly at the mercy of such a man as I saw around me. So I had to feed him now or when I came home from Toje's call. But he might be too hungry by the time I got back. . . .

I rummaged the kitchen. But there was no food, nothing cooked that my boy could eat at the time. So I took a quick decision. I could still feel the madman's eyes, searing my back as I laboured to fix my son a meal. But I didn't mind. I was content to obey their wishes, seeing I had no other choice now. If they had now decided to end the allowance, whatever might be the reason for that, then there was nothing we could do about it but wait and die. *Venture out into the market and face a determined mob one day, or stretch our feet and sit down while hunger ate us up—it would all be the same. . . .*

Our soup was finished—I could have made Oghenovo a quick *eba* and let him have a full meal. Luckily, there was some dry fish left on the ledge over the fireplace. I brought it down and broke off a fair piece. It was like a godsend. For if I had waited to cook the boy a meal before I left, that could have taken some time and I would be taking a double risk—the displeasure of my new lord and benefactor, and the approach of the curfew. So, hurriedly I set the fish down, threw two handfuls of *garri* into a plate and poured some water into it. I drained off the floating dirt, poured in a bit more water and threw a pinch of salt into the *garri*. In no time the boy was settled to the makeshift meal while I took a quick bath.

Oghenovo had finished his meal by the time I came back in. The haste with which I was carrying on told him I was soon going to be off somewhere. He looked at me, then at Odibo on the floor, who had not spoken a word since. He kept following me as I moved from one part of the house to another. Even into the room and out again. He had left his plates on the floor.

'Aren't you going to take those plates away to the kitchen?' I asked him.

He picked them up and disposed of them, unwilling that they should constitute an obstacle to my response to his questioning looks.

'Mama?' it came at last.

'Yes?'

'Where are you going?'

'Somewhere—now stop following me about like a policeman, you hear?'

He slowed down a bit. One more look at the seated Odibo made it clear to him that I was really going to be away from the house. He relaxed on the floor himself, a heavy look on his face. It had happened before, and he knew there was nothing he could do to stop me. Not even crying.

Before long I was dressed and ready. I took one more look at my son, and I swear if I could help it I would have stayed. It is a dreadful thing to be at the mercy of someone, the slave of a compulsion you know you cannot fight. That boy is all the reason I am putting up this feeble fight. Well, maybe not the *only* reason. For I think too that I must stay on to prove that I have faith in my man, that if they are truly going to do anything drastic to him in the end, his wife has a duty to live through it all. But that boy is reason enough. In him I constantly see my man before me, in him I am constantly reminded of my duty to love and cherish the memory of a man to whom that much attention is due. So I walked across to him and rubbed his head, barely stopping the plaintive tears from streaming down his eyes.

'I won't be long, my son,' I reassured him.

'Why don't you let me go along with you?'

'Odibo is here to keep you company,' was my feeble reply. 'There is no need to worry now, you hear?'

He cast a hesitant look at Odibo, then nodded, twisting the ear of his shirt and pouting his mouth.

I looked across at Odibo. I knew I had little reason to expect goodwill from a man who walked straight into my house without offering me greeting—without even looking at me—as though he had come to collect a debt. But I felt certain that, if it was the wish of Toje who sent him that he should keep watch over my boy while I stayed away, he was bound to do so. That much I could see. Beneath that seeming hostility of the man was the unquestioning servility of a dog. Or maybe his crippled arm was the reason. For as he sat there before me I could also see that he was making every effort to hide his defect, casting furtive glances now and then as though he thought someone was about to unveil his stump of an arm.

'Please look after Oghenovo,' I said. 'Make sure he doesn't stray from the house.'

He merely nodded and grunted, shifting a bit on his seat, but still looking away. I thought to myself. *If times were normal.* . . . I knew I had made a gratuitous request. I felt so. But if I found myself face to face with the potential killer of my son I thought at least I had a right to a dialogue. *If times were normal* . . .

On my way I heard the evening cock crow, and I knew I didn't have very long to keep from my house before curfew time. I greeted nobody. Nobody greeted me. I have become used to this state of affairs. I have the Major to thank that I am alive today. If he had not openly declared himself committed to protecting the lives of people and their freedom of movement in this town, whatever of this is left to people like me, how could I hope to be up and about when the evening cock called the town to retire, confronting at every step the vile faces of people that not only ignored my presence but indeed wished I was never there, and propelled by the call to keep tryst with a kindness I couldn't refuse?

And I think too that I have the curfew to thank. For it could have been one of many things. They could have surprised my son and me in a midnight attack and despatched us with the minimum of uproar. Or they could have secretly set fire to our house. Or, these days when deadly items of war lie around bushes and footpaths like ordinary pebbles, they could have hurled one of those things into our house and blasted the life out of my son and me. But thank God, they are sufficiently afraid for their lives to know that they should not stray beyond their doorposts when the military order has said no movements after half past seven. Besides, these days a soldier guards the council hall just across the road all day and, I think, all night too. If anything threatened our lives, a desperate shriek from me would alert him to action, if only because he had a duty to combat a rebel invasion rather than save the life of a rebel.

When I finally got to Odibo's house I knew Toje was there. His bicycle stood leaning against the trunk of a tree just outside. The door was ajar. I approached it and knocked gently. There was no reply from within. I looked back to see if there was anyone in sight. There were none of the adults in the neighbourhood around. There was just one little naked girl, stooping to defecate in the yard. She was staring so steadily at me that I began to develop some feeling of guilt: whether for prying into her private affair or for perching alone at someone else's doorstep and looking round like a burglar making a last cautious check, I cannot now tell.

I quickly looked away from her, and gave the door a gentle push. Over in the bedroom to the right was my big benefactor. I could hardly believe the picture I saw before me. A big old dandy, all done up and dozing in style! His hair was combed and neatly parted from the temple right up to the crown, oiled and brushed too—very delicate and impressive. His face was powdered, and there was a generous dab of talc on his neck, with thin rings of sweat marking off the folds of it. His collarless long-sleeved shirt was of spotless white, and for a sleeping man the shirt-tails were too neatly smoothed over his wrapper. The wrapper was an eight-yard George with brilliant red checks, it too laid and folded in neat order. A pair of well-polished and heavily soled black shoes were on his feet. One leg was resting on the floor, while the other, the right, was carefully laid along the edge of the bed. Of this, part of the big hairy thigh showed slightly under the wrapper. I am ashamed to admit it, but that brief confrontation with manhood stirred the woman in me, long dormant with fear and disuse. I quickly turned my eyes from it, but at once noticed the brilliant white handkerchief resting near the right arm on the bed. The bed itself had been done up and transformed from the crude bamboo frame that I had seen the last time I had been in that hut. For it was now laid with two pillows and an overflowing spread of blue-striped covering. It was all an impressive scene, and contrasted very sharply with the rest of the setting inside the room.

During this survey the man had been slumbering steadily, and snoring. He didn't know I was there. But I didn't have very much time, and had to announce my arrival.

'I am sorry I kept you waiting so long for me,' I said.

'Eh? Eh?' the old man rustled up on his seat, rubbing his hand across his dripping mouth and blinking to full wakefulness. 'Pardon me. What was it you said?'

'I said I was sorry I kept you so long.'

'Oh no, no, that's all right. I was just—'

'*Migwo*,' I genuflected.

'*Vren, doh,*' he responded. 'I just decided to take a little nap while I waited for you. It has been a very busy day for me. Sit down,' he said, indicating a position on the bed beside him.

I pretended I didn't see him, and was walking towards a bench near the window when he called me back.

'No. I mean *here*.'

'It's all right, sir. I think this seat is fine,' I said, smiling just to soothe his possible displeasure.

'No, no. Come on now,' he insisted, trying hard by an equally tired smile to avoid being unpleasant. 'I think it is better here. Come on now.'

I hesitated, for I had a feeling of suspicion, though I cannot now swear that as a full-grown woman I did not know the ways of men. But then I quickly thought to myself, *What would I lose if I did? What wouldn't I lose if I didn't?* and so let discretion get the better of tired conscience.

Well, I went over to him and sat where he had indicated—close to him. The bamboo bed creaked under our combined weight. Toje shifted to make more room, chuckling it seemed at the poverty of the place that was now having to accommodate us. There was a little gap between us, but—my God—I could feel his presence all over me. It was probably not from his heavy breathing or the scent of the perfume which he seemed to have so generously put on his person. I think I must have been thoroughly overwhelmed to find myself in such an unfamiliar and uneasy confrontation with a man whose supreme personality circumstances had brought me to acknowledge even from a distance. I could smell it all now. After all, I am a woman, and I don't think the present situation has robbed me of my judgment yet. I was prepared to see how much I could take or mildly oppose without losing my sense of shame or his favour. It was a delicate situation, and up till that point I was still prepared to let doubt rule my mind. I had to be careful. What would I lose if I did? And if I let indiscreet valour undo my son and me, the same world would laugh at me that would judge me an incontinent whore if I let discretion prevail. And what wouldn't I lose if I didn't?

He put his head back on the bed. I was waiting, not without disquiet, to see what he was going to do next. The situation was so delicate as to be almost frightening, and I was then ready either to run or to scream if he wasn't careful what he did. I could hear his breathing. The room was very quiet, almost frighteningly so—so that when a gecko lashed its tail on the ceiling mat I looked up in panic. Yes, I could hear his old-man breathing, but it came in such smothered gusts you would think an alligator was upon you. He still hadn't made a move, but I kept waiting.

'How is your son—is he well?' he sat up to say, bearing close upon my shoulder, with his breathing and all.

'He is quite well,' I replied. 'He just has this little sore on his leg which I am nursing, but—'

'Sore? How did he get it?'

'He set up a jumping bar in the yard—you know how these children are. I kept telling and telling him he might get injured one day. But he wouldn't listen. That's how he got the wound. And he never reported it to me until it grew into a sore and the pain became too much for him. Believe me, that child has tired me.'

'Oh, don't worry. Little children. They will always play, only they are never careful enough.'

I hissed.

He edged closer to me, and put his hand on my lap. I flinched instinctively. But I didn't say a word. He must have seen from even this limited reaction that I was wavering between grudging acquiescence and unspoken protest. And I noticed that he himself was far from steady.

'How is your son—I mean, how are you? Are you well yourself?' he said, removing his hand from my lap and putting it across my shoulder.

'Well,' I said, resignedly enough to make an impression, 'I am alive. Can I ask for more than that now?'

'You don't need to worry about anything. Everything will be all right.'

'I keep hoping and praying so. But whatever happens to me now, I don't think there is anything I can do but take it as it comes.'

'Nothing will happen. Leave that to me—'

'But they have had him for three years now, and I have heard nothing of him.'

'They can't do anything to him—unless I am no longer Toje.'

'Yes, but they have guns.'

'I know. But they still listen to people like me.'

'It's all in the hands of God.'

'Don't worry. My efforts have not slackened. Do you know what is happening at the moment?'

'What?' I turned my eyes to him.

'I have got in touch with a number of army officers. And they assure me that they have really not found anything against him, and that the only reason he hasn't been released is that the authorities are very angry about the continuing air and guerrilla attacks on this town. Otherwise,' he lowered his hand again into my lap, 'it won't be long before you have your man back again.'

'Oh, my God,' I shook my head, feeling once again in my heart the usual tussle between hope and fear. At this very moment it didn't seem to matter very much to me that the man's hand was pressing more firmly into my lap.

And he wasn't very easy. I could feel it. But I didn't know what to do or say. I wanted very much to distract him, but under the circumstances I didn't know how to proceed. The man's behaviour quite surprised me. His hand was still down in my lap. Now he began to rub my thigh, and when I looked up I saw a strained smile on his face—strained both by the very effort he seemed to put into it and even by the result it seemed to force. For I could detect spots of sweat on his nose and his forehead. I don't know how it happened, but somehow it came out of my mouth.

'Please,' I said, 'Please don't.'

'Why?'

I had no answer for that.

'Hm? Why?' he repeated, as his now quaking hand dug deeper into my lap.

'Please.'

'Come on,' his voice was quaking too. 'Why won't you? Why?'

'You know how I feel. My heart is not settled.'

'I know,' he said. 'But you don't have to worry all your life.'

'Please. Think what—'

It just came out of my mouth. And because I had not reasoned it I did not have enough words to say it all out.

'Hm? You don't have—you—you don't have to brood all your life. You must give yourself some relief.'

'Please,' I pleaded again.

But he wouldn't let go of me. Indeed he seemed to be struggling much more than was necessary. For I could feel myself slowly giving in. I am ashamed to admit it, but desire in me had accumulated like pus in a boil. However much I tried to fight the man's crude advances, I knew that the most gentle touch would do to release this pent-up feeling. He did not seem to lose time about it, but now tried to take full advantage of my defencelessness, pulling me down with him onto the bed and working away with his hand on my person with the blind fumbling of a child unwrapping a sensational gift. My God, how brittle a woman can be. . . .

Something suddenly struck me. I looked up at once, opened my eyes to look at the man's face. It was streaming with sweat, and I could see his teeth behind his slightly parted lips, clenched and clattering, his breathing hard and animal-like and his eyes closed either from that wild animal ecstasy or under the pressure of the effort he so frighteningly seemed to be making. And then he let go of my lap at once. He shook his head and hissed, raising his trunk on his two arms over me. I stared on at him, with frightened wonder in my eyes, but all he did was shake his head once again and hiss. He eased up and sat at the edge of the bed, sighing heavily but still showing signs of the perturbation which seemed to have forced him from his attempt on me.

'I must be tired,' he said, dabbing his face and neck with subdued panic, so unsteady were his hands. 'It was quite a busy day for me.'

'I understand,' I said. I couldn't afford under the circumstances to deny him the rapport.

'Yes. And—and then, that talk about your husband. . . . I don't think you should have mentioned him. Because it put me off,' he seemed to gulp. 'Anyway,' he said, sighing now, and dabbing his face and neck once again, 'I think it was more the tiredness. I was too tired. A tired man shouldn't—shouldn't try to do a thing like this, certainly not—not such a busy man as myself.'

'Yes. I think you are right.'

I began to cover myself up. I sat up slowly, and smoothed the cloth over my legs. He didn't object at all. He even seemed to ignore me.

And then I began to hate myself. The anger rose slowly within me as I looked myself over. For look what a fool I had made of myself. How much, really, could I have lost if I had said no to the man? Could he have been such a fool as not to understand that, if a woman didn't want to do anything with a man, her honour, not to say her pride, should be respected? Come and meet me at such and such a place: and you came. Lie down: and you spread your wretched self on the bed. Open your legs: and you obeyed like a patient without any choice. And all this time you offered nothing that could be called resistance. You couldn't summon up the courage to tell him to his face that what he was doing was wrong and unjust. You couldn't ask him how he would have felt if he had been away three years in detention and then came back to learn that all that time his wife had been prostituting herself to somebody else for mere food and clothing! *My God, I hated myself.* And then you let him mess you up, mess you up as a child messes up his meal, and then leave you there on the bed bristling in an unfulfilled passion, an unfinished job, like a half-pulled snail, with the rest of the body left bristling inside the shell. I hated the whole world, but hated myself most of all. . . .

I hissed, shook my head and let the hanging tear fall from my eye. When I looked up I saw that darkness was setting in. The insects were beginning to cry, and the air now carried with it the smell of smoke from neighbourhood fires.

'I must be leaving,' I said, as I rose from the bed. 'The time is upon me.'

'Oh, yes,' he shook himself up, sighing heavily yet again. 'You must be going, and I'll be seeing you some other time. I'll send for you.' He dug his hand into a fold, brought out a purse, and took some money out. 'Take this,' he said without looking me in the eye. 'You may not be buying anything, but keep it all the same.'

'*Migwo*,' I said with a choked voice, genuflecting.

'Oh, don't worry. That's nothing.'

He opened the door to let me out—he seemed to be in a hurry to get rid of me. And I could not bear to look at his face any more.

'Good night, sir.'

'Good night,' he said, pushing the door shut behind me.

I stood briefly at the doorstep to look myself over, to convince myself at least that I was not wearing the shame on me. Then I stepped out. Instinctively I looked ahead of me to see if that little girl was still around. The girl wasn't there. But there was an old woman struggling to drag a haltered goat into the house. I seized the opportunity to step into the road and walk quickly homeward.

I could hardly fight the feeling of shame, now further complicated by fear at once more stepping into the unfriendly open. For when I looked at people's faces on the way I seemed to be trying hard to read their dispositions. Might they vent their anger now? Do I wear the disgrace unmistakably on my person? And the darkness kept growing. Human movement was now reduced to a trickle, and military vehicles whipped past the road.

When I got to my house I saw the door closed. There was no light inside, no sound. I stopped in my tracks. For the solitude was too much for me. Luckily a window was open, and luckily again there was still enough light to see objects if only in their faint outlines. I peeped in through the window, and—! My rearing heart settled down again. They were there, sleeping together. I went across and pushed the door open. I went into the kitchen and brought a hurricane lamp, and lit it. They still didn't stir, and I took the opportunity to take a good look at the strange comradeship. I was moved no end, seeing my son so fondly wrapped in the bosom of a man whose goodwill I could have stoutly denied.

And what a fine man he was too. In the negligence of sleep he had not covered up his stumped arm properly, for it stuck out from under a fold of the cloth with which he had so anxiously hidden it when he had first entered. But the rest of his body be-spoke a man—now that, happily, sleep had stripped him of his pretences and thrown him bare to my stolen gaze. . . .

I quickly looked away. For something inside me told me it was all wrong. My heart had been burdened enough for one evening by that forbidden encounter with manhood, and I wanted no more sorrows.

'Wake up,' I clapped. 'I am back.'

He didn't hear me. He was snoring away, with his mouth open. So I walked across the room and dragged a chair. Slowly he came to, and I could see the wild surprise in his eyes as they tried to familiarise themselves with the atmosphere around them. He shut his mouth, and swallowed. He sat up, and when he noticed I was looking at him he quickly drew the cloth over his stumped arm. I could read the curse in his eyes. I withdrew my gaze, not so much apologetically as in a manner to assure him that his deformity never really caught my attention.

'When did you come back?' he said in a clumsy, half-awake tone. And I was glad to hear him talk to me.

'I just came in. You two must have been sleeping for a long time.'

He struggled up on his feet, taking care with his one hand not to disturb his partner. I saw he was not having an easy time, and I ran to help him.

'Leave off,' he seemed to say in a warning tone.

I was slightly shaken. I knew at once I should have left him to settle the boy all by himself, for helping him would have brought home to him his insufficiency. I was sorry. And for a brief moment I was struck to notice that behind that cruelty of nature lay some amount of will.

'Thank you,' I said.

He grunted in response.

'I hope the rascal did not give you too much trouble,' I said, to relax the atmosphere.

He shook his head, as he yawned deeply and rubbed the crust of sleep off his eyes.

'I think I must be going now,' he said.

'Won't you wait to eat whatever there is?'

'No. Thank you. It's growing dark now.'

'That's true,' I said, looking outside. 'It's almost curfew time.'

He looked down at Oghenovo, and eased an ill-rested leg of the sleeping boy.

'Thank you,' I said, deeply impressed, even joyed.

He nodded.

'I'm going now. Goodnight.'

'Goodnight,' I replied warmly. 'Take care on the way.'

He didn't say a word in reply, he didn't even turn back. I stood at the door to watch him as he went, and in a short while the darkness hid him away. For a while I stared after him blankly, into the empty darkness, my mind roving aimlessly now in its own dim cogitation. It took a harsh sound from nearby—a cough from Oghenovo I think it was—to call me back to reality. I shut and bolted the door, and walked back in.

I lifted my boy clear of the ground where he was lying and carried him to the bed, bringing the lamp along. Then I sat by the edge of the bed to think again. This time it was clear to me what kind of life I was now trapped in. I could very clearly see my role: Toje's whoring mistress, bound to minister to his animal desire at the price of food and clothing, maybe even protection and occasional words of comfort, forced to remain in this town and in this house, a prisoner not so much of the present military situation as of a stubborn resolve to last out the trials of my man and prove to him that he had not lost everything. But, my God, what a price to pay—what a price to pay! I broke down and cried. . . .

Last night, Mukoro, I saw you in my dream. I said I was tired and hungry. You told me not to worry at all, told me you were going to make me all right in a short while. From out of nowhere, you fetched the most comfortable bed in the whole world, with mattress and pillows heavily stuffed with scented foam, cotton wool and eagle down, and told me the makers had even turned down an offer from the Queen of England. You laid me gently down on this bed, and let my tender frame sink cosily into the yielding upholstery, giving me a soothing kiss and caress before you took your leave. Then you rushed off into the kitchen, and in no time at all you had laid before me a mighty, steaming bowl of *ukodo*, with such a generous helping of fish and meat I could hardly see the broth. I said I would like to bathe before I ate and you said that was no problem at all. Before I could blink twice you had lowered me into a huge basinful of warm scented water, scrubbing me with the most fragrant soap in the world and drying me later with a towel fit only for princesses. You brought me back to the table, and took it upon yourself to feed me. I ate everything, cheered on no less by your welcome hand than by the sweetness of the food. Then you whisked me back to bed in your arms, and in no time at all you were covering me with hot caresses, yet with the same delicate care with which one cuddles an egg.

I was very sad this morning when I opened my eyes to the harsh reality of daylight, and wished I could have slipped back into the cosy folds of my sweet fantasy. For I miss you too much now. I miss you much more now than I ever did. I know that whatever Toje might try to do for me would only be a travesty of comfort compared to the mere presence of you. But if what he tells me about you is true, then I know that the message of my dream is clear and unmistakable and soon my life will be blessed once more with your tender loving care. Yes, I can see pleasure and good cheer coming back to my life once again! But let it not wait too long, my prince. Three years have been a painfully long time. How much longer do you think I can endure this condition, if I am reduced to Toje's plaything and all I am left with are endless memories of you?

Oshevire

'Look, Mr Rukeme,' says counsel to the tribunal. 'I can't understand you. A few minutes ago you said that Mr Oshevire was always visiting the rebel army barracks in your town. Now you are telling us that he tried to conceal his relationship with them by letting them meet him at his house all the time. Well, which do you mean—

were they always coming to him or he was always going to them?'

'He was always going to them.'

'I hope you will stand by that, won't you?'

'Yes—no—yes, sir!'

There is laughter from the gallery. Counsel throws a cold look at the uneasy Rukeme. Dishonesty never sits easy.

'Now, Mr Rukeme,' says counsel, 'do you remember the 11th of April, 1968?'

'Yes, sir,' Rukeme says, after a brief thought.

'Tell us what happened.'

My accuser takes a long look at the ceiling. Then he looks down on the ground, long and hard, biting his lower lip and screwing his brow.

Counsel sighs and looks at him again.

'If I may refresh your memory, your memorandum here talks about Mr Oshevire helping rebel troops to conduct a raid on Urukpe market.'

My eyes nearly pop onto the ground!

'Oh, yes,' Rukeme comes alive. 'It was on a Sunday afternoon— hm?—no, Monday morning—'

'Your memorandum says Wednesday afternoon!'

'Yes—Wednesday afternoon. It was on a Wednesday afternoon. The market was full, and there was a lot of buying and selling going on. Suddenly an army Landrover pulled up by the side of the road, near the market. Mr Oshevire and about three soldiers jumped out of the car and marched quickly into the market. They stopped at the beans stall and priced beans. The woman told them it was sixpence a cup. They said they would pay twopence a cup, and if the woman wasn't satisfied she should go and hang herself. When the woman protested, Mr Oshevire shouted at her to shut up, or they would beat her to death. One of the soldiers slapped the woman, and Mr Oshevire pushed her aside, and she fell down on a basinful of rice. They threw down a ten shilling note before her and started toting away the basins of rice, until—'

'Rice?' asks counsel.

'Sir?'

'Did you say rice?'

'Yes, sir.'

'I thought you were telling us about beans?'

'Yes—oh, yes. I'm sorry. Beans.'

Obanye and I look at each other, and shake our heads.

'Look,' says counsel, 'will you try to be consistent?'

'Yes, sir.' Rukeme swallows, and readjusts his sitting posture. 'They started making away with the woman's basins of beans. When they got to the Landrover, Mr Oshevire came out of the vehicle and helped them carry the basins into the back of it.'

'Mr Oshevire?'

'Yes, sir.'

'Where did you say he was?'

'Inside the Landrover, sir.'

'Oh-ho! He did not accompany the soldiers into the market then?'

'No, sir. He did not. He was sitting in the Landrover.'

At this point the chairman explodes.

'Look, are you sure you know what you are saying? At one moment you tell us that Mr Oshevire accompanied the rebel soldiers into the market and even helped them manhandle the woman. At another moment you tell us that he was waiting in the car while the soldiers were in the market. Which do you mean?'

'I think he was sitting in the car, sir.'

'Don't *think*! You've got to be certain what evidence you are bringing before this tribunal,' says the chairman, putting down his glasses on the table. 'Do you realise how much difference it would make to Mr Oshevire what you say before this tribunal—or don't you care?'

Rukeme is speechless.

'Carry on with your questioning, Mr Counsel,' says the chairman, settling back in his chair and putting his glasses back on.

Counsel flips through the papers before him, then throws Rukeme a half-smiling gaze.

'Now, Mr Rukeme, you said that Mr Oshevire was in the habit of holding meetings with the rebels in his house, isn't that right?'

'Yes, sir.'

'Can you elaborate on this—can you tell the tribunal about one such meeting?'

'One day, they were—'

'What day was that?'

'Ehm,' the witness coughs. 'I think it was in May, sir.'

'You think—or you are sure?'

'I am sure, sir.'

'All right. What date in May, and what year?'

'Twenty-third of May, 1968, sir.'

'All right. What happened on the 23rd May, 1968?'

'I was a witness myself to what happened. They—'

'You mean, you were *present* at the meeting?'

'No, sir!' the man swears.

The audience roars with laughter.

'I happened to be around the place. It was on a Sunday evening, at about six o'clock. There were about five or six military vehicles, mostly Landrovers. I think there were about two Mercedes Benz, each bearing the rebel flag. The area of Mr Oshevire's house, right up to the Council Hall and all the houses immediately around it, was blocked off, and nobody was allowed even to approach. They started off the meeting by singing one of their tribal war songs—I didn't understand what they said. Then there was silence. They started planning and scheming. It was plain they were planning and scheming to do something.'

'How could you tell that?'

'It was generally known that they were always planning and scheming. At one time it was said that they wanted to kill all the young men in the town, so that we would not have the chance of giving them any kind of resistance. At another time, when they saw that they were beginning to lose too many of their men in encounters with the federal troops, they decided they would do a wide-scale conscription of young men into their army. That Sunday meeting at Mr Oshevire's place was designed to plan such an operation in our town.'

'Are you certain about this?'

'This was a rumour I heard.'

'I see. When was it you said the meeting took place on that Sunday?'

'At about . . . eight o'clock in the evening.'

'Did you say "eight o'clock"?'

'Yes, sir.'

'I see.'

Counsel sighs and shakes his head, then turns to the chairman of the tribunal.

'I have no more questions, my Lord,' he says. 'I would now like to call on Mr Mukoro Oshevire to come forward and cross-examine the witness.'

Not me. Not me. You won't get a word from me. Does the truth not shine forth brightly enough now?

'Mr Mukoro Oshevire!' the secretary to the tribunal shouts to me. 'Will you please step forward . . .?'

The policeman by my side nudges me on the back, rather hard for my liking. *It is not your fault. . . .*

I rise from my seat and walk towards counsel. I stand before him, submitting myself to his supreme pleasure.

'Now, Mr Oshevire,' it is the chairman that addresses me now, 'do you have any questions you wish to ask Mr Rukeme?'

'I have none,' I tell him, shaking my head, not even looking at anyone's face.

For what is there to say to Rukeme? How would it alter the appointed course of events?

'Are you quite sure you have no questions for him?'

'I have none at all.' *Shuo!*

'All right,' says the chairman. 'Go back to your seat, please.'

I turn around and do that. There is silence everywhere. The looks on the faces of the soldier and the policeman tell me they would cudgel me to death if they had the chance. They might yet have the chance!

The chairman looks round at the commissioners in an invitation to further questioning of the witness. I take a brief look at him, I mean Rukeme. I cannot really explain what I feel towards him. It cannot be spite. Even if there is spite in my feeling towards him, it cannot be that alone, or I am likely to be underestimating the gravity of his statements.

For they are serious indeed. They are serious not really because they are likely to send me to my grave—that may even be a certainty now. For after three years of forced seclusion from the true joy of your life, with no hope of release, how far can you be from certain death? But there is more to it than that. Ever since we have been appearing before this tribunal, I have listened to so many people give the most damaging evidence against my fellow-detainees, watched the brazen-faced conviction with which these accusations have been delivered. And it is only now that the gravity of the whole situation is beginning to come home to me. For if indeed so many men are as innocent as I know I am, yet stand in danger of losing their freedom, and even their lives—who knows? —just because some people have the boldness to come forth and exercise a serpentine slickness of tongue, then there is fear indeed over the land. I'm just a plain country farmer, much better off tending my rubber trees in the thick of the farm dirt than seated here before a panel of clean, respectable folk to debate a cause that should never have been. If Rukeme makes his point, then I shall probably appear before a firing squad. But let them have their victory. . . .

I can now see that there are many people in my position. If this is a general trend, what safety is there for anyone? All it means is that you can suddenly be brought here to argue your life just because somebody has questioned it. What safety, I say, what hope is there for anybody? My mind suddenly goes to my wife and little son. Who knows what torment they now face. . . .

'Mr Rukeme,' this is another one of the commissioners speaking, 'what did you say your occupation was?'

'I am a teacher.'

'Where do you teach?'

'At St Martin's Mission School, Urukpe.'

'How long have you been teaching?'

'For—' he is straining his mind now, 'for five years.'

'And were you teaching in Urukpe before the rebel occupation of this state?'

'Yes, sir. Oh, no, sir. I was teaching in Ofuze then.'

The commissioner glowers.

'Are you familiar with Mr Oshevire?'

'Yes, sir.'

'How familiar?'

'Very familiar, sir. I used to see him very often.'

'I see. You merely saw him very often—have you ever been to his house?'

'No, sir.'

'Then it's obvious you are not so familiar, isn't that so?'

Rukeme lowers his gaze.

'Yes, sir.'

'Then how can you be so sure of his movements and activities?'

'Everybody knew about him.'

'Including you?'

'Yes, sir.'

'From rumours, or from personal experience?'

Rukeme is silent, staring blankly ahead of him.

'I asked you a question—from rumours, or from an intimate knowledge of the man?'

'Well—we all knew what he was doing.'

'You haven't answered my question. I said, was this knowledge based on rumours or on intimate experience?'

'The reports were all over the town, how he used to associate with them.'

'Aha, *reports* then?' the commissioner says with a challenging gaze.

'Yes, sir.'

'Mr Rukeme, have you never considered that some of these reports may have been exaggerated?'

'I—I don't know. I don't think so.'

'You don't think so!' There is both mockery and anger in the commissioner's voice. 'If you felt so certain about things you put down in your memorandum would you be wasting our time here with so many self-contradictions?'

Rukeme stares again ahead of him, morose and bewildered. His interlocked fingers loosen and his arms slip from the chair.

'Now, look,' says the commissioner. 'I want you to get this very clear in your mind. We are not obliged to believe everything you say. Because it is possible that as you tell your stories to us a few doubts will arise now and then in your mind about one or two details. And that's only natural. Do you understand? Good. Otherwise, if we were obliged to believe everything you say, there is a danger that we would be holding a lot of things against Mr Oshevire quite unjustly. And this tribunal is out to be fair to everybody. Understand? Right. On the other hand, we want you to relax.'

Rukeme startles to attention, and the audience burst out laughing. The commissioner shakes his head.

'You must try to feel at ease. Otherwise you cannot possibly tell a straight story. This is not a court of law. We are only trying to find out one or two things about what happened during the rebel occupation of this state. So feel at ease. Now,' he assumes a more serious look, his fingers interlocked on the table, 'tell us, Mr Rukeme, do you have a personal grudge against Mr Oshevire?'

'No, sir.'

'Good. Of course you have already told us that you were not all that familiar with him. Is that not right?'

'Yes, sir.'

'Which means that you could never have been so close to him as to be able to observe his day to day activities. Is that not so?'

Rukeme hesitates.

'Answer me—is that not so?'

'Yes, sir.'

'What does "yes, sir" mean? Is it so or is it not?'

'It is so.'

'Very good. Now, Mr Rukeme, what was the general feeling in Urukpe about Mr Oshevire. Did people generally like him, or did they hate him?'

'They hated him.'

'Does this include you?'

Rukeme is silent.

'Do you hate Mr Oshevire, I ask you?'

'No, sir.'

'Good. So let us now assume that you were different from the rest of the town—that while everybody else hated him you had no grudge at all against him. Is that not so?'

Rukeme is again morose. I wish he would say something. Not that I am likely to be overjoyed if he says he is in love with me—for how can he feel that way and at the same time seek to set me before a firing line of soldiers?

'Now, when did people start hating Mr Oshevire—was it before the rebel occupation, or was it since the occupation, or was it after the federal troops liberated your town?'

'It was after the federal troops liberated our town.'

'Why, do you think, did people start hating him *then*?'

'Well—he—his wife is a rebel.'

'A rebel?'

'Yes, sir.'

'I see. Of course his wife is a Simba, I understand. But didn't he marry her before the rebel troops occupied this state?'

Good question. Good question. He is confused again!

'Well, didn't he?' shouts the commissioner.

'I think so, sir.'

'You *think*, or you know?'

'He did.'

'Then it is obvious that if they hated him because his wife was a Simba, they must have hated him before the rebel occupation, which means long before the federal troops came into Urukpe. Is that not right?'

'Yes, sir.'

'That means that your first statement is not correct, but the second one is.'

'Sir?'

'What you are telling us in effect is that the people of Urukpe hated Mr Oshevire because he married a Simba woman. Isn't that correct?'

Silence. 'Yes, sir.'

'Good. But, Mr Rukeme, do you sincerely believe that that statement is right? Do you mean that everybody in your town that married a Simba woman was consequently hated by the rest of the population?'

Rukeme has no words.

'Look,' says the commissioner, 'I realise that Urukpe is a sort of border town between Igabos and Simbas, though it is an Igabo town. Is that not so?'

'Yes, sir.'

'Right. Quite understandably, therefore, there has been a good deal of intermingling between members of both tribes, as a result of that situation. Right?'

'Yes, sir.'

'Is it not therefore right for us to assume that there has been much inter-marrying between Simbas and Igabos—Simba women being married to Igabo men and Igabo women being married to Simba men?'

Rukeme hesitates. 'Yes.'

'Are you married?'

'Yes, sir.'

'Where does your wife come from?'

'She comes from my town.'

'From Urukpe?'

'Yes, sir.'

'Is she Igabo, or Simba?'

'She is Igabo.'

'Do you have any relation—brother, cousin, uncle—who is married to a Simba woman?'

Rukeme does not reply. He avoids the gaze of the commissioner and begins to look on the floor.

'I asked you a question, Mr Rukeme. Is there any of your relations that is married to a Simba woman?'

'My eldest brother is married to a Simba woman.'

'I see,' says the commissioner, relaxing somewhat on his seat. 'And where is she now?'

'She—she ran away when the federal troops came into our town.'

'All right—that's not important now. But did the whole of Urukpe hate your brother because he married a Simba woman?'

'No, sir,' says Rukeme, trying hard, it seems, to impress with the firmness of his denial.

'And would you say the same of everybody else? Did the rest of Urukpe hate anyone who married a Simba?'

85

'No, sir,' he is hesitant again. I think he is afraid to spoil his case.

'Then, what makes Mr Oshevire special? Why was he singled out for hatred on account of his marrying a Simba?'

You can't subdue the truth. However hard you try, it will always insist on surfacing like a calabash gourd pressed under water.

'Answer my question, Mr Rukeme,' says the commissioner.' Why was Mr Oshevire alone hated because he married a Simba woman —or were other men hated for the same reason?'

'I don't know.'

'Well, why was he hated for that reason anyway?'

'He was supporting the rebels.'

'Was that then why he was hated?'

'Yes.'

'Oh-ho. So, now, he was hated not because he married a Simba woman, but because he was supporting the rebels. Is that not so?'

'Yes, sir.'

'That statement of yours therefore was incorrect, that Mr Oshevire was hated long before the federal troops came to liberate your town?'

Silence again.

'Mm?'

'Yes, sir.'

'Can we therefore settle on this, Mr Rukeme: the people of Urukpe started hating Mr Oshevire during the rebel occupation— not before or after?'

Rukeme is sweating. His face now sports quite a few beads of water, produced no doubt by the rigours of dishonesty. His gaze is fixed on the floor, his legs are uneasy.

'Now, please answer me, Mr Rukeme,' says the commissioner.

'Yes.'

'Very good. At least we have been able to agree on one thing. I am very glad about that, because it means that we can look forward henceforth to cooperating with each other. Now, Mr Rukeme, were there any other people in your town known to have collaborated with the rebel troops?'

'Yes, sir.'

'Where are they now?'

'Most of them ran away with the rebels when the federal troops started attacking the town.'

'Why do you think they ran away?'

'Well—they knew what would have happened to them if they had stayed.'

'Did I hear you say "most of them ran away"?'

'Yes, sir.'

'Where are the rest?'

'They were—I don't know.'

'All right. What do you think would have happened to those others if they had stayed?'

'They would have paid for what they did.'

'How, Mr Rukeme?'

'I—I don't know.'

'All right. Do you think Mr Oshevire knew that people hated him so much?'

'I don't know. You can ask him,' gesturing towards me.

'I am asking you, Mr Rukeme!' the commissioner says, with a touch of irritation.

'I think so, sir,' returns Rukeme, staggered into discipline.

'You think so?'

'Yes, sir. He knew. He must have noticed how everybody avoided him.'

'Well, if he knew that everybody hated him, why did he not run away, like most other collaborators at the approach of the federal forces?'

Rukeme has no reply.

'All right. If indeed people hated him so much, and he was still very much around when the federal troops took the town, why did people not make him "pay for" what he did?'

Rukeme is silent, looking down again. For how can he look up, look truth in the face, when his conscience is not clean? *You cannot subdue the truth, however hard you try*.

'Mm? Why did he not run away like most of the others—answer that first? It can only be one of two things: either he was sure he was innocent, or he is a very stubborn man. Which do you think is the case?'

'He is a very stubborn man.'

'But, Mr Rukeme, how can you know so much about him if, as you told us earlier, you are not familiar with him?'

Once again Rukeme is speechless.

The commissioner shakes his head. He turns to the chairman, indicating that he is through with his questioning, and settles back finally in his seat.

There is a kind of uneasy silence throughout the hall. A low but persistent murmur ranges through the gallery. The chairman is consulting quietly with his commissioners. Rukeme is using the respite to scrub his face clean of the perspiration. When I turn to look at Obanye at my side, I find that he is lost in thought, eyes fixed unblinkingly downward in a mood that obviously does not wish to be disturbed. Maybe he too, like me, is perplexed by the madness of it all. That truth should be so brazenly challenged. That a man should leave his home, more than a hundred miles away, and heap charges upon another man—and these are charges that he cannot substantiate even with the faintest hint of certitude. And, indeed, that the very life of a man should seem to depend on such an outrageous exercise.

'Now,' says the chairman, pausing briefly to let the murmur die down completely. 'I think this is enough for now. But before we rise today I wish to remind everybody here of what His Excellency the Governor of the Black Gold State said recently. In his own words, "Without prejudice to the work of the Tribunal of Enquiry, I must say that it would be very unpatriotic of anyone to bring up fictitious charges against his fellow-citizen, whatever his motivation, because we are trying to build a society in which truth and justice prevail, and in which no man seeks to oppress his neighbour merely because he happens to wield some kind of advantage."

'Now, Mr Rukeme, in saying this I am not at all trying to pre-judge the issue. But there seems little doubt that you have not taken care to tie up your case neatly. You have clearly not been in con-trol of your statements—they have lacked consistency. I am not saying you have been lying: I am only saying that if you are telling us the truth, you certainly haven't taken care to put it across in the appropriate sort of language. It seems to me you have slightly misunderstood the purpose of this tribunal. I think you must have been looking upon this place as a court of law. If that is the case, then I can understand why you have been lacking in that ease of mind that is necessary for a clear, orderly and logical exposition of your points. That is all we can ask of you in this exercise. We have no doubt at all that you are willing to help the tribunal in its investigations, but you must appreciate that inconsistencies in your statements can only lead us to conclude that you have been motivated by a certain amount of vindictiveness and are therefore not qualified to help the tribunal fulfil its purpose. We thank you for the effort you have made to help the tribunal, but I am afraid we have to close your evidence.

'This tribunal is taking a break, and this particular case is adjourned indefinitely. When we reopen it, at a date to be announced later, we would wish to hear the evidence of Mr Mukoro Oshevire.'

We all rise. The chairman and the commissioners depart, and everybody else leaves after them. My fellow-detainee and I are herded out of the room to the Black Maria, waiting outside to take us back to the place of detention. There is already a crowd waiting to take a look at us. I refuse to look at anybody. I think I have had enough of ill-will for today, and am unwilling to look at either the spite or the condemnation which these bystanders are certain to be wearing on their faces. My right arm is tightly gripped by the policeman, and I have little room therefore for such a luxury as looking at people's faces. I am helped into the Black Maria, where the policeman's determined push tells me I belong. Indeed I must observe that, once seated in the welcome darkness of the van, Obanye and I are comforted to be secure from the possible wrath of the crowd.

Yet I do not know how much comfort I can really have. Who knows now what is happening to my wife and child? If Rukeme is right in what he says, that the whole of Urukpe hates me, how can my family hope to be safe? Even if they have not been visited with any physical harm, though that now seems very remote, it is plain that, starved of attention, starved of comfort and love, they cannot hope to survive very long.

But let that be. Whatever comes upon them will be my perpetual sorrow, for I could have wished that, if I should suffer for what I am convinced was an act of humanity on my part, I should bear my suffering alone, and not drag along with me the only people for whose sake alone life for me is worth living. Yet nothing—nothing at all—will deter me from the path of truth and integrity. I will forever stand up like a man.

Part two

Except by rooting,
who could pluck yam tubers from their base?

CHRISTOPHER OKIGBO

Ali

A terrible air raid it was! The rebels meant business this time. A haunting peace still pervades this town, uneasy, as after a tremendous storm or a ripping outburst of gunfire. It is only to be expected. This is by no means the first time that the town has suffered an attack. But people can hardly be expected to get used to a calamity such as this. Still, we are in a war, and we have got to learn to expect the worst at any time and take things as they come.

I feel a little relieved to see that the worst fears are over. After three days we seem to be getting close to normalcy here. I could have wished that people stayed indoors for a while: who knows how many such visits we should be expecting from the rebels, now that they have continued to receive further supplies of aircraft and other armaments from Europe? The curfew regulations stay as before, no tighter than they have been. But I am strengthening the military vigilance, posting anti-aircraft guns at a few more strategic points in and around the town, reinforcing the defences against possible guerrilla incursions.

As soldiers, of course, we know that anything can happen at any time. But for the villagers here, unaccustomed as they are to such harsh surprises, a thundering air raid proves a bit too much to absorb. *Allah*, the rebels meant business!

It all happened at twilight. Captain Olayinka, Captain Usman and myself were discussing the deployment of the new recruits. There wasn't any more peace than there should be in an army camp, with trucks roaring past and N.C.O.s blasting the usual orders. Suddenly we heard the faint buzzing of light craft. We knew at once by the sound that they couldn't be our planes. We rushed out of my quarters and came out to verify. Sure enough. From the eastern horizon three Minicons came in formation, skirting the tops of trees, threatening to whip off the foliage. They have to fly so low, these moths, to achieve anything like a hit.

We didn't wait any further. We quickly dispersed, and in a short while the camp came under the familiar mood of panic. Orders shouted. Rifles cracking. Anti-aircraft guns booming at their locations. Presently we heard the distant blasts of bombs dropped by the invading planes; I think they must have come on a determined mission, for they dropped many bombs. *Diimm! Kpoai! Toai! Diimm! Kpoai! Kpoai!* Our guns themselves never stopped in their replies, I can say that for the readiness of our soldiers. As usual, the raid was brief. In no time at all the visitors had disappeared beyond the trees and the foliage whence they came, satisfied that they had done their intended havoc.

I have not had time to study any report, federal or rebel, about the situation—I have been too busy to do that. Nobody seems to have heard anything yet from our radio, but early this morning Captain Olayinka informed me that the rebels claimed to have set the whole town on fire and put *me* to flight. *Shege!* These people are really something! But of course this is a war, and everything is a weapon. I don't expect our side to be too honest in their report either.

Still, the truth lives here with us in a stark and undeniable presence. As I drive through the town with my batman now, at ten o'clock in the morning, on an inspection and condolence tour, I am under no illusion at all but that considerable damage has been done to the peace and happiness of this town. Six poor lives were destroyed in that raid; fourteen persons injured—most of them critical cases; four houses blasted to the ground, all of them completely burnt by the resulting flames; and the entire population driven once again to the limits of anxiety and despair. The raid brought back all over again the kind of atmosphere that I have been trying to contain, for what promise or hope can you give to a woman who has lost her husband and possibly her children too? But their protection and welfare are as much my concern as the military purpose.

My batman and I are driving through a near-empty street, saved from total and haunting loneliness by the presence of a few foraging goats and fowls. A dog stops to urinate by the side of the road, unperturbed even by our Minimoke as it bumps along the sandy path with urgency. . . .

We drive off towards the local Red Cross office. I have little doubt that the Red Cross is capable of coping with the job of helping the injured and the bereaved; they have the resources of food, medicines, clothing, maybe enough goodwill and sympathy too. They are supposed to be assisted by the Government's Rehabilitation Commission, and even the Civil Defence Unit here in Urukpe. But these two bodies can scarcely be counted on for co-operation. The Rehabilitation people never come to this town—I suppose they would claim the place was too far from the state capital and the journey too risky. And ever since the Civil Defenders taught people how to take cover, nobody seems to see them around on any sort of active duty. But this town is not just a town affected by the war. It is a border town harbouring two tribes and perhaps two sympathies. And why should I, a soldier equipped no less by the present circumstances than by military training with a strong sense of danger, allow my defences to stand in jeopardy by letting civilian bodies, who are in no position to assess the military situation in these parts, to take sole charge of ensuring the goodwill of the people of this place? I think I know better than that.

As I step out of the car, I am met by the head of the local Red Cross, Mr Eziregbe, a fine man.

'Good morning, Major,' he beams in his usual manner.

'Good morning, Mr Eziregbe,' I shake hands with him. 'How is everything today?' We walk into his office.

'Well, we are trying to do the best we can. Please sit down.'

'I know. It's a difficult situation. But you are doing a great job.'

'Thank you, Major. I must say I am receiving a lot of cooperation. The Anglican School has allowed me to use one of its blocks for the refugee centre.'

'Who is the headmaster there—Mr Egboge?'

'Yes. He's a very kind man.'

'That's right. He's very kind.'

'I just wish I could have some peace from that place.'

'What's the matter?'

'You know that old woman, whose son was killed in the air raid, and whose house was shattered?'

'You mean Madam Dafe?'

'Yes. Every night she goes into endless wailing about the misfortune, and the next morning she comes here still crying for her son to be brought back to life for her.'

'Poor woman. I know how terrible it must be for her.'

'Yes, Major. But you know how difficult it makes our work. That sort of thing puts us off here.'

'I know. I know. It's a pity about that. I think I must go and talk to her.'

'That would be very kind of you.'

He calls one of his assistants to take away a letter or something like that.

'Any news about the injured people?' I ask him.

'Oh, yes. You know of course that those slightly injured have been treated in the dispensary here and sent home. Now, this morning I got the news that two of the serious cases died on the way to the hospital at Okere Town.'

'Too bad,' I say. 'Have their people been informed?'

'No. I intend to do that later today.'

'Terrible. But that's life.' The whole thing is beginning to get a little sentimental. 'Well, let me be on my way, Mr Eziregbe,' I announce, rising from my seat and hitting my swagger-stick a number of times on my hand to fight the sentimentality. 'Any time you need our help, don't forget to let me know. I'd be only too glad to help.'

'That's very kind of you, Major.'

'Take care of yourself—don't forget to lie flat on your belly when you hear a strange sound!'

'No, Major, I won't forget!' he acknowledges the joke.

'Goodbye.'

'Goodbye, Major.'

We shake hands and I go back to the Minimoke. I start the car and my batman and I head towards the refugee centre at Anglican, a short distance away. I quite clearly have an option not to go to see anybody at all—I don't have to spend my time going about consoling bereaved people or comforting the afflicted. But it seems to me that the people of this town do specially need to be assured that the army, the federal army, is on their side. Confronted by two military forces—Federal and Simbian, though one is surely more open than the other—neither of which would be said to be pleasant or welcome company in the normal life of a people, they demand of us, as the visible power in their midst, every assurance of protection and safety as well as a touch of humanity and simple fellow feeling in our relationship with them. Otherwise, we are quite plainly an enemy—and Allah forbid that they should look upon us as such!

Most of the refugees we have in this town don't actually come from Urukpe. They come from villages much closer to the fighting front and so in more serious trouble from endless guerrilla raids and exchanges of fire between us and the rebel forces. They form by far the majority, these outsiders. The rest are natives of Urukpe whose houses have been damaged at one time or another by rebel air raids such as the one we have just experienced, or who have lost, in these raids, members of their families who provided for them. You should see the faces of these people. *Wallahi!*

As we draw up at the Anglican School building, we are met at the entrance by Mr Eziregbe's assistant, Johnson Oviri, a hearty young man with a cheerful face.

'Good morning, Major,' he greets me briskly, stiffening to attention and saluting.

'Good morning, Johnson,' I return. 'How is life with you?'

'Trying to manage, sir.'

'Well, we're all managing, aren't we?'

He laughs and rubs shyly at his left arm.

'How are your inmates?' I ask before we go in.

'Well,' he is less cheerful now, his face dimming with seriousness and his gaze lowered, 'they are managing. They had their meals this morning. Some of them left with their belongings after break-fast—their relatives offered to take them into their homes, thinking it a shame that their own blood should be housed in a refugee camp. Some of the others have gone out, for a walk I think, just to escape from the boredom of the atmosphere here. Some others are sleeping. A number of the children are, of course, playing in the backyard—thank God. The main problem is that old woman.'

'Madam Dafe?'

'Yes, sir. She refused to have a bite this morning. And as usual she did not sleep last night, wailing endlessly, even into this morn-ing. When we passed her the food, she just took a look at it, hissed and shook her head. And tears started streaming down her face.'

'Ah! Does she want to die of starvation?'

'Honestly, I don't know. I have tried and tried my best to console her—even some of her fellow-refugees have helped, in spite of their own sorrows. But—no good.'

'Terrible,' I sigh. 'Is she in now?'

'Yes, sir.'

True enough. As we walk in, there is Madam Dafe by the corner of a wall, looking out of a low window in mournful and absent-minded seclusion from the rest of the crowd, some of whom are stretched out on their mats in sleep or plain rest. I am slightly at a loss what to say to attract her attention. My presence in the long hall has already drawn towards us a good number of the refugees, adults and children, trailing after us and crowding round us, a gaze of smitten hope in each pair of eyes. It is this crowd more than any-thing else that seems to have pulled the old woman a little now from her long and lonely stare, for she turns towards us and fixes me with dim, woe-weary eyes.

'Mama,' I call. I'm trying to talk to her.

She makes no reply. She merely looks down, cups her brow in one hand and shakes her head. Beneath her hand her face seems to be swelling with feeling, and I fear that she may soon be overcome by the access of sorrow that has been reported by both Mr Eziregbe and Johnson.

'Mama,' I try again, touching her lightly on the shoulder, hoping that a little warmth and tenderness will take away at least some of the heavy feeling within her.

But she breaks into sobbing, and as she takes her hand from her face she reveals two trails of tears running down her cheeks. Presently she lets out a long tormented cry, and her wailing is upon her again. I cannot understand the words of her dirge, which are all touchingly delivered in the native Igabo language, and I look to Johnson.

'What is she saying?'

'She says the world should leave her alone to lament her fate . . . for what is left of her when . . . when the only son that meant life to her has gone.'

More wailing from the old woman. Johnson listens, half-disdainful. He doesn't like what he's doing, I think. But neither do I—*Kai*!

'What was that she said?' I ask again.

'—that she might as well be killed herself . . . that there is no use in her remaining in this world. That's what she keeps crying every day, Major. We've been unable to get her to stop.'

The woman then descends to a low moaning sound. She now sings her lament in a subdued but still unyielding tone.

'Tell her,' I advise Johnson, 'that everything will be all right, that she shouldn't cry any more.'

Johnson translates it to the woman, who continues in her subdued lament, not even looking at us.

'Tell her that too much crying won't be good for her health.'

He does.

'—that we will do everything possible for her.'

Johnson still can't get her to listen.

'—that we are sorry her son was killed . . . that since there is nothing we can do about the dead we should give our attention to the living.'

Johnson translates, but she still doesn't listen.

'Tell her I too feel very sad about the death of her son . . . but that if we all have to think about it every day our sorrow will never leave us, and that's not very good.'

He tells her.

'—that I am very hurt to hear that she has refused to eat her food

. . . she should try to eat, and remember that we have not forgotten her.'

The whole thing seems to have worked, I can tell now. For as Johnson translates my last exhortation, I can see Madam Dafe slowly rubbing her eyes with an ear of her cloth. The wailing has stopped and she is now merely shaking her head and blowing her nose.

'Mama,' I put in, thinking it the right moment. 'Stop crying. Everything will be all right. Sorry. Don't worry now. Sorry.' And I pat her shoulder to reassure her.

The circle of refugees is still around us. Where do I start with my words of reassurance? No use anyway. They know even from my eyes alone that I wish them comfort, and I smile at them to drive home the point. As I step away from Madam Dafe the crowd retreats somewhat, forming a path for me.

'Thank you very much, Major,' says Johnson.

'That's all right. I should sympathise with you on the trouble you are having every day trying to keep this kind of situation under control.'

'Well, what else can we do? We are only managing.'

'Yes. Tell me, Johnson, does she not have any relatives who could take her with them?'

'That's part of the whole problem, Major,' says Johnson. 'They have come several times to take her away, but she just refuses to budge from her place. You should have seen the amount of trouble we had dragging her to this place from the ruins of their house. After her son was buried on the site she refused to leave the place, though there was not the least shelter in the midst of the ruins—saying she would remain there until her life was overtaken by the same fate that took her son away.'

I can see the outlines of stubbornness, from her narrow jaw and unblinking eyes. But sorrow too wears strange shapes, transforming contours of joy into features of ugliness and despair.

'I think she'll be all right after some time. Continue to soothe her whenever she goes into her moods. She'll forget about it all soon.'

'I hope so, Major.'

'That's all right. I think we'll leave now.'

'Thank you very much, Major. I'm grateful.'

As I walk along the path formed by the morose crowd, I try to do the best I can to comfort and cheer, saying 'Sorry, Sorry' all the way down and rubbing the heads of children straddling their mothers' hips.

Outside the hall I feel a little relieved. I exchange a few more words of greeting with Johnson, then drive off with my batman. My next place of call is the house of the *Otota* of Urukpe, the old chief.

The entire landscape is as cheerless as the looks on people's faces —sombre, retractive, bleak. There is a very mild wind, and leaves and grasses sway dully as though labouring in slumber. We are now driving through an almost empty area, with hardly anybody in the front yards of the houses. Some of these yards are proudly advertised by ambitious signboards—'Idhigu's Technical Radio Works' . . . 'German Medical Company (For Superior Medication)' . . . 'Franco's Cut (International Barber)' . . . 'Delta Massage Clinick (For Relief of Backy-ache and Instant Pregnancy of Woman, A Triall will conceive You)' . . .

I stop by a sign which I recall very well. This one is called 'Godinheaven Oniemorame's Herbal Home—Cures Epilepsy, Paralysis, People possessed by Water Devil, Witchcrafts, Eunuch, and Prevention for soldiers; we are also Fortune Tellers, and can help school children who are not brilliant. (Registered No. 227/69, Black Gold State Central Union of Herbalists). Try and See.'

Godinheaven is a funny character. There is also some legend attached to him. The incident happened before I was posted to this town, when Major Akuya Bello was in command of the forces here. Because Godinheaven has advertised himself as possessing and providing 'Prevention for soldiers', a lot of soldiers went to his place and paid good money for charms, which the medicineman assured them would turn bullets to water on hitting their bodies. And then something happened one day. For some reason, either by mere chance or due to a lull in action, there was for some time no encounter with the rebels which could have put the efficacy of Godinheaven's charm to test. So it happened that one day one of these 'protected' soldiers fell into an argument with a companion who was not yet convinced that the business made any sense. It

all came down to bluffs, and the 'protected' one challenged the un-
believer to shoot him in the thigh. He had his God to thank that he
chose the thigh, because the bullet tore clean through the unpro-
tected hide and, as if to prove the point further, ripped the earth
behind him!

No further proof was needed. Godinheaven has still not dis-
claimed that qualification, and indeed took pains to explain to
whoever cared to ask that the efficacy of his charms should not be
made the subject of careless bluffs, and in any case it was only a fool
that went around bragging about anything he had! But he was
thrown into considerable fear as to his fate with the authorities, and
lost no time in running up to Major Bello and tendering his apolo-
gies. When I took command here, he was one of the very first to
welcome me with bottles of local gin, and to this day he has spared
no effort in reasserting his solidarity with the army.

His signboard was, unfortunately, a casualty of the recent air
raid. One of the rebel bombs had landed some yards away from it,
on the open path, and the resulting blast had claimed one of the
wooden posts on which the signboard stood. So now, standing on
one leg, it nods downward. It all looks curious! I shake my head in
amusement, and as I am about to kick off Godinheaven runs out of
his house and hails me.

'Hello, Major!'

'Godinheaven!' I reply, switching off the fire of my Minimoke.

'And goodwill on earth!' This is his regular reply.

'How now?'

'Well, what can I do? I'm still alive.'

'I can see that. So the rebels came all the way to seek out your
sign?'

I step down from the car to meet him. A middle-aged and very
short man, Godinheaven. His figure has to it a mixed touch of
humour and pity. He extends a sinewy arm to me now in greeting
and bares his tanned teeth in a broad smile.

'Good morning, Major.'

'Good morning, sir. I was asking if the rebels had nothing better
to think of than bothering your innocent signpost.'

'Isn't it strange?' he says, readjusting the heavy fold of the wrapper on his waist, with the bristles of his groin clearly showing. 'When those planes visited, my family and I did as the Civil Defence said. We lay with our bellies flat on the floor, under the bed. And then those blasts sounded. After they had departed we all came out, and the next thing I saw was that damage. I thought to myself, what a stupid raid!'

'Indeed. Indeed. Well, how is your family?'

'We are all well, hoping, praying.'

'Well, there's no worry. Just tell them to mind their movements, and keep out of trouble's way. And nobody should pick up or even touch any strange objects anywhere.'

'I will make sure they avoid that kind of foolishness. It won't all start with my household!'

'Good. Good. But I never expected you to be affected in any way by that raid—a whole Godinheaven!'

He can read what I mean, of course!

'Well . . . well,' he says, scratching his head in fake bafflement, contemplating a defence, 'you see, some of these things are unprovided for sometimes. But I can assure you that it won't happen again—I give you my word on that.'

'But aren't you thankful they stopped only at the signpost?'

'That's true,' he says, 'that's true. But if they come again they won't bother my signboard. It will be different—I promise you that!'

'Very good. Godinheaven!' I hail him, patting him on the shoulder in warm reassurance.

'And goodwill on earth!'

'Let me be on my way. Take care.'

'Thank you very much, Major. You, too.'

I get into the car, and we are once more on our way, past the cluster of market stalls immediately next to Godinheaven's omnipotent pharmacy and a handful of bystanding neighbours, to whom I smile and wave in sympathy and solidarity.

I have a few more calls to make to families who suffered harm or bereavement during the raid. But these must wait till later in the day, when I have attended to the necessary military duties without which my position here would be untenable. We are now fast on our way to pay our reassurance to the *Otota*, the traditional guardian of his people whom the present circumstances have compelled to abandon much of his traditional role. My call must of necessity be brief, for reasons of major urgencies and the fact that I cannot communicate with the old and illiterate chief except through an interpreter. . . .

My apprehension is confirmed. As we approach the *Otota's* house, I can see a number of bicycles standing in the front yard, some rested against trees. I am fairly certain that the Chief is in council with his men, and I have no wish to go through all the traditional protocol and lose all the time I could use for more practical engagements. I think my visit can wait for the evening. So I redirect the Minimoke, taking care to avoid anyone noticing my 'disrespectful' change of mind. There is still a little time left to spare, and I don't mind stopping by briefly at the house of our most honourable friend Chief Toje.

I am well aware how far this brief stopover could be stretched—trust the Chief for that!—but I'll handle it all nicely and in a way not to hurt the grand citizen's ego.

'Hello, madam,' I'm greeting the Chief's wife, who is busy around the yard. 'Good morning.'

'Good morning, Major.'

'Is the Chief in?'

'I think so.'

'Who is the fool that "thinks" I am in?' roars Chief Toje as he storms out of the door, bristling with fury, his lion chest bare and his hand gripping the fold of his wrapper well under the greyish bristles of his groin.

'Take it easy, Chief,' I exhort. 'It's madam. I think maybe she wasn't very sure.'

'How could she not be sure—in my own house?'

'Well—'

'That's how they mislead people who come to see me, telling them I'm not in when everybody knows you cannot mistake the presence of a man like me. *Bugger!*' he curses, spitting. 'I'll teach all these rascals a lesson, just you wait. Come in, Major.'

'There's nothing to worry about, sir. It was just a mistake.'

'It's happened too often, and I'm not going to let it continue in this house which I built with my own sweat.'

'It's all right, sir. Good morning.'

'Good morning, my son. Sit down. I'll join you in a moment.'

The man is simply wonderful!

The sitting room has hardly changed. Above the front door is balanced a huge and aging photograph of the Chief in full chiefly regalia—a feathered bourdillon on his head, an assortment of beads hanging from his neck, a white collarless long-sleeved shirt, a smartly carved walking-stick, and a flowing wrapper with the insteps of his shoes showing under it. There is a stern, no-nonsense look on his face and menace in his heavy shoulders. At a corner of the photograph, but prominently enough, is inscribed in ink the words, *Chief London Toje Onovwakpo of Urukpe Town*. . . .

The only new item in the whole setting is a longish almanac, issued under the title of *The Igabo Progress Union* and subtitled *Great Sons and Daughters of Igaboland*. I step closer to this, and am engaged in looking at the pictures and the names under them, when the Chief reappears.

'Welcome, my son,' he says, with a shirt on now.

'Thank you, sir. Chief, your picture doesn't appear to be in this almanac?'

'Don't mind those stupid people. I don't know how they judge their important personalities. Imagine omitting me from that kind of list! Who are the big names in the whole of Igaboland, if not people like me? There is something wrong with their heads. I almost tore that paper to pieces when it was given to me, but I was given a firm promise that my picture would be the first in the next issue. A big rubber magnate like myself, who alone would be sufficient to guarantee this town a name, and they omit my picture and any mention of me, leaving in the list only small and insignificant rascals who cannot boast any wind up their arses. Surely something is worrying their heads.'

I chuckle in agreement.

'Sit down, Major.'

'I am sorry, Chief, but I have very pressing duties this morning.'

'So pressing you can't even sit for a minute and take a tot of something with me? Come on, Major!'

'No, really, sir, I merely wanted to stop to—'

'No, no, no, no! Look, Major, you can't come to the house of a man like me and refuse to take something. My people don't do like that. Robinson!' he rises and calls to one of his children.

'Please, sir, I really cannot—'

'Robinson!' he ignores me, looking out of the door for the boy. '*i—Robinson—ioh!* Where is this scoundrel? No sooner do you look away than they—*Robinson!*'

'Sir!'

'Come here quickly.' He rejoins me. 'It won't take any time, Major. Just something to greet the day with.'

Robinson appears at the door, a boy of about six, naked, and wearing all the dirt of play on him.

'Bring the gin and two tumblers, quickly.'

The boy hurries into the room, and in no time at all sets before us the bottle of local gin. It has in it a number of cut roots that have given the liquid a tinge of yellowish-brown. He then hurries off to get the glasses.

'As I was saying, Major, it's a great shame if the importance of a man is not recognised the way it should be. Because very soon something happens in which the word of that man would have served some useful purpose, and then the people who should have known better begin to bite their fingers and regret their foolish neglect. You understand what I am saying?'

I nod, scarcely aware in which direction his wisdom is tending this time. The boy serves the drinks.

'It was not so long ago that we were all in council with the *Otota*, and I raised the point that, now that the House of Chiefs no longer functioned as a result of the military regime, some kind of contact should be maintained between the government and us, so that government could from time to time consult our wishes. I suggested that the *Otota* should pick a couple of people or so, say myself and one other man like Chief J. J. C. Ukoli, who could talk with sufficient authority for this town and be sure of a hearing with the Military Governor. I suggested that the *Otota* should send us to the Governor to make a representation along these lines. . . . Cheers, Major.'

'Cheers, sir.'

'I feel the local brew is better for the mornings, don't you think?'

'You're right,' and we laugh over it.

'But the blockheads refused. The idea would have been laughed out of court, if I hadn't been who I am and if they hadn't realised that nobody ridiculed me with impunity. But look what's happening. Our town is an endless target for rebel raids, and nothing serious is being done about it. Do you understand what I'm trying to say, Major?'

I nod again, this time faintly and with much less intention to indulge him. I am holding the glass between my teeth, and I can feel my grip on it tightening. It's not just that the man's statement amounts to an indictment of my own military efforts. Bad enough as that is, I am willing to let it pass as the product of frustrated concern. What bothers me more is—*Allah*, it's an insult even!—that the old man should go so far as to delude himself into thinking that constant conferences between the Military Governor at Iddu and local civilian leaders from far out in the country would result in outstanding military successes for us. A few shots of whisky or gin, a few nods, a few laughs—and the rebels would be routed for good, and the war would end, and we would all go home and sleep peacefully on our beds! *Shege!* The man is in a class by himself. But there is no use arguing with him. That would waste my time. So I attack the drink in my glass with undisguised urgency, so that he can understand that I have no wish to tarry. He has been waiting for me all this time.

'And he has called us again today for another meeting.'

'Yes, I saw a few bicycles outside his house on my way here.'

'Don't mind him. *Bugger!* I can't go and waste my time there so early in the day. What purpose would it serve talking to foolish men who don't understand anything? Have some more, Major.'

'Oh, no, Chief. I'm sorry, but I really must be on my way,' for this seems to me the right point to do so.

I think he is considerably overcome. He knows he can't keep me now. As I pick up my cap and swagger-stick, and am about to rise,

I can see some panic in his looks, as of someone pleading for a last desperate chance. He does not rise at once with me.

'These must be busy times for you, Major.'

'Yes, sir. I have just been to the Red Cross office and the Refugee Centre at Anglican. I just thought I should drop by here and see how you all are. I'm happy all is well with your household.'

'Very kind of you, Major. Very kind of you,' he says. 'That was a bad raid, wasn't it? I don't think we ever had it so bad.'

'Yes. It was bad,' I say, trying to fight down within me the piqued suspicion that there is still a tone of indictment in the man's words. 'It was bad.'

I can indeed see him watching me from the corner of his eye. I advance towards the door, putting on my cap, determined now to get away from here, not without menace in my bearing. He still hasn't risen from his seat.

'Tell me, Major, what are we going to do about all this?'

'About what, sir?'

His question has actually pulled me to a stop, and I turn to face him. He avoids my direct stare.

'You know . . . all these raids. Are we going to continue to suffer like this for ever?'

'Well, we are doing the best we can. The Simbians are well prepared, you know. They have arms, and we can't stop them from using them. But we are trying to fight back, and drive them to a point where they cannot use them and will ultimately have to surrender. It's not easy. They are well armed.'

'I know. I know. You don't understand what I mean. You see, we don't hear of these raids happening in other towns around us the way they happen here. Surely something must be behind it all.'

'How do you mean, sir?'

'You remember the last time we met and I was telling you about collaborators?'

'That's right, sir.'

'Well, it seems to me we are beginning to suffer the results of the seeds they sowed.'

'I still don't understand.'

'Look at it this way, Major. Every time they take off from their base out in the rebel jungle somewhere and come to these parts, it's always this town that they visit. They are always hitting us and hitting us hard, they never miss. How is it that they are so accurate?'

'They are very well equipped. They know they are fighting a war and they are not taking any chances. They have studied all our positions. They have the map of the whole country, and they know exactly where to hit.'

'Exactly! Who tells them this where to hit? Surely somebody does?'

'Yes, of course, they have their spies. This is a war, sir, and they are prepared to do everything, take every risk. And they send out spies now and then to search out our locations and pry into our plans.'

'That's right, Major. You are coming round to my point. Spies. *And* collaborators, too. Look, Major, I want you to understand one thing.' He rises from his seat now. 'You can be pretty certain that we both share the same anxiety and wish to put an end to this menace, the rebel menace. We cannot therefore afford to take any chances at all. That means that we have to take some very drastic steps, no matter who gets hurt in the end, even if it turns out to be people whom we feel bound to love and protect. You remember I told you about collaborators—sit down awhile, Major. This isn't something we should talk about standing by the door. Please sit down awhile.'

Reluctantly, I take off my cap again and sit down with a sigh.

'You know, Major, the last time I raised this point about collaborators, I was a bit reluctant to press you, lest you would misunderstand me as having a special interest in incriminating somebody. But we can't overlook the matter any further. And I think it is in the interest of the safety of all of us, and your own military efforts none the less, that we put our fingers on the real problem. Our people have a saying that, if you spare your scabies the harsh scrub of the sponge, merely because it will hurt your skin, you may later be faced with a malignant boil. You understand what I mean?'

I nod, looking down on the floor and twirling my moustache.

'I'm talking about this Oshevire who is on trial at Iddu.'

He pauses briefly, thinking I will say something. But I don't even so much as move my head.

'I think people like him have the clue to our problems, all these air and guerrilla raids—otherwise how could the rebels be striking with so much accuracy, and why our town in particular? I think if the right questions are asked him, and the right methods employed, he will be made to confess his activities and, what is more, he will be made to reveal the names of people like him who may still be hiding their faces in this town under the guise of good citizenship. Unless you are enjoying these harassments, Major, I think this is a sensible course of action in the circumstances.'

I can almost imagine Mr Oshevire pointing his finger at the Chief as one of his accomplices! *Wallahi*, I'd like to see the look on the Chief's face if that happened! But I am at a loss as to what's at the back of the man's mind.

'I see what you mean, Chief. I think you have a point there. But I'd like you to understand one or two things. In the first place, I am totally incapable of influencing the tribunal's proceedings at Iddu, and I do not see the least chance of them asking me to come and give evidence in Oshevire's case.'

'But suppose you were supplied the necessary information by a respectable citizen of this town, would they turn it down?'

'Well, in that case that citizen has to deposit a memorandum with the tribunal and be invited to testify. Frankly, Chief, it seems to me that if you personally have anything you wish to bring against Mr Oshevire, you should step forward and make your points known to the tribunal—that is if fresh memoranda are acceptable at this stage. I think that would be practical aid.'

'Oh . . . well, Major,' he says, retracting now. 'You know our people. They will start saying I am being vindictive, or that I am envious of his rubber business, and all that sort of thing.'

'That's unfortunate, then. For if you really mean to contribute something towards the safety of us all, and are prepared to damn all that public grumbling and tell what you know, no matter what the result, I think that this is your chance. And another thing, Chief. The rebels don't need any collaborators to bomb us. We just happen to be close enough to them—if they had the necessary planes they would go right up to the federal capital and drop bombs there. In any case, as I said, we as soldiers are trying to do the best we can to counteract the rebel activities. It's not easy in the least, but I can assure you we will continue to fight them effectively. That's what we're here for. Now, if you'll excuse me, sir, I really must go.'

I don my cap again and rise. He rises reluctantly after me, rubbing his neck in unspoken but clearly uneasy resentment at the abrupt end to our conversation. The man is irrepressible, but he is wasting my time with pointless talk.

'Well. Major,' he says, with a touch of inconclusiveness in his voice, 'let's leave it at that. Let's leave it at that.'

'That's all right, Chief,' I say, approaching the door now. 'Oh, Chief?' I stop and turn.

'Yes?' He is rather shaken.

'How is Mrs Oshevire?'

'She is all right,' he says, with something of a frightened question in his eyes.

'Nothing of course happened to her?'

'No, nothing. Nothing at all, Major. She's—she's quite all right.'

'I just wondered, Chief. About what you told me—that she generally felt very insecure any time a thing like this happened. So I thought, well, wouldn't it be a terrible thing for her to continue in that state? You see, we can't guarantee that the rebels won't visit us again, and I think it's unkind to let her live with a perpetual feeling of insecurity and fear when we could have given her more certain protection, until her town was liberated and she could be given an escort home if she wanted to go.'

'Well—'

'You know, I was thinking of putting her in the refugee camp, but then I reflected that she might not feel any safer there. And then I thought seriously again of putting her under military custody, which would be a more assured protection.'

'Oh, no, no, Major. There's no call for that. No need for you to do that.'

'You think not, Chief?' The doubt in my mind is now growing stronger.

'Yes, she's all right. I tell you, Major, she's all right. I said I was looking after her, and I am. Her husband and I . . . we were in this rubber business together, you know, and . . . I tell you, Major, she's all right. I'm taking care of her. I promise . . . nothing will happen to her. Nothing at all.'

He looks rather small now. The picture has certainly changed, the great big chief, the grand citizen and leader of his people, now pleading with almost puerile panic to be left custody of a woman towards whose husband he cannot be said to feel the greatest good-will.

'Well, all right, Chief,' I sigh as I move outside again. 'If there's anything I can do to help, just let me know.'

'Oh, thank you, Major,' he says with sudden elation, looking all the more puerile. 'I realise we share the same concern. I mean, I'm as worried as you are about the lot of helpless people like her. And that's why I thought I should do the best I could. After all, she's as good as any citizen here, being married to one of us.'

One of us. Oh, indeed? I could turn now, to challenge him on that remark. But what's the use?

'Thanks, Chief,' I say. 'I'll be seeing you again. And thank you for the drink. I must admit it limbered me up.'

'I told you, *ha, ha ha!*' he says, bursting with jubilation. 'Didn't I tell you it would? *Ha ha ha!* Nothing like gin and root for whipping yourself up in the morning, *ha ha ha!*'

'That's right, Chief. That's right.'

'Very good.'

'Goodbye, sir. Tell your family to be careful.'

'I'll do that, Major. I'll do that.'

'Goodbye.'

'Goodbye, Major.'

Even as we drive away and the view of his premises gets smaller and smaller in the rear-mirror, I can see him standing in the door-way, perhaps waiting to be absolutely certain that we have gone.

Something in me tells me all is not well. Honestly, it all looks very unreal, this thing about the Chief and the woman. How can an honest man live with two inclinations so thoroughly opposed to one another? You feel so deeply convinced that a man is a rebel colla-borator and you would even be prepared to supply evidence to the tribunal that could seal his doom, yet you are so very concerned about the welfare of his wife and her comfort. Of course I have no personal stake in the Oshevire case. If it is convincingly proved that he collaborated with the rebels during their stay in this town, then —God help him. Though, as the newspapers seem to report of the proceedings, there doesn't appear to be any solid basis for the charges brought against him—still, if in the end he is shown to have aided the rebel occupation, in the name of justice he should consider himself responsible for whatever the government decides to do to him.

But that's for the tribunal to find out for themselves, and no amount of pressure from the Chief would make me offer unsolicited services to civilian exercises far away at Iddu, when the severe realities of war confront me right here in Urukpe. *Lai'llah!*

Now I don't like all this fishy business about Chief Toje and Mrs Oshevire. His intentions may well be sincere. If he is the respectable man that I have always seen him to be, then he may yet maintain his integrity—after all, there is really nothing so seriously incompatible in him feeling so strongly about Oshevire's collaboration with the rebels (if he is truly convinced of this) yet at the same time having enough human stirrings within him to want to help the man's family. He is probably right then, that we share the same concern. But I don't want to be too certain about anything. First I must find out exactly where she lives, just in case. . . .

Oghenovo

the big soldier is standing very close to the small soldier. he is much taller than the small soldier, and his red cap is slanted with his face as he looks down on the small soldier. the small soldier is standing straight and looking straight, not at the big soldier, his gun by his side. the big soldier is talking to him, and knocking his cane on his own leg, and the small soldier is not looking at him yet. i think he is afraid of the big soldier.

i want to be like the big soldier, so that i can give onome a good beating. calling my father a thief. saying the soldiers took away my father because he stole something and the soldiers don't like people to steal anything because they want to keep it all to themselves. but my mother says my father is a good man. she says my father did not steal anything.

now the big soldier is walking around. he goes away from the small soldier standing straight with the gun, and he walks round a little, looking about him. he stands at the door of the hall now, then looks round again. he comes down from the steps of the door, and walks again round the place. he goes to where the little motor car is standing, with another small soldier standing near it. the soldier that came with him. he talks to this small soldier that came with him. the soldier is standing straight too. then the big soldier shakes his head, and walks away from the small soldier that came with him, knocking the cane again on his own leg. then the big soldier walks again to the other small soldier. the one that didn't come with him. the one standing straight with the gun.

he is afraid of him now. why does he not shoot him with the gun. i think he is afraid of the big soldier. then the big soldier stands again near this small soldier. he is talking to him again.

and now they are looking towards me. they are pointing at our house. the small soldier is showing the big soldier our house. and the big soldier is pointing too. then the small soldier—

oghenovo! the big soldier puts his hand down, but is looking straight at our house still, his eyes dark under the peak of his red cap, and he does not—

oghenovo! my mother shouts.

ma, i answer her.

where are you, you little wizard, she says.

i am here, ma, i say.

come in quickly before i open my eyes, she says.

and my mother comes out from the door and draws me away by the collar into the house. *what will the big soldier do to the small—*

what do you think you were doing there, says my mother.

it's the big soldier, i say.

what big soldier, she says.

the one with the open pleasure car, i say. the one that—

what about him, my mother says.

he is there, mother, i say. he is outside with the small soldier.

what small soldier, she says.

the one that—

do you want to bring more sorrows upon me, you little devil, says my mother. do you not see what has been happening.

but i only—

shut up and listen to me, she says. do you want to go outside and bring your destruction in, when it would come into the house looking for you anyway.

i was only outside the door, mother, i say. i never went beyond the door.

if you stay at home where you are supposed to be, you won't have to bother about any big soldiers and small soldiers until they come and get you.

then she doesn't say anything. she looks away from me, looking down at the grains of rice that she is picking in the calabash bowl. she is angry, my mother is, not looking at me now. *she says my father is a good man. therefore onome is a liar. i want to be like that big soldier so that i can beat onome.*

will they come to this house, mother, i ask her.

if they want to, she says.

when will they want to, mother, i say.

when they get tired of you looking at them, says my mother.

perhaps they will come now, i say.

perhaps, she says.

i think they are talking about us, i say.

yes, says my mother, they are saying they will catch you because you won't let them be. do you want them to catch you.

I shake my head. *the small soldier is afraid of the big soldier, but why does he not shoot him down with the gun.*

mother, i say, i saw them looking at our house, pointing this way.

what, says my mother, raising her eyes at me now.

i saw the small soldier pointing to our house, i say. showing our house to the big soldier. and after some time the big soldier begins to point this way too. do you think they are coming to catch me, mother.

my mother does not answer me. she gets up from her seat, putting the calabash bowl of rice down now. then she goes quickly to the door. she opens the door a little, and peeps out. i run up to her, and peep too from behind her.

go away, says my mother, pushing me back with her behind. go back into the house quickly.

i leave her there, standing with the door slightly open and peeping out through the long crack of light. i run to a window and peep through a hole of light. i can see the small soldier, pacing now. the big soldier and the other small soldier that came with him are walking into the little open pleasure car. then they enter the car, and drive away.

my mother comes away from the door. but i have already left the window, so that she doesn't notice that i have been peeping too.

will they come and get me, mother, i ask her.

but she does not answer me. she walks slowly from the door now. slowly, picking her steps, towards the bowl of rice. she does not look at me now. i think she wants to cry. holding one hand against her chest, and letting her unsmiling and untalking face gaze straight at the calabash bowl on the floor near her stool. she picks up the bowl and starts picking the rice again, not talking to me. maybe she too is afraid of the big soldier.

mother, will they come and catch me, i ask her.

perhaps, she says. if you won't keep indoors.

what was the big soldier telling the small soldier, mother, i say. what was he saying about us.

i don't know, says my mother.

maybe the big soldier and the small soldier were talking about my father. maybe onome told them about my father, that he stole something. but mother says that my father is a good man.

were they talking about my father, i say.

i don't think so, she says. why would they talk about your father. they don't know your father, she says.

but onome said they took my father away, i say.

they did not take him away, she says. he travelled with them, but not these ones. tell onome that.

which ones was it, i say.

they are no longer here, she says.

where are they, i say.

i don't know, she says. but not these ones.

then who will bring him back, i ask. is it not the ones with whom he travelled.

i don't know, she says. but not these ones.

my mother says my father did not steal anything because he is a good man. onome is a liar. i want to be like the big soldier so that i can beat him.

when will my father come back, i ask her.

i don't know, my mother says. but he will come back soon.

onome said he would never come back, i tell her. he says the soldiers will never let him come back because he stole their things. and if anybody steals—

stop telling me what onome says, my mother shouts. onome says this, onome says that, what does onome know about your father. if onome calls your father a thief, then call his father a thief too and stop bothering me about what onome says. if you stay indoors will onome have the opportunity to tell you that your father is a thief.

my mother is very angry with me. then she bends down and begins to pick the rice again and does not look up. i don't want my mother to be angry again.

onome's father is a thief onome's father is a thief onome's father is a thief onome's father is a thief onome's father is . . .

go into the room and lie on the bed, my mother says. when the food is ready i will call you to eat.

my mother hisses, and begins to murmur something. then her mouth stops moving, and her untalking and unsmiling face does not look up again from the bowl of rice. *my father is a good man and onome's father is a thief.*

i lie on my mother's bed, and look at the thatchleaves of the roo sketch restless shadows on the wall. there is a wall-gecko crawling across slowly, down towards the far end of the wall. now it creeps slowly, now it darts fast towards a fly. the fly runs away, and the gecko stops and waits to let it perch. and then the gecko steals across again, slowly, slowly. on its back the patches of light and leaf-shadows sketch moving dapples. but the fly does not wait for it to come.

mother said if i slept she would wake me up when she finished cooking, and when i have eaten, i will hide away from my mother and go to the small soldier standing with the gun, and i will ask him when my father will come back, and i will ask him who took my father away, and i will tell him what onome said, that my father stole something and . . . for that reason . . . the soldiers . . . *shut up says the big big soldier with the fat club in his hand and the thief lying on the ground begins to cry and to beg the soldier to let him go home and the big soldier beats him again on the head with the big stick and onome sitting on top of the high high tree begins to laugh at the crying thief lying on the ground and i begin to cry and to feel very sorry for the thief and the big big giant soldier says catch that little boy and the ten small small soldiers carry their guns and walk quickly towards me and i try to run but i cannot because my feet are stuck to the ground and the sky begins to turn round and round and suddenly it begins to rain and there is a lot of rice in the rain and the big big giant soldier leaves the crying thief on the ground and begins to swallow all the rice and refuses to let me have any of it and still i can't run away because my feet are stuck to the ground and all i can do is cry and cry and cry. . . .*

Toje

I have always known it. Small men must always think small and act small, whatever happens. You give a man good money to go down to Iddu and argue a case, and even furnish him with sound, convincing arguments to bear up the case: yet let the judge merely open his mouth to yawn, and your little scoundrel loses no time in collapsing on his rump.

It wasn't that if I had looked around the town for people with guts—at least guts enough for the kind of job I wanted done—I could not have found them. Add a little money into the bargain, and you'll get a man ready to stand up and tell the chairman of the tribunal to his face where his father's father was born. Now look what this wretch has gone to do before the tribunal. What bothers me is not so much that he went up there to expose himself to ridicule as that he seems to have made nonsense of the whole case. For what the chairman has done amounts to practically telling him that his evidence is useless and cannot be upheld. Now was I expected to go there by myself and put forward convincing and well-argued points in the way in which any sensible man ought to have done? It's a curse to be a small man.

Who could have been better qualified than Omonigho Rukeme to argue a case against Mukoro Oshevire, knowing full well that this was his best and indeed only good chance to avenge the disgrace brought upon his father by Oshevire?

It wasn't long before the war came to this state. Everybody remembers the incident. Oshevire had long known from reports brought to him by his tappers that someone was stealing the latex from his rubber plantation. It was also known that Uduefe Rukeme's was the next plantation to Oshevire's And it was also known that Rukeme was in the habit of going to his farm much earlier than anybody else did. And of course being a poor wretched farmer, with only a very small plantation, he either went alone to his farm or took a son along. There aren't many people like me who can afford to pay labourers to do the job. So one day a trap was laid, and it caught! Rukeme was cornered practically emptying the latex from the cup on one of Oshevire's trees into his bucket. Well, he tried all he could to browbeat the labourer who caught him, but the man made the report to Oshevire, who went straight to the *Otota* and was barely restrained from taking the case to court. When the case was brought before council—what didn't the wily old fox do to disengage himself? He swore by the grey hairs of his head and penis, by his long-deceased grandfather, even by the cunt of his own mother—may he not live to hear the next cock crow if he ever so much as stepped close to Oshevire's latex! Of course everybody knew that Uduefe Rukeme was a thief. But council gave him the benefit of his oath and of the vigour and conviction with which it had been sworn. We even found ourselves blaming it all on the visual error of the labourer, asking the man, on Rukeme's invitation, to produce concrete evidence of the theft!

Yet for the people at large, Rukeme's past record alone was enough to determine a verdict; before the week was out a song had already been composed and popularised, about ten aging but slick little fingers sticky with rubber!

Yes, I am not ashamed to admit it. I would not go about noising it to the wind or whispering it to anyone. But I can admit it to myself: I called Omonigho Rukeme to my house and in secret elicited his cooperation in incriminating Mukoro Oshevire. Yes, there was too an atmosphere of suspicion and distrust all over this place after the rebels had been cleared from Urukpe, and even the military authorities, and the Commander of the federal forces here then, Major Akuya Bello, were prepared and eager to listen to the words of prominent and distinguished sons of Urukpe like me. Anybody who noticed the entries and exits of any number of rebel soldiers in Oshevire's house would be prepared to believe anything said about him collaborating with them, particularly if it came from the mouth of a respected citizen like myself. Yes, I exploited the situation and secretly reported Oshevire to Major Bello, and thereafter Oshevire was whisked off into detention at Iddu. And yes, I later got together a number of trumped up charges, and proceeded to suborn the son of Oshevire's old enemy to appear in evidence against the man who put the shame on his father only a few years back. Yes, I did all these things, and though I won't tell anybody else, at least I am prepared to stand by myself in defence of my act— whether of bad faith or of realism, call it what you will.

And why did I do all this? For a number of reasons, bearing not only on civic concern but also on pride of place and on plain old survival, if the severe truth should be told. For one thing, after the federal troops liberated this town—thanks no less to the subtle resistance organised by good citizens like myself than to the military efforts of the fighting men—the military authorities realised that it was in the interest of their security that unreliable elements in the town be exposed and contained. So they went about asking questions or at least demonstrating a willingness to listen to useful advice. And who in this town was, and is, better qualified to enjoy the confidence of authority than myself and maybe a handful of others? All right—so I volunteered my information to Major Bello unsolicited, though he could have asked me all the same and the fact may have slipped his attention. But I was acting like a good and important citizen by doing what I did—and who is there that can challenge my civic responsibility, let alone my place?

Yes, I informed on Oshevire, or I exercised my civic duty—it all amounts to the same thing. But the whole town saw him—was there anyone who didn't know that rebel soldiers went in and out of Oshevire's house, even if they could have gone there to ask for a drink of water? *Ehn*, if Oshevire knows he is such an innocent man and that was all they did in his house, let him go ahead and prove to the tribunal that he was the only one in Urukpe with a pot of water clean enough and fit enough for rebel soldiers to drink. *Shuo!* If they can believe him then he is a free man, and we can line the streets and welcome him back with singing and dancing.

And I cannot view my survival and pride of place lightly. I was in this rubber business before Oshevire came into it. Mention my name in any rubber circles in this town, this whole area, the whole state, and even the whole country, and if there is anyone who can come forward and claim that he has never heard about me, then either he is not in rubber or I am not Toje Onovwakpo! And then Oshevire came. Before he entered into the business, I was conducting mine quietly, without any molestation or doubts. I'm not against younger men getting into the business. After all, they are the ones who will take over after we older ones have left the scene. But there he was. I was doing my business very well and successfully. Rukeme is nobody till today—nobody thinks of him when rubber is mentioned. Chief Ukoli has a moderate plantation, but he is not well organised in the business. Chief Dafinone Arigbe is a drunkard and could have done much better than his cups have left him to do now. Akpotobo Onoge is too involved in politics—when he is not fighting land cases far away in Okere Town—to have sufficient time to tend his trees. There is hardly anybody else worth mentioning.

So I could have enjoyed a long and unchallenged supremacy in this business if the upstart Oshevire had not pushed himself into the scene. Of course he inherited a plantation almost as big as mine—but that's not the point. Before long he was already attracting labourers away from me, because he paid better, or so they thought. *Shuo!* Not much later the government came up with all that nonsense about unadulterated latex, and in no time the buying agents began to turn their faces away from me. Even when I took the lumps up to Iddu myself the assessors at the Marketing Corporation tossed them about as though they were cow dung. 'Too much sand,' they said. 'Too much dirt. Too impure.' And Oshevire began to enjoy increasing attention. Oshevire began to receive the agents more and more often, and they avoided my house as though it had an epidemic of smallpox! Oshevire began to grow bigger and bigger, and even to throw his weight about! One day I made the mistake of asking him if he bought his coagulating acid cheaper, and from the way he answered me he left me regretting my folly in asking that question: 'Well,' he said, dragging his tone, and you could see the condescension on his face, 'well . . . it depends how strong you want the acid, you know. There are many types of acid, you know, many grades. Which grade are you talking about?'

Haw!

Anyway, I made up my mind that I wasn't going to sit down and fold my arms and legs and let myself be pushed out of my rightful place of prominence. For, think how it would sound if people suddenly began to hear that Toje Onovwakpo could no longer make ends meet! Think how it would sound if the word went around that Toje Onovwakpo had nothing and was nobody after all! Think what it would look like if nobody respected my word in council, or people started to make fun of me, when not so long ago you hardly heard the name of Urukpe without hearing the names of people like me attached to it!

The absence of Mukoro Oshevire therefore gives me the opportunity to set things right. It gives me the opportunity to re-establish my prominence, my power, and the respect that everybody in this town ought to show me.

But look what a mess the accursed Rukeme has made by his most inept appearance before the tribunal. I could hardly bring myself to believe what I read in the newspaper had to do with a human being with brains in his head.

The air raid on this town had disrupted our contact with the outside world, so it wasn't possible for us to get the newspapers. Just before the raid I had vaguely heard from the radio the points that the chairman of the tribunal had made at the close of Rukeme's evidence, and I had waited to get the papers to be able to read the proceedings in full. But the air raid came. So, after the Major visited me in the morning two days ago, I set out for Iddu so as to inform myself better on the matter. On getting to Iddu, I first called at the house of a friend, and there I was able to get hold of the issue of the *Zonda Observer* that reported the proceedings in detail. My God, what ineptitude Rukeme displayed! It was all there in the newspaper.

I didn't wait long at my friend's place. I set out at once to look for Rukeme, and later found the scoundrel at a drinking bar which was said to be his regular haunt. When he saw me coming into the bar, he shuddered, and I could see that if he had his chance he would have taken to his heels. I motioned him to an isolated table, and even before we sat down there, he was already in a panic.

'I tried my best,' he blubbered. 'Believe me, Toje, I—'

'Sit down first,' I told him. 'Let's not be too hasty. What was it you were drinking?' He had an empty glass on his table when I saw him.

'Honestly, Toje, it wasn't easy for—'

'I said what was it you were drinking?'

'Fanta.'

I looked at him in wonder.

'You came all the way here to drink Fanta? Come on, man, what will you drink?'

'Beer.'

I called one of the bar boys.

'One beer,' I told him.

Rukeme was restless in his seat, I could see that well, his hands rubbing nervously at his knees and his eyes wearing a frightened plea.

'Now, Rukeme, tell me what happened,' I said. 'I don't mean narrate the proceedings to me, for those are clear enough from the papers. I just want you to tell me how it came about that you lost your bearing before the tribunal.'

'I . . . you . . . I . . . believe me, Toje, it wasn't easy. I tri—'

'What wasn't easy?'

'All that crowd. And the panel. Their eyes. I could hardly . . . it was almost as if *I* was on trial. The way they looked at—'

'God! Did you go in there thinking they were going to smile and shake hands with you for bringing them good news?'

'I swear . . . it wasn't easy . . . it wasn't.'

'But of course—what did you expect? Did you think the panel was there on a holiday? The government has called them to preside over the freedom and maybe the lives of a number of men, and you think for them it is a very cheerful assignment?'

He avoided my face completely, looking aside all the while, still nervous. I didn't know what to say to a fool of this kind, and I found myself regretting having entrusted the assignment to the creature.

'All right,' I said. 'What do you think is going to happen now?'

'What?' he half-raised his timid eyes.

'What do you think we are going to do now? Of course, you don't need to be told that the evidence you presented to the tribunal has been totally rejected. So what are we going to do now, since all that remains is for Oshevire to tell the tribunal that he has done nothing?'

'Well. . . . I suppose he still has to prove it.'

'Well, that's a brilliant thing for you to say now! It was left to *you* to give all the proof, and look what you went up there and did. Even my little Robinson could have stood boldly before that panel and told them that Oshevire lavished food and drinks on rebel soldiers. And if they asked him what that proved, he would still have the courage to retort that nobody else in Urukpe gave the rebels that much comfort. And it would be left to the tribunal to decide for themselves which way Oshevire's sympathies lay. Now was that asking too much of a man in your position, when you had all the reason in the world to want to take your revenge on him, and when you got good money even in spite of this—how much was it I gave you?'

'One fifty pounds.'

'One fifty pounds! And you couldn't stand on your two feet before that rotten crowd and tell them with a straight face how you felt? And you knew you were backed with that much money and even the knowledge that you had been sent by no less a man than me! Now what do you think will happen next?'

'If . . . I don't know—'

'You don't know? I think we have heard that sort of language too often from your family lately. The other day your father was caught in the act and all he could swear to the world was that he didn't know what his accusers were talking about, when the rubber had barely dried from his hands.'

'That's not true,' the scoundrel said. That's what he said!

'Don't give me any of those lies again. We know all about these things—never mind that we sometimes keep our mouths shut out of sympathy for you wretched things.'

'It's not true,' he said. 'And you know it. You were there when the case was brought before the council.'

'Yes, yes. I was there. Of course I was there. But so what? Maybe I composed those songs too?'

'It's all a lie, Toje, and you know it.'

'*All right!*' I banged on the table, upsetting his drink, which he hadn't touched and now fought to save. 'I'm not discussing this any further. But get this quite clear. If that man goes free, then it means I haven't received the services for which I paid one fifty pounds. And I must have that money back. Otherwise, I promise you that a lot of people are going to be sorry. Don't forget that I am still Chief Toje Onovwakpo of Urukpe. You can enjoy your holiday now in Iddu, but don't forget to pray every day and every night that Mukoro Oshevire does not win the judgment.'

I rose quickly from my seat and left him. I could see some faces turned in my direction as I was making my way out, but I wasn't bothered at all.

I was hardly at the door when the steward ran up to me.

'Oga, money for the drink?'

'Out of my way!' I bawled at him. 'That bastard there will pay you. He's got all the money.'

I stormed out of the god-forsaken place.

One hundred and fifty pounds—and even that couldn't get the goat to sit straight on his arse! My God, poverty is a curse. And his excuse: that he was made to feel as if *he* was on trial!

I was too angry and too confused to think constructively, trying to fight my frustrations and at the same time to sort out my priorities. I finally made up my mind to try once more to save the situation. So I took a taxi and made for the headquarters of the Second Division of the Federal Army at Iddu, where I was sure Major Akuya Bello would be. He it was to whom I gave my information in the first place concerning Oshevire's collaboration with the rebels. He knew very well how strongly people felt about such an issue at that time, just after the federal forces came into our town. Sitting now on the panel of the tribunal, he should, I reckoned, be able to view the menace with even greater seriousness than when he led the forces into Urukpe in the wake of the fleeing rebels. And I reckoned also that, if he felt enough respect for me at that time to want to throw Oshevire into detention at my instigation, he should be moved to an even greater feeling of awe at seeing a respectable man like myself doing all that distance from Urukpe to Iddu just to press a case.

At one point the driver of the taxi stopped to pick up a woman with a load. *The dog!*

'What do you want to do?' I asked him.

'Why—to pick up the passenger.'

'Move on at once,' I roared at him.

'Are you then chartering the taxi? If you are, then it would come to fifteen shillings from the point where I picked you up to the Army Headquarters.'

'No,' I said. 'Ten shillings.'

'No, sir,' he returned, turning off the engine and removing his cap to scratch his scruffy head. 'The distance is too much. Fifteen shillings or nothing.'

The woman came up to us, dragging her load, a bag of yams. The driver sat back nonchalantly, and sighed.

'What do you say, sir?' he asked.

One look at the woman was enough to arouse revulsion in me—I couldn't bear to share the car with such common sort.

'All right. All right,' I told him. 'Go on. And be quick about it!'

We were off again. I did not wish to spend the night at Iddu. I came into the town with the lorry that was to transport the yams for the federal forces at Urukpe, and I wanted to go back with it. Besides, my misadventure at the whorehouse had created in me sufficient aversion for this town, and I had resolved that I was never going to lay myself open to the kind of thing a man could do under a careless itch of passion.

We were barely fifty yards from the gate of the Army Headquarters when the driver stopped, and turned off the engine. I couldn't understand the man.

'We're there,' he said.

'Where?' I asked. I couldn't understand the scum.

'The Army Headquarters,' he replied, turning round to look at my face. 'Wasn't that where you wanted to go?'

'Yes, but you're not quite there yet.'

'This is as far as I can go.'

'Why?'

'I don't want any trouble,' he said, glancing towards the guarded gate.

I gazed at him for a moment. This time it was not so much that I didn't understand him. I simply resented having to be made to walk that distance to the gate so unbefittingly, like one approaching a shrine in supplication! I thought I was too big for that.

However, I sighed in resignation and carefully opened the door at my side. Carefully also I stepped out of the taxi—first my walking stick, then, holding my plumed bourdillon on my head, one gentle foot after the other. I preened myself to order—I had to. These soldiers are discourteous enough to any man: how much more so if a man did not bear himself admirably and respectably. I paid the driver, who in his impatience—*the fool*!—had turned on the engine again, and I faced my task.

The gate was closed. One soldier sat with his back against it, facing the military premises. Another was leaning against one of the posts, his gun slung across a shoulder and his cap tilted over his eyes. Two more were inside a booth, playing a game. None of them paid me any attention as I walked up to the gate, though I felt certain they knew I was there. I was rather disturbed. If a beggar came to the place, I thought, then they had reason to ignore him. But I was definitely not one, nor did I look like one. So I coughed for deserved notice. Before I was through, one of the players threw out at me:

'What do you want?' He didn't even raise his head from his game.

'Is Major Bello here?' I asked him in return.

'What do you want with him?'

'I have urgent business to discuss with him,' I said.

The soldier sitting with his back to me turned round slowly and surveyed me from foot to head, and turned back again. The one leaning against the post tipped up his cap just enough to run his bloodshot eyes down me, from head to foot, then let it settle again over his eyes, and resumed his posture. *Haw!*

'What kind of business is that?' the player asked.

'It is between the two of us,' I said. 'He'll understand if you just let him know I'm here to see him.'

At this he stopped playing to look at me, quite piercingly.

'Look here, old man,' he said, 'you can't just come here and demand to see an officer for some vague reason. What do you want— what business is it you want to discuss with him?'

I was perplexed. It's one thing to probe a man's mission and another thing to do so with such blatant and oppressive rudeness. I dabbed my sweating palms with my handkerchief.

'A—ah,' I said. 'I have told you—'

'You haven't told me anything. Look—where is your pass?'

'Pass?'

'Do you also not know that you can't get into this place without a pass?'

'I—'

'All right, go away,' he said, turning back to his game. 'Go away, and stop wasting my time.'

'But Major Bello—'

'You heard what he said,' intoned the tilted cap, still unmoving and without losing any of his silent menace. 'Go away.'

I did not wish to press the issue. I looked ahead into the guarded premises. The military air of the place was stern. I resolved to save myself further embarrassment and perhaps more.

As I walked away to look for a taxi, my anger swelled up in me. It was bad enough that I had failed to achieve my desperate mission. But it was much worse that I had to do so with that much disrespect and outright rudeness from brats whom I could feed tenfold. And look at all the trouble I took, a man of my position!

Yet, perhaps it was much better that I did not see Major Bello. For these soldiers could be a strange set! Take the case of Ali here in Urukpe. Whatever the reasons for my approaches to him, it seems to me that his judgment and good sense surely elude him sometimes. You are constantly confronted by the danger of rebels overrunning your post and perhaps destroying you, and you refuse to take the initiative in helping to track down known and identified rebel supporters—even when you receive an offer of assistance from a highly-placed citizen like myself whose word can hardly be questioned. And your reason is that you are unwilling to let a probe in Iddu distract you from your tardy soldiering here!

So how could I have taken it if Akuya Bello, from the same misguided self-delusion, had suddenly begun reading me his lessons on a tribunal's search for justice, on fair hearing, on evidence of doubtful credit, and other such nonsense—when not so long ago he knew no better than to obey rude impulse; all I had to do was point to a man and say 'He's a collaborator!' and he lost no time in throwing chains around the man and hustling him off to detention more than a hundred miles away?

However, somewhere in the midst of my loaded feelings lurked a conviction that my mission would yet be accomplished. For, in the first place, I was—and still am—convinced that Oshevire was going to infuriate the panel into a hasty condemnation of him. A man comes forward and heaps charges upon your head, though he cannot prove his points; and when you are asked if you have any questions to put to him, you reply that you have none—what kind of courage is that, that invites the fate of a dog? Also, I was sure—and still am— that something was going to happen to Ali. One good shattering blast from the rebels, and I would dare him to persist in his misguided refusal to have anything to do with the tribunal!

Hard though it was, I swallowed my exasperation at those unruly ruffians at the military gate, and sought a taxi to take me back to town. All I was going to do, while the chattered lorry loaded the yams, was buy a few articles for Oshevire's wife and child. . . .

For that other victory has to be won also. It occupies no less a place of importance in my mission of self-reassertion.

Okumagba

Only the consequences of such an action deter me from sticking the barrel of my gun through the window and blasting the brains clean out of that woman and her child. For that is what they deserve, like all rebels. But I know what a crazy major we have here. Get only so near as to touch the hair on the body of anyone who doesn't wear a gun, and he makes haste to tie you to the stake and despatch you with a spray of burning lead. Justice, even the swift justice of the gun, has gone mad in his head.

Here I am—a soldier of the Federal Republic of Zonda. I went into the Army by my own choice, when the nation summoned the willing to arms; nobody conscripted me. All right—soldiering pays better (if you live through it) than the job of a tailoring apprentice, which I had before the war. But all the same I went in of my own accord. Once in, I swore loyally to defend this country, with my own life if need be, against any form of violation. I have taken part in many campaigns, faced the risk of certain death in the worst encounters with the rebels, and am more than happy that I took part in the push that chased them out of this town, my own town, Urukpe. Now look where I have ended up. A lone and ineffective guard, performing not the duty that I pledged myself to but a most unbecoming chore: detailed to preserve the life of a rebel and her child and even make certain that no loyal citizen comes close to causing them the least concern!

Look what this stupid detail has exposed me to. 'Stay right

there,' said the Major, 'rain or sun, every day up until twelve midnight: and make sure nothing happens to that woman and her child.' All right. I couldn't refuse, for as a soldier I shouldn't. But look what my stupid loyalty has exposed me to.

First, there's the question of rebel raids. If anything happens, I am confronted with the double task of saving my own life and making sure that nothing happens to Oshevire's wife and child. That's what the Major said. And if any determined guerrilla attacks happen in the night, I will be too hopelessly outnumbered to put up any resistance, let alone try to save the lives of two other people for whom, God knows, my heart feels not the least sympathy.

Take the other day, when we had this rebel air raid. I was pacing round the council hall premises, as has now become my painful custom. It was just like any other day, with the sun rising, blazing and setting as usual and people going about their several businesses with no more fear of danger in their hearts than would be normal for a crisis such as we are in. Suddenly, out of the twilit horizon and from beyond the surrounding woods rose their planes, in deadly formation. I knew this was it—it had happened more than once before. I cocked my gun, and edged carefully well by the front door of the council hall. Within seconds their bombs boomed as they dropped, and all over the town you could hear the cries of human beings amid the frenzied bursts and crackles of anti-aircraft fire. One rebel bomb dropped not very far from my position and I rose to the challenge and released a determined volley of fire towards the plane. That bomb-blast claimed the life of Omonigho Dafe and the little house which he occupied with his aged mother (who at the time was just coming back from the stream). But to this day it remains for me a matter of deepest regret that my foremost concern at the moment of the disaster was with the danger I *thought* confronted these accursed creatures that our crazy Major had put under my protection—not the real tragedy that threatened the lives of honest citizens. While that bomb dropped and put an end to the life of a true son of Urukpe, my trigger-finger was driven on by the anxiety to save the lives of people who have shown by their collaboration with the rebels that they never meant Urukpe well!

And then there is this toing and froing between the woman and the cripple Odibo. It is beginning to happen with such frequency these days that I am wondering if the whole thing is genuine. The cripple sneaks in, either empty-handed or with a basketful of things or a wrapped-up parcel. Moments later the woman appears, all done up in so much splendour you begin to wonder if this really is a woman supposed to be grieving over the detention of her husband, about whose return she could not be too certain. She stands at the door for a while to preen herself, like a duck, unfolding her wrapper to tie it in better order or giving her headtie a few last gentle pats at the sides. Then she proceeds, whither I do not know. She comes back much later, very close to curfew time: empty-handed sometimes, and at other times with some bundle trussed under an arm, yet at all times wearing signs that the missions he had been on could scarcely be described as honest. She enters the house, and a few moments later the cripple comes out and slinks his way home.

'Leave them alone,' said the Major. 'They are trying to help her.' All right. But the trouble with the Major is, he is crazy. He doesn't know anything. Besides, he's a stranger from up-country and he doesn't understand our people down here. A rebel woman and the wife of a known rebel collaborator—and he is determined to extend to her the benevolence and protection that should be reserved for true citizens, and (what's worse) has set me here to police the madness! He thinks these people are trying to show her kindness. What sort of kindness is it, that could not be shown in daylight, that happens only towards the end of the day, when all good people should be thinking of retiring into their homes to avoid the danger of being seen out and about at curfew time? *If I could just blast open this lie, this madness. . . .*

But—here comes Odibo. I should have guessed that this was his prowling time. Here he comes, the cripple. Making his way once again to the woman's place, face downward, never looking up, like a pig. And again in the evening. This can hardly be genuine. Or a kindness. *Oh, for a chance. . . .* He walks right up to the door, and knocks. Still looking downward. The door is opened, and he sneaks in. . . .

Leave them alone, said the Major. I'll leave them alone. But one of these days my patience will be spent. One of these days I'll find I can no longer contain this anger. Perhaps something will give me a good chance. Like a rebel guerrilla raid at night while I'm still on guard. If they don't get me, and we succeed in beating back the raid, I'll take the opportunity to empty a few rounds into that god-forsaken house, and save myself once and for all from this hateful detail. Nobody would know what happened. Our authorities would be too busy sorting themselves out to stop to investigate whether it was a federal or rebel gun that did the job.

A rebel is bad enough. But a whoring rebel! *Hm*. . . .

Toje

It's only fair exchange. She needs food, clothing, maintenance and protection very badly. With her husband far away and under the firm grip of detention she cannot help herself, alone and unattended. I am in need of self-reassurance. I need very badly to confirm to my-self that I still possess within me that natural power without which a man has no claim whatsoever to the qualification.

Come to think of it, I stand to lose more than she does in the matter. There's no question but that she needs a man. A woman who has known no man for over three years must be feeling the burning itch of desire, and she is too young to let her groin suffer that long torment. I therefore mean her no small service; and she should be thankful to know that, if she must give herself away, it won't be to any common scum but to a respected celebrity of Urukpe.

Whereas, if I should fail to achieve what I have set out to do, it will be no small tragedy. For how would it sound in people's ears, that Chief Toje Onovwakpo of Urukpe is an impotent man? How would the news be taken—that the big rubber magnate, whose name and enterprise alone are sufficient to guarantee Urukpe its reputa-tion as a major rubber producing town in the Black Gold State, is devoid of manhood? Surely that would be a big blot on the name of this town. I am too aware, not only of the grandeur of my name, but indeed of my deep civic concern, to let such news get around. Perish the thought! And if it takes my manipulating a forlorn woman into adultery—though she knows she stands doubly to gain by the act—I am convinced that no sacrifice is too big so long as the disaster can be averted.

So here I am, in Odibo's unbecoming hovel once again, waiting for Oshevire's wife, ready to wait for as long as it takes to achieve a noble purpose. This time I am not prepared to take any chances. Too often, in my attempt on the woman, have I permitted my powers to fail me by letting the thought of the matter prey too much on my mind. I have therefore brought along with me a full bottle of gin. Before she arrives I am going to see the bottom of this bottle—and my energies, unencumbered by all too conscious worry, will be driven on by a mad animal urge.

Odibo

I saw it. I saw it! I swear to God—I saw it. And though I should never—dare not—mention it, I saw it with my two eyes, in full view, right from where I'm sitting now. The naked form of the woman! By God, I saw it!

I came in here not so long ago, and delivered the usual invitation. 'He's waiting for you at my place,' I said. 'He says you should come.'

She wasn't doing anything. When I had knocked, and she'd come and opened the door for me, there was that look in her eyes that seemed to say she knew what I was there for. But she didn't seem to show too much interest. She merely sighed, weakly I thought, removing her hand from the door-post to let me in.

'Sit down,' she said, 'while I get ready.'

She went into her bedroom, and later I heard her getting ready to take her bath. The jingle of the bucket as she walked to fetch the water from the pot in the backyard. Then later she came into the bedroom again, through the parlour. I was still sitting, in the same position as I am now. As she passed by I eyed her furtively. It wasn't my fault. Toje had before tried to get me to look at the woman—until he thought I was looking too much for my own good. So somehow my eyes have become used to stealing occasional glances through no fault of mine.

I watched her pass by to the bedroom. She had a wrapper tied to her body, reaching from the breasts to just below the knee and exposing the upper part of the breasts and the beautiful legs and toes. She didn't see me looking at her, but I was. I swallowed as I saw these things.

And then her son came over to me, squatting by my side and drawing on the floor with a little piece of dirty wood.

'Shall I go with you today?' he asked, looking up.

At first I looked at him. I was getting a little worried about him being left out of it so often. I merely looked at him, showing by my blankness that I couldn't help. I had no hand in the matter.

'Hm? Shall I?' he asked again, looking sad and perhaps ready to cry if I said the wrong word.

'I don't know,' I said. 'Why not ask your mother?'

'My mother will not let me go with her,' he said.

And I said, 'Why don't you try? Maybe she will let you today, for a change.'

He looked down, diffident, and continued scratching on the floor.

'You'll ruin the floor,' I said.

He ceased scratching, then broke the stick, angrily, and threw the pieces away.

'Don't you want to ask her?' I said.

And he said, 'She won't let me. She will shout at me.'

And I said, 'Maybe she won't today. Go on and try.'

He rose up, with diffident slowness, and walked to the bedroom. I felt sorry as I looked at him.

He pushed the door open—and there it was. The full naked form of the woman! Once drawn to the sight, my eyes could not of their own natural will detach themselves from the wonder that confronted them: a trunk smooth as a pebble, bristling womanhood and a lot of hair where it should be! She was pulling a dress over her head, standing near a bed and facing the doorway. As soon as she heard the door fly open, she quickly turned round and put down her arms, covering herself with the dress.

'Shut that door at once!' she shouted at Oghenovo. 'What's the matter with you?'

The boy recoiled in fright and retreated from the bedroom, shutting the door as he did. I too quickly looked away. But something went through me that I had never felt before. . . .

As I sit here now, still waiting for her to come out, I can scarcely rub the mark off my mind. *My God.* . . .

The mission bell rings. The day is advancing gradually to a close. Curfew time is not too far away. I only wish that—

'I'll be going now,' she says as she reappears from the bedroom. *She is quite well dressed. What beauty she sports underneath that dress God knows what she looks like when she takes off everything and is about to go to sleep she must be undressing completely to go to sleep does anyone see all this why did Toje always ask me what she looked like maybe he sees her sometimes maybe she undresses for him at my place at my place undresses in my house—*

'I said I was going now,' she repeats, stopping briefly.

'All right,' I say. 'Go well.'

She smiles at me. *What is she smiling at now? Or is she laughing at me? Why should she laugh at me?*

'Please don't try to give Oghenovo anything to eat,' she says. 'He had a very heavy meal this afternoon and I don't intend to give him anything until late this evening.'

'All right,' I say, still looking at her.

She looks at the boy in the corner where he sulks, but ignores him and opens the door. Only when she has gone out of sight do I look away.

I turn to Oghenovo, and I see that he is sobbing, with a film of water covering each eye.

'Come here,' I tell him.

But he is in no mood for fellowship. He shakes his shoulders, sitting where he is.

'Come,' I persist. 'I want to tell you something.'

He rubs the tears from his eyes, and rises slowly. I stretch my hand in encouragement, and he walks to me, rubbing his eyes some more, face downward.

'She won't be long, you hear?'

He nods.

I rub his head with my hand, and then I take the opportunity to have a good look at him. The child will never know why I am looking at him. I am not even in total control of my own thoughts. For already my mind is beginning to draw a connection between this boy and the figure that hit my eyes only a while ago, the picture of which now can never leave my mind.

'Teach me a new game today,' he says, brightening up.

He almost catches me staring at him.

'What do you want to play?' I ask him.

He is confused. He puts a finger into his mouth and stares out.

'Shall I call Onome here, to come and play with me?' he asks.

'Your mother doesn't want you to leave the house,' I say. 'So you can't go and call Onome.'

'But their house is not far away.'

'Even so,' I say. 'Your mother will beat you if she hears you went anywhere.'

'Will you tell her?'

'I won't, but she may see you on her way back.'

'I will run.'

'She may still see you,' I say. 'And then she will beat you.'

That seems enough to subdue him. He looks down, and fumbles with an ear of his jumper.

'Let me bring my bottle-top, so that we can play it together,' he says.

'All right.'

He runs into their bedroom. His mother comes back into my mind.

In a moment he reappears with his stringed bottle-top. He holds one end of the string, while I hold the other, with the bottle-top balanced in the middle of the string by the hole bored through it. We swing the string round and round till it is sufficiently taut. Then we stretch it out at measured intervals, giving the bottle-top a fine whirring spin on each stretch.

After a while he gets tired of the game, like myself. I suppose the thought of his mother puts some sadness upon him. He slumps back against the wall, and looks out through the open door.

This time I try to reflect on the whole situation. My distaste for Toje is gradually deepening. There is no doubt about that. It is not merely that he makes a fool of me and tries to make me believe that I am less than a man. But I am beginning to be sick of his mean old ways, and my aversion is now strengthened by a growing feeling that I am being degraded merely because he is carrying on a sinister affair with Oshevire's wife. It is all very plain. I can no longer be fooled about it all. I can no longer be convinced that all this show of goodwill is not aimed at something. Hair well done, dress elaborate, shoes shining, face and neck well powdered, and the wooden rack in my hut all finely draped and decked just to give it sufficient grace for an occasion. I cannot be fooled any more. I may have too little sense or ability to help myself, but I am certainly not a child and I cannot be fooled as to what all this adds up to.

I don't mind what they decide to do with each other. It is not my place to question the movements of two people who have chosen to have an affair. But what I do mind is that I should be made to suffer any indignities that I know I do not deserve.

'Dress up the bed and get lost,' he often tells me, and 'Did I hear you mutter something? You should consider it a favour that a a man of my stature should bring himself to set foot in this hovel.' And to the woman he would say, 'Oh, he's just a fool. All he's got is a big body but hardly any sense,' and all that kind of language. And I wonder why, if he has all that stature that he so often talks about, I wonder why he does not take the woman to his own house and put that great big stature to test. Can't he do her all these favours in his own house too?

I know it is an unfortunate thing to be crippled. But God will help me one day. One day I shall be able to stand on my two feet, and I will no longer have to be at anyone's mercy or be made to suffer disgrace in front of a woman. Someday I shall find something to do, and I may yet be my own man. It wasn't so bad before the war and before we came into contact with Oshevire's wife. I then took my insults without complaint. But it's not the same now, with me being shamed in front of a woman. All my life I have avoided women, because I know they would not stop short of calling me a cripple.

'Shall I show you my gun?' says the boy, rousing from his boredom.

'Gun?' I ask, slightly puzzled.

'Yes. I made a gun yesterday.'

'What kind of gun?'

'Let me show you.'

He runs into their bedroom again. When he reappears he hands me a thick stick, carved narrow at the fore-end. A string is tied to both ends of the stick, and hangs loosely, like a gun-strap. I look up at him and smile. He grins widely with pride, then settles down by my side as though all he was waiting for was my approving smile.

'I made it yesterday,' he says.

'Very nice,' I say. 'Who showed you how to do it?'

'Nobody. I saw that soldier's gun.'

'Which soldier?' I ask.

'That soldier outside there,' he says, pointing to the soldier guarding the Town Council.

'I see. What are you going to use it for?'

'I will use it to shoot Onome,' he says.

I laugh under my breath. 'Why? What has Onome done to you?'

'He calls my father a thief.'

'What?'

'He says—he says my father is a thief, and that he stole something, and the soldiers carried him away and locked him up, because the soldiers don't want anybody to steal anything, because they want to keep everything to themselves, and that is why they carried my father away and locked him up.'

'Did you tell your mother about it?'

'Yes.'

'And what did she say?'

'She said that my father did not steal anything, because my father was a good man.'

I look at him for a while. *Poor boy.* When he looks back I look away, not wishing to recreate any sorrows.

'Well,' I say, 'don't shoot Onome, you hear?'

He nods, looking downward and rubbing at his stomach.

'And if he abuses your father again, tell me, so that I will beat him for you, you hear?'

He nods again.

'Does your mother know you have this gun?'

'No,' he says. 'I hide it.'

'Good. Where do you hide it?'

'Somewhere inside our room. Come and let me show you.'

He beckons me to follow. When I rise up he holds my hand, and leads me into their bedroom. I am a little hesitant, because I don't want to be caught exploring her privacy. I know what women are like. I don't want to be called any names.

'Come,' he insists.

I follow him into the bedroom. In the middle of the room and close to a window is a huge metal bed. Oghenovo leads me on to the head-end of the bed, and points underneath the bed.

'Here it is,' he says, pointing behind a huge metal box under the bed.

'Put the gun there and let me see.'

He slips the stick gently out of sight behind the box.

'Very good,' I say, patting his head. 'She'll never see it.'

I look round the room, while Oghenovo rolls on the bed. It is a big place. At the far end of it is a rack on which many clothes are hanging, including some men's clothes. At another end is a pile of yet other boxes. There are many other things besides, including a picture of Oshevire on a table near the bed. I walk up to the picture and take it up. Oghenovo rolls over to the edge of the bed, near where I am standing.

'That's my father.'

'You know him?'

'No. But my mother says so.'

I gaze at him, and he blushes and rolls away.

'Do you miss him?' I ask.

He shakes his head. *Poor boy.* He hardly knew the man before he was whisked away.

'Does your mother miss him?'

'I don't know.'

'Does she cry at night?'

He thinks a little, then shakes his head.

Maybe she doesn't miss him. Maybe she is so steeped in an affair with Toje that she doesn't even remember her husband, and this picture is just lying around like any other object that hasn't been moved for a long time.

I put the picture down.

'So this is your mother's room?'

'Yes,' he says.

'And she sleeps here?' I ask, touching the bed.

He nods.

'And you—where do you sleep?' I ask.

'I sleep beside her here.'

'It's a nice bed,' I say, feeling the bed, while a slight sensation runs through me. *Maybe she sleeps naked. And she would be quite a sight. Could she ever want me near her?*

I sit down at the edge of the bed. *What can Toje be doing now with Oshevire's wife in my place?* My hatred for Toje grows more and more every minute. I wish I could hurt him. I wish very badly that I could do something that would really hurt his pride. And then he would know what it means to make me feel the way I do when he does those things that he does to me.

Oshevire

It is evening now, gradually growing dark. All of us detainees are sitting down peacefully, hardly saying anything. We have stayed here long enough to get used to the routine of changing moods, at one time recoiling within ourselves to nurture our minds on the things that touch us severely deep down and far away, at another time seeking to relieve the boredom by cheerful remarks and light talk.

Right now there is hardly any talk going on among us. There is no guard around. The soldiers and policemen are off amusing themselves in another section of the huge prison. We know no life outside these walls other than the open sky, the horizon, the changing light and shade of night and day, and the faint sounds that manage to float over the impenetrable walls to us. We have all had our supper.

All, except our angry young friend, Agbeyegbe. He hardly touched his meal. When he received his dish—we were served beans with boiled yam—he turned it this way and that, a cold sour look on his heavily-bearded face, one hand in his pocket, and hissed. Sitting down at his corner, he tossed the two pieces of meat into his mouth and pushed the plate away with the rest of the contents totally untouched. He paid not the least attention to the good words of Mr Ogbe, the oldest among us, a truly old man, whom we call Baba.

'Look, my son,' Baba had told him, 'it won't do you any good. What use is it trying to starve yourself to death? It may yet happen that the tribunal will find no case against you, and set you free. But what chance do you have of realising this freedom if you die of hunger now? I know how you feel about having to be brought here. We all feel the same way. Look at me—am I not too old to be taking sides in any cause? It was my kindness that dragged me into this. But I do not complain, because I know that my innocence will be vindicated—so what would I gain by trying to lose my peace and my sanity over a temporary setback? Eat your food, and leave the rest to God.'

All of which went unheeded. Agbeyegbe simply sat there on the floor, talking to no one, a restless gleam in his youthful eyes.

He has been sitting like that for a long time now. Suddenly he springs up and begins to pace up and down, his hands in his pockets, his restless eyes downward. He continues to do this for some time, without changing either his course or his posture. Then all at once he stops, and squats before us, screwing his brow and tensing his knuckles.

'Look, gentlemen,' he addresses us, stopping briefly to secure his squat more firmly, and pulling in his trousers at the thighs. 'You've got to try to understand, all of you. I do not think you fully appreciate this world-wide struggle that some of us are carrying out for the benefit of humanity. You see this military thing that is happening in our country today? It is only wasting our time. It can only succeed in retarding the course of the destined confrontation, but it *cannot* stop it. *Never!*' he shoots a clenched fist upwards, springing up again yet fixing his gaze on us. He brings out a cigarette from a crumpled pack in his shirt pocket, and lights it.

'And what is this struggle that I am talking about?' he continues. 'It is the determined fight to free the masses of the workers, the poor people, from their shameless and inhuman exploitation by the rich.' He begins to pace slowly among us, his eyes still trained on our puzzled faces. 'Do you think that God has created mankind with the intention that one section of it should be subjugated and enslaved by the other? Do you think it was God's intention that some people should recline in comfort and abundance while others are for-ever hewers of wood and fetchers of water, destined only to minister to the shameless debauchery of those sitting over their heads, while they themselves languish in penury and pain? Do you think that some people are born to rule, as some have claimed for reasons best known to themselves, while others are born to be ruled, mani-pulated and exploited for the benefit of their oppressors, beyond all reason and justice? No, my brothers. Give it just one moment's thought, and you will see the irrationality and madness of the vast exploitation of no small section of mankind that is going on in the world today.'

He puts to his lips his cigarette, fast diminishing with neglect, and blows out a column of smoke into the wind. The vanishing mist returns to his face. A soldier approaches us with the gun dangling from his hand. Agbeyegbe suspends his speech and pretends to be just walking around, with one hand in his pocket and the other hand nursing the bare stub of his cigarette. We relax our uncompre-hending faces. But the soldier is recalled by his companion, and walks back again to where he has just appeared from. With one contemptuous glance at the disappearing soldier, our learned speaker returns to us and resumes the old squat.

'As I was saying, gentlemen, the bane of the world today is exploitation, the exploitation of the lower classes. And they are lower not because they chose to be, but because their oppressors have constantly kept them in that position and blocked every chance they might have of rising to greater positions.'

He pauses. Some of us sigh and look at one another. Nobody says a word. We resume our unbegrudging audience, this time staring at him less with puzzlement than with a readiness to be enlightened or at least freed of our incomprehension. He starts pacing again.

'Now take a look at all of us here being detained. Is there any rich man among us? I ask you—is there? Of course not! And I am sure you are gradually beginning to see what I mean by the continued oppression and suppression of the poor.

'Let us examine a few of us. Baba, you told us you were a farmer. How much were you able to get from your farming? *Nothing!* Nothing at all, except the mean benefit that you were able to feed your family—though I do not need to place before you a comparison between your level of feeding and that of our big men. And your benefits were always limited because the rich men in our country have consistently clamped down on the prices they paid you for your crops—just to keep you from being one of them!

'Mr Emeni, you were a court-messenger, and according to you, you were that for thirty-two years. Thirty-two years—now how about that! Do you mean that in all that time you did not deserve any promotion? For it is clear that if you didn't do your work well you would have been dismissed. But leave that aside. You were in court every single day of your life, so none of us here can tell better than you the injustice to which the less privileged citizens of our society have constantly been subjected.

'Mr Oshevire, you said you owned a rubber plantation. You really had a chance of being a big, rich man. But that greatness has eluded you, and you were in not much better station than the labourers who tapped your rubber for you. And why was this so? Because a determined conspiracy of the forces of oppression all over the world has put the price of rubber in fluctuation—and, believe me, there is nothing anyone can do about that.

'I am sure that it is the same with every one of us here. But for how long must this continue?' He stops pacing to declaim, raising his agitated arms in the manner of a preacher, wide-eyed with passion. 'For how long must we suffer this burden of oppression and exploitation? How long must we suffer our tormentors on our backs and at our throats?'

He resumes his pacing, looking at us with unflagging concentration.

'You can therefore see that only a drastic and bitter resistance can put an end to all these unbearable indignities. These things have gone on so long and with such determination that we would be deceiving ourselves if we thought we could talk our oppressors into reasoning with us. No, no—there is no such thing! Reasoning? Why, if they ever got down to reason all these years they would never have contemplated such atrocities, let alone sought to perpetrate them. No, gentlemen. The revolution must have its course. There is no talking with the enemy. Until he can be made to suffer the bitter consequences of his crimes, he will never agree to sit down to talk things over with you.

'So, gentlemen—*comrades*, rather. For that is what we all are: comrades in oppression. So let me address you in more fitting terms. Comrades, that is our case. This was what I was busy trying to preach in my little station at Okrukpe, where I was teaching. I was trying to organise the workers there into a front, and I never ceased to do this, not even during the occupation of this state by Simbian troops. The enemy seized upon this, and as soon as he found the opportunity he reported me to the military authorities, saying I was a rebel collaborator! You see?'

'Pardon me, but . . . who is this . . . *enemy*?'

The question is from Emeni, and it throws our man quite out of balance.

'How do you mean, who is this enemy?' he retorts.

'I am sorry to be so stupid. But we have had so many words thrown about these days—enemy, rebel, this and that—that my ears are beginning to grow words.'

I want to laugh, but I'm not sure I will be joined by anyone.

'*The* enemy, of course—*the* oppressor. Who else have we been talking about?'

Emeni is not quite satisfied. But how can you argue with a learned man?

Agbeyegbe looks at us for rapport, manoeuvring within the bristly bush on his face what looks like a grin. Some of us sigh and shake our heads. And now at least it seems likely, from the prevailing mood among us, that he can count on some measure of understanding. At this point he squats briskly again, fixing us once more with a sharp and challenging stare, and when he resumes speaking his tone is subdued, controlled, yet no less pressing.

'Now, comrades,' he says, 'the time has come for us to take positive action.'

Some people come closer, to hear him better. There is an atmosphere of rapport bordering on conspiracy. Night has now taken almost total control of the day. Everyone waits to hear Agbeyegbe drop the word. The surrounding darkness seems to have allowed him a little halo of light, and in that light, the last dying light of day, his figure is cast in an awesome silhouette.

'So, listen carefully,' he continues. 'I believe it is possible for us here, even as small as we are in number, to contribute our own small share to the worldwide struggle to liberate the small man, the poor man, from the devilish control of the oppressor. And do not think that we would be acting in isolation. No, comrades, far from it! Even as we are here now, the struggle is going on irrevocably in the whole world—even in our own country, right now—for this liberation. The forces of the revolution are marching on relentlessly. You cannot know of it because you are confined within these walls— these walls thrown around you by the enemy. Stir yourselves just one bit from these confines, and you will see that we are not alone in what we are trying to undertake now.'

'Do you mean . . . a fight is going on now outside this prison?' someone else makes bold to ask—it is Ozegbe—and all eyes turn on him.

'Of course, Comrade Ozegbe,' returns Agbeyegbe.

'And heads are being broken, and people are—'

He is interrupted by laughter among us. Agbeyegbe raises his arms to plead for calm. This does not look like the kind of reaction he expects from us.

'Silence, comrades! This is no laughing matter. The confrontation with our oppressor is nothing for us to make light of—particularly as he wields very dangerous weapons, though by no means insurmountable,' he takes care to add. 'Now let us try to answer Comrade Ozegbe's question seriously, because it is plain that he is seeking enlightenment. Yes, a fight is going on outside these walls—and a determined one too. But of course there are several fronts on which this fight is being undertaken. One of these is doctrinal or ideological. It is necessary to educate the masses of the people on the need for this revolution and the ideals for which the struggle is being embarked upon.

'Linked closely with this is the intellectual front. In this respect, it falls to the more enlightened ones among us to engage the champions of oppression in endless contests in the press and on platforms, by producing books and pamphlets, and by all other means that the educated mind can employ. The purpose of this is to seek, more by verbal confrontation than by any such compromising contact as dialogue, to knock down all those baseless and immoral arguments that our oppressors have constantly sought to use to justify their inhuman exercise.

'Thirdly, there is the strategic front. In this regard certain institutions are set up for the training of young, able men—able in mind and body—towards the eventual confrontation. In these institutions, they are taught how to organise revolutionary activity in their several areas of operation, how to disseminate revolutionary thought, how to organise pressure groups. They are even instructed in the arts of offence and defence, in preparation for the inevitable physical struggle.

'Last, but certainly not the least, of these fronts is the physical front, the *fight*—breaking of heads, as Comrade Ozegbe has so vividly put it.' Appreciative glances turn to Ozegbe, and he now sits back to acknowledge the recognition and drink in his well-won pride. 'And this, comrades, is the struggle in which you, all of us, are being called upon now to play a part. We shall not sit down and let ourselves be rolled over, like unaccountable grass by the road-side, or like dogs and goats which are crushed every day on our roads. Yes, comrades, we shall all rise like one man. We shall take the initiative, and carry death to the oppressor—which is no less than he intends for us.

'But first, we must escape from these confines to be able to achieve this. We shall elude arrest, and the oppressor is going to be baffled and frustrated. For it is a cardinal factor in this do-or-die struggle that the enemy should be frustrated at every point and at every turn.'

He takes out another cigarette and lights it, throwing down the extinguished match and crushing it under one of his bare feet.

'You see these walls, how high they are and how insurmountable they appear? Well, we are going to do it! For therein, comrades, lies our only means of realising the essential part of our mission. We *must* escape. And tonight! I have thoroughly explored these grounds, and I don't think there is anyone who knows these walls as well as I do. I know where the weak points are. We must exploit these tonight in the dead of dark, in the very early hours of to-morrow, somewhat after midnight tonight, when these armed guards—these stooges of the enemy who don't know any better than to serve his evil ends—when they are drowned in insensible slumber and so completely ineffective against our clever moves. And we need everything we can get hold of—cloth, wood, wire, stone, everything. Don't ask me how it will be done. When the time comes I shall give full instructions, and the rest will be smooth and easy. We also need a few men to lead the way.

'However, some of you might shudder at the thought of the whole of us—the whole twenty-five of us detainees—leaving this prison in one go. Well, I think there is a very strong point there. Apart from everything else, the exercise raises a few operational problems. I am fully aware of these, and I have made allowance for this contingency in my planning. I have therefore thought of an alternative. And this is that at least one of us should be helped to escape, if only to com-municate to our comrades outside these walls the overwhelming support with which the inmates here have greeted the cause of the revolution. I offer my humble services.'

Agbeyegbe puffs at his cigarette, perhaps to let his message sink into his audience. And that message is not lost at all on us. There are a few sighs, and a few groans. Some people scratch their necks, stretch their bodies, and wear telling looks on their faces. Some people yawn loudly and cough, rather meaningfully. Of course, it must have been clear to many of us for some time during the lecture that this sort of news was coming. I for one have been watching the contortions on the boy's face, the drama of his delivery, and have been left in a bit of doubt as to the sincerity of his message. Somehow I feel now that I am not alone in my suspicion. But what has baffled me, especially now at the end of this long-winded talk, is how such a small boy, who is far younger than any one of us, could hope to fool the whole lot of us and be certain that we would swallow whatever he thought fit to feed us.

My doubts seems confirmed by the atmosphere that now prevails. It is as if a great earthen pot has dropped from an unreachable rafter on which it has been resting for a long time, and all its hidden contents are now exposed to general view. A few more coughs are heard.

Lights are switched on.

'Jiggers are funny insects.' It is Emeni that breaks the controlled silence, stretching himself and yawning wide.

There is loud laughter among us. Agbeyegbe shoots him an aggressive glance.

'What was that?' he queries.

'Mm? Oh, I was talking about jiggers.'

'What about jiggers?'

'I was saying what funny creatures they are. So hard to understand.'

'What have jiggers got to do with this issue?'

'Oh, I was just thinking. . . . You see, I was in court every single day of my life, and every single day of my life I was bitten by at least one jigger, because I had no shoes on. So I was always worrying about jiggers. And now that I think of it, I think the reason I never got that promotion after all was because I always had jiggers either on my mind or in my feet.'

Agbeyegbe hisses and looks away. There is another outburst of laughter, and Emeni is careful to conceal his mocking face from its object.

'I see,' says Agbeyegbe, and there is silence again, 'that some people are not ready for our cause. But we should not let them drag us back. We have no time to waste, and we must tackle our problem, *fast*. Comrade Okoro, what do you say about helping to organise this thing tonight?'

'Who, me?' asks Okoro.

'Yes.'

'Oh . . . em . . . I have a pain in my neck, and I am feeling a bit sleepy already.'

There is more laughing.

'Please, comrades!' Agbeyegbe pleads, standing up to press his point. 'There is no reason for all this.' Turning again to Okoro, he says, 'I sympathise with you, Comrade Okoro, but I feel sure that you fully associate yourself with the noble cause of the revolution?'

'Oh, I'm with you—I'm with you!' Okoro says. 'Just take it that some of us are not physically ready for the revolution. A pain in the neck is quite a drawback, but I am certain that you made an allowance for this contingency in your planning.'

And simulating a stiffened neck and a face contorted with pain, Okoro groans to good measure and rests his back on the floor. The laughter from the group is barely muffled.

Agbeyegbe sighs and shakes his head.

'*Chei!*' shouts Eboh.

'What was that?' Agbeyegbe swings round at him to question.

'I thought I heard a sound. It was quite a heavy sound—didn't you hear it?'

'No.'

'Oh, sorry. I thought I heard one of those guards let out a fart, and the sound of it was so loud you would have thought it came from over the walls.'

'Well?'

'No, I just thought. . . . If the enemy or his stooges decide to attack us with farts, we should all rise like one man and outfart them all.'

'I think you are trying to make light of the issue, and I declare the revolution has no place for this sort of behaviour.'

'I agree with you—*comrade*!'

This time we can hardly contain ourselves.

Agbeyegbe is frustrated. His lips tighten. His eyes flash. He puts his hands to his hips, sighs vehemently—and the sound resembles the snorting of a cornered ram.

'Look, gentlemen—'

'Comrades,' someone reminds him, amid more laughter.

'*Listen!* This is totally uncalled for. Perhaps you think that I am bringing this whole thing up merely for my own benefit—or even amusement. I think you are quite mistaken. It is unlikely that I should devote my whole life to a cause of such overwhelming importance simply to fool people. Yet I sincerely believe that you are reasonable enough to know that the things of which I speak deeply concern the lives of millions of people who deserve better fortunes than they have at the moment.'

He sighs, and starts pacing slowly. We all watch him.

'I know how difficult things have been for all of us. It's not an easy thing for men to sustain normal reasoning after they have been secluded for so long from normal life. I know how hard it is. But we are all men, and like men we should defy this setback—which is nothing compared to the terrible misfortune facing the wretched of the earth. We must face our task with fortitude, and that is all I ask of you tonight.

'All right, then. I offer to stand aside. Let someone else from among us undertake the responsibility. But someone has to escape tonight. The only reason I volunteered to do it was that I considered myself better qualified to spread the message, since I have all the contacts. You can let someone else do the job, if it is your wish.

'Baba, what do you say?'

The old man is startled.

'Me?' He can hardly believe his ears.

'Are you prepared to play a part in this?'

'Do you mean . . . help to organise the escape, or do the actual escaping?'

'Whichever one you choose.'

Baba sighs, and shakes his head, with a sick look on his wrinkled face.

'Look, my son,' he says. 'What can you expect of an aged wreck like me? Can you imagine me summoning up sufficient energy to help construct a ladder, let alone scale these mighty walls? Give it a thought yourself. If I should slip off and tumble to the ground, and my already weak body was reduced to a pulp, what kind of message do you think I would be spreading within these walls, let alone outside of them? No, my son. Look to firmer limbs. I am sure the revolution can do without ineffective fogies like me, who may not after all survive the kind of turmoil that you have outlined for us tonight. Pass along, my son.'

'I think you can be excused. Comrade Oshevire?'

I cannot swear that I didn't see it coming. I have known all along that he will come to do this kind of headcount, and I have been waiting for him. My head is rested on my interlocked hands against the wall, and I am staring straight into his face—actually, into his mouth, which is a big black hole in the midst of an overgrown bush of hair. I am particularly hurt by his assumption that he now has the authority to appoint this man, or excuse that man—merely because he has treated us to his learning. So from where I sit I have been staring straight at him. He has been avoiding my eyes. But now he has come to face me squarely, and I am still staring at him. He is rather uneasy, but I refuse to take my eyes away.

'Why do you stare at me like that?'

He becomes aggressive. We are now the focus of all attention. Nobody says a word.

'Well, stop staring at me and say something!' he spurts. 'Or do you have nothing to say?'

I sigh, and ease off my posture.

'Agbeyegbe, sit down,' I tell him, calmly.

'What?' he says, with growing agitation.

'I said sit down.'

'Why should I sit down? Answer my question first.'

'All right,' I say, 'I'll answer your question.' I sit up straight, fixing him with a more unyielding stare. 'But first of all I'm going to ask you a few questions myself.'

'Go on,' he says, moving back a step, clenching his fists as if we are about to exchange blows. 'Ask your questions. Go on.'

'Good. Most of us here have been in this place for years. You have only been here a few months. Now do you think we enjoy this kind of life, when we would be much happier at home with our families? And is it fair of you to expect us to put ourselves further into trouble, particularly over a cause we neither fully understand nor can ever hope to defend with the slightest pretence to conviction or enthusiasm?'

'*Fair?*' he counters. 'Who talks about fairness in a cause like this? If we are men we must be prepared to brace ourselves to the situation and not ask—'

'Brace ourselves! I didn't notice you bracing yourself when that soldier approached us a moment ago.'

'I—I—I wasn't scared of him. You think I was scared of him? I wasn't scared of him.'

'How could you be! But leave that aside. Suppose we actually succeeded in helping you over this wall, and you got across and eluded escape; and then you got together your crowd and started raising confusion, and you were arrested and taken away a second time—do you think any mercy is going to be shown you?'

'A true revolutionary is not supposed to worry about the safety of his own life,' he says. 'The ultimate victory of the common people should always be his concern and his consolation.'

'You know, Agbeyegbe, I think you are a truly noble man, and truly noble words issue from your mouth. But somehow I don't think you'll find many of us prepared to share your sentiments, because we have got other things on our minds, things for which we would be prepared to give our lives the same way, perhaps, as you seem prepared to surrender your own. But we want to be sure that when we give our lives, we do so in the way we know *real* men should. Besides, our circumstances may not be quite the same. Tell me, Agbeyegbe, are you married?'

He stares at me without a word, his fingers closing in and fanning out alternately.

'I asked you a question—are you married?'

'I don't see what marriage has to do with this.'

'Perhaps not—but are you married?'

'No, I am not.'

'There you are. You see, not being married, and without a family of your own, you are not likely to appreciate the restraint that most of us here are having to apply to our several indignations.'

'Calm down, my children,' says Baba. 'Calm down. There is no need for all this.'

'But that's nonsense!' Agbeyegbe is bristling at me. 'Hear him talk about wife and family. What good does having a wife and family do you now? Are you any better off than me on that account?'

'Perhaps not. But at least the thought of them saves me from the type of rashness that you are now inviting us to perform.'

'But what good does that do you—I mean thinking about your family? Whether or not you think about them you are going to languish within these walls, just because you lack the initiative to get up and do something about it. So what good does it all do you?'

'Certainly not the kind of good that you are offering me. But I'll tell you something. Suppose I attempted to scale these walls and I was seen and suddenly shot down, what kind of life would my family live hereafter, knowing that their man died the death of a coward, a dog? Or even suppose that I got off safely and escaped to my family. What kind of life do you think I would be living—knowing every moment of it that somebody was after me, and living in perpetual fear of re-arrest and even more severe incarceration. Is that living? But more than that, what kind of example would I be setting before my family, with my son growing up in disgrace and in the unworthy shadow of a father who lacked the courage to stand up to his problems like a man? No, Agbeyegbe, I think I know better than that. Besides, why should I escape? Would my trying to escape not be sure proof that I was guilty of the charges brought against me?'

He looks at me, long and hard, and swallows, breathing hard and still betraying uneasiness on his fingers. I settle back into my recline.

'Men like you are not fit to live!' he declares.

'Calm down, my children. Calm down,' says the old man, and others join to counsel restraint.

'I say men like you are not fit to live,' Agbeyegbe continues, though I am no longer looking at him. 'Hear him talking about his family. Do you think they are wasting their thoughts on you? Tell me, do you think they care the least bit for you? If so, why hasn't anyone ever come here to visit you or ask of you or bring you anything?'

'These are hard words,' says the old man. 'Calm down, please. There is no need for—'

'Leave me!' Agbeyegbe cuts in, fulminating. 'Let me tell him what he seems not to have noticed yet. Wife, children, family— *nonsense!* Why hasn't your wife come to see you? Have you not seen others' wives and children coming to see them?'

'These are hard words. Please, now—'

'Let me tell him! For maybe he doesn't know. Or he is pretending. Wife! You think there is anything they would stop at—I mean the people who put you here? They'd stop at *nothing*, including your wife. And here you are thinking about her, when she has not even sent a word through anybody, let alone come to see you herself.'

'These are hard words—'

'Yes, but he should know them.' He brings out his handkerchief and blows his nose into it. 'There is no place today for people like him, thinking all that nonsense about wife and family when there are more serious things plaguing mankind.'

Two of the guards reappear, soldiers, walking towards us with their guns over their shoulders. Agbeyegbe starts pacing about once again. He brings out another cigarette and lights it, smoking frantically, one hand firmly stuck into his pocket. The silence puzzles the soldiers as they stop before us.

'What's the matter now?' asks one of them.

Some of the men get up and walk into their cells, showing the desire to go to sleep.

The soldier casts a look at Agbeyegbe.

'Mr Book,' he says, 'What is it now?'

Agbeyegbe waves him down in contempt, and walks into the cell without saying a word, throwing off his half-burnt cigarette.

'What's eating him?' the soldier asks, looking round to us.

'Book, what else?' Emeni answers him. 'Or do you know what else could eat a man?'

The soldiers laugh. They continue their walk round the precincts. Baba excuses himself, and goes in. The silence continues . . .

The thoughts that go through my mind transcend Agbeyegbe. He is hardly a problem, certainly not one on which I should spend my feelings. He is too young and is only the victim of misguided exuberance. Though he said enough to throw a man into a fit of anger, I don't see why I should have traded venom with him beyond the reasoning that was intended to dissuade him from the path of madness. I see no reason why he should be taken seriously in his vile display of emotion. If he knew any better he would understand that running is only the mark of a coward—and it is a coward that is not fit to live.

I am thinking about my family. We have a Rediffusion box in our cell, and when it is not relaying music it talks about the war. Every announcement of an air raid or guerrilla attack on Urukpe has always struck me with pain. For if what Rukeme said in the tribunal is true, about me being hated all over the town, what hope of protection can there be for a woman and child deprived of the presence and security of a man and exposed to the resentment of a whole population?

Of course, if Agbeyegbe implied that Aku was letting herself be used, then he was talking nonsense. I know what women are, but I also know my woman. My only worry as far as that is concerned, is that if anyone sought to visit any dishonour upon her, she might try to do a desperate thing, perhaps not even short of taking her own life. Every Simba woman that I knew of in Urukpe deserted her family and escaped to save her life at the liberation of our town by the federal troops. Now would a woman who stood through all the horrors of that moment, when devil-driven citizens of the town took the law into their own hands and tormented the lives of innocent people—would such a woman, who stood through it all just so she would stand beside her man, submit her honour to base desire when things were relatively calm? But let that be meanwhile. . . .

I rise from the ground and wipe my seat. As I walk into the cell, preparing to go to sleep, my mind is occupied now by thoughts of my impending appearance before the tribunal. Somehow I seem to look forward to it with eagerness, if only because I intend to let my enemies understand that they cannot gloat over my misfortune with ease. For what man would submit himself to such cheap defeat, when he knows he has truth and integrity on his side—whatever the odds are against him?

Aku

It is nearly morning now, and still I cannot sleep. There is a strain on my eyelids, and my body feels half-cooked. But every time I close my eyes and pray for sleep to take control of me, I feel my ears straining with stubborn keenness to catch a sound and my mind fighting its way through a mist of doubts and questions. Not that I am unaccustomed to all this. For over three years now since my man has been away and I have been left to make the best of lingering uncertainty, I have known periods like this when I have had to keep anxious vigils, waiting for the worst to happen any moment, though knowing only too well that when it came I would be helplessly un-prepared to meet it. But this is a new kind of anxiety that I feel now.

It all started yesterday evening. I had gone to meet Toje, in the usual place and on the usual mission. What transpired between us was no different from other occasions. I had succumbed to his demand, saying not a word in protest. But I was shaken to find that I was facing a new kind of beast. For this time he had drowned himself in alcohol by the time I got there. The bottle lay on the floor beside the bed, and the drooling figure of a man was sitting on the bed with his back against the wall, hardly making a reply to all my words of greeting.

But I was prepared for anything. Then of course we got into the usual processes. He asked me to sit near him, and I did. He started working his restless hands all over me. This was nothing new, except that now under the influence of so much alcohol (there was nothing left in that bottle on the floor!) he was ravishing me with such coarse lack of direction that he could have torn my clothes to shreds. I asked him to let me take off my clothes, and he welcomed the suggestion with sottish guffaws—but he could hardly stay his hands as I was undressing. When I got back in bed he fell over me, and gradually levered his slobbering mass over my body.

The rest of the story is again nothing new. Panting heavily, like a fallen lizard, he let me have full measure of his drunken breath and old-man smell, all of which I tried hopelessly to avoid by turning my face to the side and holding off my breath at intervals. Then too with his hand he explored my groin with such blind vigour that, at the end of the whole affair, not only was I left with a passion only rudely tickled, but indeed not even the little resistance that my body put up could save me from the resultant trickle of blood.

As usual, he did nothing beyond that. When the handwork was over, I sat up on the bed and wept. He did not say a word in sympathy. He simply turned his face towards the wall and let me have my fill of crying. Not even after I had dressed myself again and told him I was going did he offer any response.

As I opened the door and stepped outside I was struck with sudden fright at finding that the day had grown very dark and it was certainly past curfew time. There was not a single soul that I met on my way home. As I ran towards my house, my heart beating very fast, I prayed anxiously that three years of grudging luck be not terminated by one brief luckless encounter with gunfire.

Fear had taken control of me. Fear had dried my tears as I ran homeward, and had sat squarely in my heart where a moment before sorrow had been. Yet as I stepped into the house, back once again to the secure prison where for over three years now I have lived a life of programmed uncertainty, I suddenly felt that fear give way to a kind of desperate abandon. Fighting hard to get back my breath, I cared little now what came to me next.

And then a strange thing happened. I was standing with my back against the closed door, panting for breath. Suddenly Odibo came up to me at the door, wanting to get past and go.

'Wait,' I said, still panting.

'It's late,' he said, 'and I must go.'

'Wait,' I repeated.

I had instinctively raised my hands to his shoulders for support, and rested my head against his chest. He did not move. He just let me hold on to him like that, not objecting in the least. And then a quick sensation went through me. It had to do with both the way he let me hold on to him securely, and with the smell of his body. For over three years I had not known this security and ungrudging support, and the smell reminded me of those times when my man had come home in the evening from the rubber farm with his body all wet and greasy yet inspiring in me a surge of passion. I held on for a long while to the body of Odibo, imbibing fully a hot billy-goat smell that revived in me a feeling I had not known for years. It did not last very long, but the impression had been made. I raised my eyes to Odibo, but he turned away his face, and tried to disengage himself.

'I really must go,' he said.

'But you can't,' I said, letting my hands slip gradually down from his recoiling body. 'It's too late, and they will get you.'

I was still standing against the door. I could see he was nervous and unprepared for the alternative that I now offered.

'I must go. What would I be doing here?'

'I'm sorry,' I said, after a brief reflection. 'It's my fault. I stayed too long. But you can't go. It's too late, and the soldiers will surely get you.'

'What then do you want me to do?', he asked, his eyes turned downward and unwilling to confront me.

'Well,' I said, 'you can stay here for tonight.'

'Stay here! That's impossible. I can't do that.'

'But if you step outside there a soldier can shoot you for breaking the curfew. Would you want that to happen to you?'

He still had his eyes to the floor. But I could see the message was beginning to get through to him. I seized the opportunity to reinforce my argument, by flinging the door open.

'Look,' I said. 'Can't you see it's very dark? I was very lucky to escape their notice, and even if they had caught me they could have had mercy on me because I am a woman. But you may not be so lucky. And you know they don't ask many questions.'

He looked confused, turning his head this way and that and still avoiding my gaze.

'Stay the night,' I said.

'But—'

'But what?'

'What . . . what do you think Toje will say to that?'

'What can he say to it? He made me stay this long, and you'd just plainly tell him that by the time I came back it was too risky for you to venture out, for fear of the soldiers.'

He sighed deeply, and made for the bench by the wall. I had my eyes trained on him. By this time I had got much of my breath back.

'Stay with us for the night,' I said. 'There is a room where you can sleep. I will get the bed ready for you shortly.'

'All right,' he said after a while.

I quickly went into my room, but stopped briefly by the door leading into the room. As I turned round I noticed that he was staring at me.

'Won't you have something to eat?'

'I am not hungry,' he said.

'Please eat something. I'm sure you have had nothing this evening since you left your place.'

'Thank you,' he insisted. 'But I'm not hungry at all. I never eat much.'

'Not even a little something before you go to sleep?'

He shook his head.

I hurried into the room, closing the door behind me. Oghenovo was sprawled carelessly on my bed, with his clothes on. I tucked him in properly.

'Did he eat anything before he slept?' I reappeared abruptly to ask.

'He ate some remnants of boiled plantain that he found in the kitchen, with oil. He said he was very hungry,'

'I see.'

Back in the room, I took off some of my clothes, and proceeded to make the bed in the spare room for Obido. Doing this gave me a certain cheerfulness. It had been a long time since I felt called upon to give hospitality, and the presence of a guest in the house was almost beginning to fill me with a false feeling of normalcy.

When I was done I went across to announce to him that his bed was ready.

'Why not let me sleep here?' he asked.

'What? In this bare open place, and expose yourself to the cold in the middle of the night? No, that is not proper. The bed is all ready. I have never heard of a man lying on the floor when a more comfortable place has been offered him.'

He demurred, but rose anyway. I showed him into the room. We bade each other goodnight. There was no lock to the door, but he closed it. A short while later I heard the bed creak under his weight.

Not long after, I proceeded to take my bath, rustle up a quick bite, and retire to bed. I had locked all the doors and windows. As usual, I did not put out the hurricane lamp, but turned the wick down to a low flame which faintly illuminated the little table near my bed. I had completely undressed myself, and now lay on the bed, with only my wrapper drawn up over my body to just below my breasts. Everywhere was silent. The only noise around was the shrieking of the insects and geckos and the gentle monotone of Oghenovo's snores.

I began to go over in my mind the painful life that I had been subjected to living since they took my man away. Luck has certainly not been on my side. The endless loneliness. The lack of protection. The interminable anxiety. The loss of all comfort. The fact that I was now having to crawl on my knees—and spread my legs!— for a living. The total shame of living under the shadow of the animal lust of a man who merely tantalised desire in me, causing me to live only by thrift of passion when passion would want to overflow. . . .

My thoughts rambled on. Could Toje have deliberately wished to bring shame on me, merely to gloat over my misfortune? Or was it that he lacked true manly powers? I've heard that some men lose their manhood after a time. But it seemed to me a cruel act of fate that I should be made the victim of that sort of malady, condemned to live perpetually at the brink of desire and to be led on and on

without any hope of achieving a fulfilment. If it was now my lot to
be Toje's whore, did I not have a right at least to be purged of my
desire—unwilling as I might be—as often as it suited him to invite
me to play the role? Fate, I insisted, had no reason to treat me to such
undeserved sadism, and—the shame of it!—I found myself praying
deeply in my mind that whatever had come upon Toje should turn
out to be a passing thing! I found myself wishing that someday he
would summon up the power to slake the desire that he was con-
tinually working up in me!

Still, sleep would not come. The night had gone far deep. The
cries of the little creatures were becoming fewer and fewer, the
silence now almost total. The usual anxiety in my mind was gradually giving way to the adulterous longings that now strove to over-
power me, when—for shame!—I felt my own hand playing with
my groin! And it was in the midst of this act of self-disgrace that I
heard the door of the other room creak.

I stopped. My eyes turned slowly towards the direction of the
sound, but I was careful not to let my body betray my attention. So,
though I was lying supine, my eyes were directed at that door.
Slowly it glided open. I waited. Soon after, I saw the dim silhouette
of Odibo slowly emerge through the door. He was picking his
steps, very carefully. As he came nearer and nearer, I noticed that he
was bare to the waist, with his cloth wrapped round his loin. He
came closer and closer to my bed. I could now see him in full view.
The stump of what should have been his left arm. His imposing
build. The swell of his shoulders and of the biceps of his right arm.
The taper of his trunk. . . . He was every inch a man—his manhood
scarcely faulted by the unfortunate loss of an arm.

He came to the foot of the bed, and stopped. I narrowed my eyes,
so as not to betray my looking. I waited to see what he was going to
do. He moved on, slowly, slowly. He came over to my side, and
stopped. I could feel his eyes all over me. I was completely nude.
Only an edge of my cover-cloth sheltered my groin. Slowly he bent
his head over me, and then proceeded to run his nose over my body
—now over my thighs, now over my breasts, over my belly, then
down again to my thighs. He raised his hand, and was about to run
it over me, when on sudden instinct I jerked. He quickly withheld

his hand, and raised himself to full standing position. I rolled over on my side, facing him fully now, but still pretending to be asleep and unaware of his presence.

It was at this point that my son went into a fit of coughing. For a while I did not move. But my son's coughing increased in intensity, and I stirred fully now and turned to steady him. The movement seemed to have dislodged my visitor's intent. Now he began to back-step, somewhat faster than he had come. With my hand massaging the chest of my son, I maintained a watchful eye on the retreating Odibo. Before I was through with my nursing attentions to my boy, the prowler had slid gently past his door and pulled it shut.

I waited and waited. He never came back. But it was clear to me what he wanted. For a long time I had been witness to the look of a defeated man that he walked about with. But events since yesterday evening seem to have thrown a light on another side of him, or perhaps an aspect of him that had since lain concealed under what I had always seen of him: natural human desires encumbered only by his subjugation to Toje. Was it my fault, therefore, that I should be drawn towards a man who, like myself, was a prisoner of circumstances—that I should be driven to seek comfort in a feeling of fellowship compounded, to be sure, with an increasing tug of desire? As the moments passed, my mind gloated over a picture that brought back cherished memories: the hot, manly smell of his body, the bristling physique that was sure to be housing eager powers. . . .

My eyes are strained and my body weak with forced wakefulness. Now and then my mind stops in its self-indulgence to ask where my desires will lead me. I can hear the crow of a cock, announcing the nearness of day. Whatever it brings will find me waiting.

Emuakpor

It was I who circumcised the tortoise!

It was I who scaled the elephant's rump to scoop the curative flea from my crotch!

It was I who caused the mad dog to stray to damnation, by pouring poisoned broth on his urine-spots that could have traced for him his homeward journey!

In my forty-seven years of practice no one has had either the cause or the courage to question the efficacy of my medicines. It is an art I inherited from my father, whose father had practised it before him, his grandfather and his great-grandfather and even his great-great-grandfather. It goes right down our line. Nobody else has it the way we have done—in all Igaboland down to the tribes beyond who speak through their noses—and I would wager my medicinal staff for anybody to come forward and prove me wrong!

It therefore came to me as a shock when Toje Onovwakpo rolled himself to these doorsteps to ask if I was sure I gave him the right sort of medicine for the venereal infection that sickened his manhood. At first I was dumb-struck to hear a man talk to me in that fashion, and barely withheld my anger. But then I took pity on him, for on a closer look he seemed to me like a cock shorn of his comb.

Yesterday, it was. I had just had my supper, and had stretched myself out in an easy-chair in the yard, smoking my pipe. Suddenly I noticed a figure cycling towards my house from a faint distance. I took the pipe from my mouth and raised my head from the chair, peering steadily with squinted eyes so as to get a better view. Everybody in this town knows I don't do any work in the evenings. Besides, these are uncertain times. So if anyone rode towards my house at the close of day with what looked like urgency, I had reason enough to want to know who he might be and what could be his mission. As the figure came to within a few leg-strides of me and the identity became all too clear, I settled back into my chair and stuck my pipe back in my mouth.

'Toje Onovwakpo,' I greeted, 'son of Umuko-of-the-unblunting-blade who alone accounted for a hundred heads in the fight between Urukpe and—'

'Save your chatter,' he said, braking to a halt and resting his bicycle by the wall of my house, 'and come in to answer a few questions.'

'So urgent that you cannot even let me exhaust my catalogue of praises for your valiant father?'

'Skip your chatter, I say. There are more serious things to talk about.'

'All right. All right.'

I rose from the chair and knocked the ashes from my pipe. There was an unfriendly look on his face as he preceded me into my chamber. His business was indeed urgent, from the way he walked.

'What might the matter be?' I asked, as we got inside.

'Sit down, you mischievous little man, and tell me what kind of dirty tricks you had the nerve to play on me.'

'Ah-ah-ah-ah!' I cautioned him, raising a hand in protest. 'I raise a decent family here and I run an honest trade. In all my years of practice nobody has treated me to any kind of abuse, and I have no stomach for your bullying. Now this is *my* house and it is *my* place to give the invitation to sit. So *you* sit down and tell me what this is all about.'

He sighed heavily, but sat down just the same, placing his plumed hat and his walking-stick on the floor beside him. I took my seat on a bench opposite him.

'What is your problem?' I asked again, staring him straight in the face.

He was looking at the floor, and his eyes seemed furious.

'Look here, Emuakpor,' he said, suddenly looking up at me. 'When I pay a man good money I expect good service.'

'Yes,' I replied. 'And when a man pays me for any service he gets his money's worth. You still haven't told me what your problem is.'

He could scarcely believe his ears, from the way he looked at me. But Toje is like that. Give him one step, and the next moment he'd be wanting you to move out of your own house. I kept my eyes on him.

'A few months ago,' he resumed, 'I came to you with a problem, and after all you did I thought all was well with me again. I didn't know you were merely indulging your—'

'Save your tongue, my boy,' I intercepted. 'Let's put it in more direct and proper language. A few months ago you came up to me with a venereal disease. You complained of a terrible pain, of pus, of malignancies here and tumours there. I took a look at you and knew you were in a bad way. You were honest enough to tell me, on enquiry, that you had been fooling around with prostitutes at Iddu. I then set about devising a cure for your trouble, and not long afterwards you were a whole man again. Now if you have the same trouble all over it can only be that you have thrown away your good sense yet again. So let's have your story in as peaceful and as decent a language as possible.'

'Come now, listen—'

'I'm listening all right. I just want you to take a good look at me before you talk to me. I'm an old man, even older than your late father while he was alive. It was I who nursed his wound from that gruesome fight with our neighbours at Okhukhu—and your father could never have stormed into my house to call me names. So you be very careful how you address me, because if you are sure that I have played any cruel jokes on you, then you might as well believe that I can do worse. I say, what is the problem this time?'

He sighed again. I thought the atmosphere suited me. I have always held that so long as you don't beg a man for money or anything you can force him to respect your integrity.

'It just won't do what it's told,' he said dejectedly.

'How do you mean, it won't do what it's told? You mean it gets there too soon—sooner than you want it—or it can't get started at all? Which is it?'

'It can't get started.'

'O-ho! You mean to say, your shaft has gone limp?'

'Well . . . if you prefer to put it that way . . . yes.'

'E—hen!, I said. 'Now you're talking. It seems we are getting closer to the problem. Now let's hear how it all came about.'

I stuffed some more tobacco into my pipe and struck a match to it. Spots of sweat appeared on the man's brow. He brought out a handkerchief from his shirt pocket and wiped his face. My eyes were hard on him. He was hardly looking up now.

'Well . . . you know,' he began, 'I was glad the pain was over. For as long as it lasted I kept away from my wife. But as soon as I felt the relief I called her over and tried to make it with her. Well . . . you know how it is. . . . .'

'No, I don't!' I cautioned. 'You had better tell me how it is. Too often have men brought ruin upon themselves by not telling the whole story—whose fault is it then but theirs that they have gone away with the wrong sort of prescription? You are not a child, so stop stuttering and tell me everything.'

He coughed and swallowed.

'Well . . . there wasn't much to it. I got astride her and—and tried, but—but, it just wouldn't work. *It just wouldn't work.*' He wiped his sweating face again. 'Then later I called her to me and—and I asked her—I was just trying to find out—I mean, I wasn't trying to accuse her. All I did was ask if she thought she had anything to do with all this. Because it—it had never happened to me before. I had never mounted my own wife only to feel my powers flawed by something I couldn't explain. I had thought the pain was over—and it was. I wasn't feeling any of the heaviness or rigour of the previous months. So I tried to ask her. But you know what women are like. She flared up, calling me this and that. I didn't touch her. It never entered my mind to do anything, though I could have strangled her there and then for daring to make me feel less than a man.

'But then I have tried other women. And it's all the same story.'

'What women was it you tried?'

'Forget about that,' he quickly countered, raising his voice, 'and just be content to know that I went to other women. And they are decent women too. But it was all the same thing. At one point I was sure the burden lay in my mind, and I even soused myself with alcohol in the hope that my mind would be free of the burden. But that too didn't work. Nothing seems to have worked. Look,

Emukapor, you can't consider your work completed until you have done something about this.'

'Don't push me now,' I told him, readjusting my sitting posture. 'Don't push me. The first time you came here you complained of a disease, and I went ahead and cured you of that. What you are complaining of now is totally different and has nothing at all to do with the first. It demands a fresh cure, and calls for fresh charges.'

'I knew you would come to that,' he said, almost shouting now. 'And I warn you that if this is the way you exploit people who come up to you like this, you are not going to have a good future with this trade.'

'I have conducted this trade for forty-seven years in exactly this way—and if I ever need your advice I'll say so! Now if you want to have this cure you must be prepared to pay fresh charges. Otherwise you have the option of stalking the whole town like a castrated lion until everybody gets to know about it. Well, which is it?'

He sighed again, and scratched his head.

'What is your charge?' he asked.

'Good. Five pounds down now, so I can buy some of the things I need for the medicine. Then you must come back later with a ram, a billy-goat, and a cock—I need their testicles. You can leave the rest to me.'

He put his hands in his pocket and counted out five pounds. He seemed to be in a hurry about it, either because the curfew was fast approaching or because he wanted to get away from my place. As soon as he had given me the money, he picked up his stick and his hat, and stood up to leave.

'Toje,' I said, 'business is business. But you and I are no strangers to each other. So let us not part this evening in such an atmosphere. Sit down and let us share a drink together.'

'You can save that for another occasion. I didn't think you had any left.'

'Just as you please!' I said. 'You can always count on my hospitality when the occasion warrants it. Give my regards to your family.'

'Goodbye,' he said, stepping out.

'Goodbye.'

I looked at him as he rode away, and shook my head. Was this the omnipotent giant? I felt sorry for him. At one point during our discussion I was sure that if a little child pushed him with a stick, he would fall over!

But he has himself to blame for whatever happened to him. I have always said that money makes a fool of a wise man. And some of the men we have around here don't strike me as the best example of wisdom. Look at a man like Toje. He has money all right. But at his age does he not know any better than to go all the way to Iddu and start scrubbing around with prostitutes? Now he ends up impotent. What good has all that money been?

Yet at his age he should know that it was all in his mind, and try to relax. But he is too full of himself to accept any kind of handicap. That's all right by me. All I am going to do is gather some thyme, alligator pepper and lemon grass. A pinch of salt and a pinch of dung. Make a mash of the whole thing in palm oil and let him rub the grease on his shaft—maybe that will settle his mind for him. But the cock and the ram and the goat will be most welcome on hungry days! I could do with some of that money he sees fit to throw away to prostitutes. In time he will have learnt his lesson.

Part three

I know
Of flowers unseen, and they
Distil beatific dawns
But tares
Withhold possession of our mangled lawns

WOLE SOYINKA

Toje

It hurts my image to be riding through this town smelling like a buzzard's crotch. I know it is not the patient's place to question a medicine-man on the ingredients that he uses to concoct his medicines. But it leaves a nasty feeling in me to know that I am wearing a detestable stench on my person. For as I ride now, I have to avoid every passer-by lest the wind carry the odour to his nose—and then he would turn round to sniff scornfully at Toje!

That lame-brained Emuakpor should have known that I was no ordinary patient. If things were as they should be, I would have had him come to my house and attend to my complaint, rather than take my respectable self to his wretched hut and submit my person to his lowly scrutiny and his irreverent remarks.

When he gave me the bottle, and I opened it, I was shocked by the odour that hit my nose. I immediately corked it again, and spat on the floor. He was sitting in one corner smoking his pipe, his back rested nonchalantly against the wall, staring at me.

'What in damnation have you put into the bottle?' I asked the scum.

'The medicine—what else?' he answered, the pipe still in his mouth.

'I know it's the medicine,' I said, spitting again, 'But what is it all made of?'

'Medicinal things—what else?'

'*What* things?'

'I can't tell you. It's against the code, you know that.'

'Damn your code! There've got to be some exceptions. I want to know what it is you expect me to rub on my body, especially on that part of it where decency is expected most. What is it?'

He refused to answer. He just looked away, smoking on without a worry.

'Listen—'

'*You* listen to me, Toje,' he broke in, removing his pipe. ' Which do you prefer—your decency or soundness of body?'

'That is not the point—'

'Well, it *should* be to you. If you are so worried about wearing a decent smell on your person, then I will be content to give you back your money and throw that medicine into the fire. And . . . if you really want to know what went into the medicine I can vouchsafe that bit of information—it's got dung in it, sheep's dung.'

'Sheep's dung!'

'Yes. Sheep's dung. Now are you satisfied?'

'But who would be so happy having to rub sheep's dung on his body?'

'Well, give me back the bottle then, and I'll refund you your money,' he said, holding out his hand. 'Come on, give it to me.'

Of course I couldn't. I sighed, and settled down on a chair. The room was dark, as it was almost evening. I didn't want to argue on.

'Well,' I said, 'what are your instructions for the use?'

He rose to spit a lump of saliva through the door.

'That should have been your first question anyway,' he said, eyeing me. 'You didn't have to come that sort of bully over me—I am too old for that.'

'All right,' I said, 'skip your lessons and tell me how I am to apply the medicine.'

He sat down again, and cleaned his mouth.

'It doesn't take much. Before you go to sleep at night, drink a lot of gin, then massage your penis with the medicine. Don't smear too much of it on. Just enough of it to give the skin a thin coating. And shortly before you go to bed with a woman, rub that same amount of it on the same place.'

'What!' I found myself asking. 'Meet a woman with this kind of smell?'

He eyed me again, then blinked and looked away, resuming his smoking.

'It's your problem, not mine,' he said. 'This medicine has worked perfectly well on a lot of people with the same complaint, and I don't see that you are any different from them. If you take my advice, it does help the efficacy of it if you believe that it will cure you, rather than walk around with a complex imposed upon you by a stupid craving for sweet fragrance. You should know better than that.'

He coughed, and spat again through the door. I could do no more than stare, now at him, now on the bottle in my hand.

'However,' he continued, 'if I were you I should give the medicine some time to build up its effect, before going on to lay a woman. . . .'

That was what he said. Give the medicine some time. But how much time have I got? How much time do I have left? Already the misguided officials at Iddu are beginning to release men from detention. How do I know that Oshevire is not the next man to be freed? Thanks to the imbecile testimony of Rukeme before the tribunal, anything could happen now. I know that his stubbornness may yet ruin Oshevire when he appears before the tribunal; there is little doubt about that. But I can scarcely take any chances now. I had rather that I had full sexual knowledge of his wife before he was released, than miss the prize and face the double shame: to be exposed to the whole community of Urukpe as a shameless adulterer, and yet live on with the deep personal knowledge that the most important man in the town is impotent. God, I have no time to spare. . . .

I glide slowly towards Odibo's hovel. I lean my bicycle against his wall, and push open the door. He is sitting on the floor, his back against the wall, dozing away.

'Wake up,' I say. 'What kind of human being sleeps at a time like this?'

He stirs, and rubs his eyes. He takes his time to rise from the floor, readjusting his cloth. The scoundrel does not even offer a word of greeting. And I am shocked to see him eye me briefly, then move towards the tiny window and push it open. Could it be the smell?

'Why do you open the window?' I ask him.

'To let in some air,' he says.

'And what do you need air for?'

He does not answer the question. Instead he turns his back on me and walks into the room. When I notice that he is taking too long, I begin to feel impatient.

'Are you going to take all evening in that room?' I ask him.

Again he doesn't reply. But I can hear him muttering something. I walk over to the door of the room, wanting to know what he is doing.

'Be quick, you fool,' I say. 'What's the matter with you?'

'Nothing,' he drawls.

'Then why are you so lazy?'

I can scarcely contain my temper. A damned cripple, who feeds from my hand!

'I've had a busy day,' he says.

'What busy day? Just because you went to Iddu and back with the lorry to bring down rice and yams?'

'It's not such an easy journey. My back aches.'

'I don't care if it breaks!' I bawl at him. 'Now come out of that room and go over to Oshevire's place to call his wife. And don't you waste any time about it. You should learn to move your mass a bit faster.'

He shuffles lazily out of the room, past me at the door and with such irreverence on his face and in his gait. *Shuo!*

'Where are the shoes I asked you to buy for her child?'

'Over on that bench,' he points, in the same slovenly style.

'Now take it quickly and get over there as fast as your legs can carry you.'

He picks up the packet of shoes, and ambles out. What! Odibo of all people—taking my orders at an easy pace, when he knows what it would cost him! If I should descend so low as to take anything, it won't be such irreverence from a damned cripple that feeds from my hand!

I sit down on the bench, to await the woman. I can already feel the smell of this medicine weighing on my mind. . . .

Oghenovo

odibo closes his eyes again, to sleep. his big nose rises and falls, rises and falls, making the noseholes bigger on each rise, the hair sticking out, the nose now like that of the big black goat that always comes to our backyard. the one that got its head covered yesterday in our cooking pot, the eyes all hidden underneath, like that of the little soldier outside there with the big iron helmet.

that is how odibo's nose rises now in his sleep. *why does he not want to look at my shoes.*

odibo, odibo, i call him now, shaking his leg.

he opens his eyes slowly and looks at me. he sighs very loud, and yawns. his mouth is black and red.

what is it, he says. don't bother me now, he says. i want to rest.

won't you look at my shoes again, i say.

they are very nice, he says, closing his eyes again.

but you haven't looked at them, i say, shaking his leg again.

he opens his eyes again.

very nice, he says. wait, you have got them on the wrong feet.

and he sits up properly and changes my shoes, putting them properly on me. there you are, he says. now let me sleep.

will you let me go out in them for a while, i ask him.

where to, he says, raising his head and staring hard at me.

i want to show them to onome, i say.

why do you want to show them to onome, he says.

i want to show him that my father has bought me a new pair of shoes, i say. he is always showing me things that his father has bought for him. and he tells me that my father can never buy me things because my father is in prison. i want to show him what my father has bought for me.

who told you your father bought you those shoes, he says.

my mother did, i say. my mother tells me that my father buys me things and sends them through you to me.

odibo looks on at me, saying nothing. then he shakes his head, and rests it again on the wall, closing his eyes once more.

wasn't it my father who bought me the shoes, i ask.

if your mother said so, then she was right, he says.

he opens his eyes a little to look at me, then closes them again, shaking his head.

will you let me show them to onome then, i ask him.

no, he says, you are not going anywhere. your mother says you should not leave the house. if you do, that soldier outside there will catch you and throw you into the hole of his gun. and you will not be able to see or breathe any more. and you will die, and he will eat you.

i want to show onome that my father is a good man and buys me good things. mother says my father is a good man.

odibo begins to sleep again. every time his big chest rises and his nose rises, his noseholes become bigger. and then they all go down again. i watch him very carefully i am waiting for him to be far asleep. and then i will open the door qui-et-ly and sneak out.

his mouth begins to open, slowly, slowly. finally his mouth falls open, showing the black teeth and the red tongue and innermouth. he doesn't wake up, and his mouth stays open. now i know that he is far asleep. slowly, slowly, i pick my steps, carefully avoiding his feet so i don't knock against them and wake him up. i grab the door-handle and turn it gently. as the door opens, it makes a harsh creaking noise. suddenly odibo shakes awake. he opens his red eyes, and peers round for me. i let go of the door at once.

come back here, he shouts, where do you think you are going.

i'm not going anywhere, i say.

then what are you doing standing by that door and opening it, he says, rubbing his eyes and mouth and sitting up.

i was only—

you were trying to steal out, he says. come back here and sit beside me. and don't you get up again.

i walk over and sit by his side. it is beginning to grow dark.

when is my mother coming back, i ask odibo.

very soon, he says. and if you try to go out again i will report to her when she returns.

then he settles down again and closes his eyes. he places one of his legs over mine. but when he sleeps far again i am going to take the leg off, gently, stand up, and sneak out through the kitchen door. then i will run quickly to onome's place and call him out and show him the shoes that my father has bought for me. and then i will run back home quickly before my mother returns.

Odibo

How much does it take to be a *man*, besides knowing that someone takes good and healthy notice of your manhood, and you can come out and receive the fresh, beautiful morning air full in your face without fearing that some other man would take you to task for it? For too long I have felt my body encaged in fear. Ever since I grew up to be aware of my physical deformity, I have lived a life of slavish caution, hiding the stump of my arm, talking very little, giving human beings a good speechless distance, and—what's worse—avoiding women in the strange fear that they would make little of my manhood, and of me. Besides, growing up in the shadow of my late father's words, that God never does a job half-way, I have always carefully restrained my impulses in the belief that I could never achieve anything however hard I might wish to try. I have lived a false existence, a prowling shadow, bashful, timorous, without a voice, without a face, without any kind of identity.

Now all that is gone. *Gone!* Now I know that I am a man like any other man. I have desires that should be satisfied, impulses that should be realised, and my big strong body is no longer there for nothing—'ineffective', as Toje has always told me to my face. For after that woman let me into her body, and I experienced a release of my long pent-up passion, I felt my whole body—my whole personality—loosen, and my entire being change. Now when Toje calls me a useless mass I am simply going to swallow his words without a care, for I know the world has been thrown wide open to me.

She had come home late again last night, for the second time. When she invited me again to spend the night there, I did not object. I was compelled to stay both by fear of possible danger and by the lustful hope that I was getting another chance to observe her naked form in the dead of night. At that point it had not entered my mind that I would do anything beyond that. I was still too afraid!

Then finally my chance came. All the world was hushed. This was the atmosphere I needed. And I rose to make use of it.

I had on just my wrapper, hugging my waist in a fold, and that not too tightly. I went to the door and pushed it gently open, avoiding all noise. As I looked into her room I again saw that lamp by the side of her bed, with the flame turned low. I was slightly worried, but not put off. Everybody leaves his lights on in one way or another when he goes to sleep. So I pulled myself together, leaving my door ajar just in case I had to hurry back in.

Then slowly, slowly, I began to step, at tiptoe, towards the woman, skirting the walls meanwhile, so that my sneaking figure did not catch any stray beams of light from the lamp. There was still no movement from either her or her son Oghenovo. He wasn't even snoring this time. I walked on and on, picking my pace. The situation demanded utmost caution—and caution was all I have ever known.

When finally I got to the side of her bed, I was thoroughly bemused by the figure that hit my eyes. The light from the lamp was very dim, but it fell on her body enough to describe it in clear and ungrudging outline. My mouth fell open! The last time I had visited she had an ear of her cloth stretched over her groin. But now she was all bare. I felt the temper rise in me, and my whole being quiver. With avid eyes I explored the rise and the fall, the luminous swell and the shaded dip of her glorious contour. My whole body was quivering in full fever. I could no longer remain standing upright. I bent over her and, my hand rested on the edge of the bed, I began to run my hot lustful breath over the length and breadth of her body. I took in the now familiar yet fresh fragrance in full

measure, losing my head in the welcome reverie. But that was not
enough. I lifted my hand and, still bent over her, I proceeded to
run the tips of my fingers over her warm skin and particularly over
the glowing mounds of her breasts, then down to the pebble-smooth
roundness of her thighs. I thought I felt her skin succumb under my
agitated touch. And I was not far wrong. For suddenly I heard the
woman breathing hard, the sigh and the gasp rising with each
moment. I stopped. But not so she. I looked at her eyes, and they
were slightly open, and so too her mouth. I was about to lift my
frame and retreat, when she suddenly shot out her arms and held on
to me.

'Please!' she gasped.

'What?' I said, quivering.

'Don't stop! Come on now.'

'No. No. I can't—'

'Now,' she cut in. 'Now.'

'But your child—'

'*Now!*' she all but yelled.

With one hand she suddenly grabbed hold of my member, which
had scarcely lost any of its agitation. She threw her legs wide apart.
My natural impulse, all too long contained, now rose to full bound-
less peak, and, my mind still teetering between fear and a scourging
compulsion to obey, I fell upon her lap and knew desire.

When it was all over, she sighed deeply, and said 'Thank you.' I
felt rather mystified by those words, and even more so by the smile
that I saw on her face. I sighed, myself, but I was still lost in the
mystique of the moment. I rose quickly and, still unbelieving, I
scuttled off to my room like a dog fresh-loosed from the halter, and
shut the door at once.

I lay on my bed and tried to pull myself together. The outcome of
my visit to the woman had exceeded my wildest dreams—if I had
ever had any. Something had happened to me that even my dreams
could never have entertained. For a brief spell I was gripped with
fear that I had set myself on a dangerous course and that I was
doomed if Toje ever got to know what I had done.

But then—! I shook myself up. Gradually I began to feel my
mind, my whole thinking, liberated from its habitual prison. The

mist was clearing now, and things started to appear in full relief. I became quite certain, beyond the shadow of a doubt, that Toje had been using my place for adulterous meetings with Oshevire's wife. Yes—there was not the least question in my mind about that now. For why all that gaudy, scented appearance? Why let the woman come alone, rather than with her child? Why choose my place to exercise his *benevolence*, when it could have been more effectively done in hers? And worse still, why treat my bed to such regal drapery ever so often?

Anyway, I had a raw deal from Toje far too long. I had too long taken a beating I never deserved. It was he that made me so painfully aware of my defect. If it wasn't for him the saying that God never left a job half-done would have had an entirely different meaning for me. It was he that had chained my mind, my whole being. And now that I knew better than I ever did, I was glad to have taken my revenge on him—glad to have registered the mark of my personality on at least one thing that seemed to have put him in such an awesome advantage over me. I took a resolution right there on that bed. I was never going to let Toje know what I had done with Oshevire's wife—she herself would be a fool to divulge it. But if he ever got to know, well, I couldn't help it. It had happened, and that was that. If he had any sense in his head, he had better just let bygones be bygones, and leave the matter well alone. Otherwise, if he made the mistake of wanting to call me to order for it, I would not mind in the least letting the entire population of Urukpe know to what shameless defilement he had been subjecting the forlorn wife of an unfortunate son of the town. He had much more to lose than I did. And if he dispossessed me, I would seek my own independent means of existence. Thereafter he could procure himself some other place for his adulterous rendezvous. As a matter of fact, it was becoming clear to me that my independence would be meaningless so long as I let such things go on in my place, under any circumstances!

The war is still here, and many of the old chances of paid labour are now closed. But as I reflected further, a few places came to mind. Labour was needed to weed and sweep the *Otota's* compound. Labour was needed to keep the town's market clean. Labour was needed to reconstruct and rehabilitate some of the essential services here affected by the war. No doubt there must be a few other openings which I could explore. In time I could save up enough money to start a small farm or something like that. I knew life was not easy for a man with one arm, but it certainly wasn't hopeless. God was sure to lend a hand at some point. With a little help from Him, I might yet achieve enough for my needs and work out my own life like everybody else. God, indeed, never left a job half-done!

As soon as the first beams of daylight hit the room, I got out of bed quickly and put on my clothes. I opened the door quietly and stepped out of the room, trying to leave with as little noise as possible. But no sooner was I at the door leading into her room than I heard the woman's voice in a soft whisper.

'Are you leaving now?'

'Yes,' I whispered back, stopping briefly in my steps, though I didn't want to look at her.

'All right. Take care.'

'Thank you.'

'I'll see you again soon, won't I?'

'Y—Yes,' I said, with hesitation.

Yes, my mind insisted, urging firmness and fearless certitude. *Yes.* . . .

As I approach my house now I can feel the gentle caress of the cool morning wind on my face. I can feel countless little dew-drops settle on me. I can see little birds flutter freely and fear-lessly in the air to which they are entitled like everything else and for which they don't need permission from anybody. And I can see my little house stand out independently on a spot of its own. That wall over on the left side seems to be deteriorating. Today I am going to mix the mud and cut the beam and mend it with whatever else I can use.

Aku

Can I swear that I never saw it coming? Frustration had driven me to the point where I would rather live the fact than the fiction of sin. Loyalty and devotion had been strained beyond all possible endurance, and neither the mind nor the body could any longer fight the overwhelming presence of temptation. The passive resistance of the body could no longer be supported by the will of the mind, until the entire defence came tumbling down, like an unsheltered mud wall under the relentless downsurge of rain. And can I now swear that I never saw it coming?

My dear Mukoro, I am sure that—wherever you may be—you still love me as much as I have always loved you. Nothing, and I mean *nothing*, will ever erase you from my heart or from my mind. Why, I stood by you when the going was tough. I gave you a good hand at the rubber business, and everybody in this town noted my tireless cooperation and applauded yet again the acknowledged industry of my people. At the entry of the federal troops into this town, when every Simba took to his heels in the wake of the unspeakable persecution conducted by lawless hordes of people, I refused to do what the normal, natural instinct for survival would have urged. I hung around until you came home, because even in the frenzy of the moment I could not contemplate any kind of life without you. For you are all I ever felt bound to.

You must therefore understand that whatever made me fail for even one moment in my bond to you must have been too great for me to fight. Three years and more of waiting for you to come back, without the least chance that my prayer will be answered, have steadily nibbled away my patience. The ever-present fear that your enemies might yet seek to visit their ill-will on what is left of your household has made me a prisoner of my own unflinching will to uphold you and everything that is yours. My unfortunate dependence on Toje for maintenance has gradually taken away much of the integrity that was needed to keep that will going. And, worst of all, the relentless assault on my chastity, which can hardly now be upheld by a flawed integrity and a beaten will, has bred in me a desire that with the passage of time has grown from passive submission to an active longing for satisfaction. Now who, my beloved, who is there that can stand up to all this and pull through unshaken? Yet, if I should be allowed even this one frivolous excuse for last night, it was that Odibo had about him something that reminded me so much of you. The urge to cling to that something has now proved my enduring shame. . . .

But be that as it may. Though I am reluctant to make the confession, I must say that now I feel some amount of relief. I do not know what all this will lead me into, but I am prepared to face the future with resignation. The day is now wide awake. I have thrown my window wide open. I can see that sphere of burnished gold in the distant horizon, and together a web of tree-leaves and the joyous frolic of birds form a glorious interception between my window and the charred sunrise.

Oshevire

'Look here, Mr Oshevire,' the chairman throws in. 'Are you quite sure you don't need the services of a lawyer? For one thing, a lawyer would make your points in as clear a language as possible and would concentrate on the essential points. For another, we would be able to avoid the irrelevant diversions that you have constantly led us into since we started questioning you yesterday. Now, are you sure you don't want to take a lawyer?'

'What would I need a lawyer for?' I ask him in turn. 'Does an honest man need a lawyer? If what I say here before you is not sufficient to make it clear that I am innocent and have been brought here for no just cause, then I am content to surrender myself to whatever interpretation you give my case and to whatever penalty you appoint for me. I do *not* need a lawyer.'

There is dead silence throughout the hall, even in the gallery.

'Carry on then, Mr Opubor,' the chairman turns to say to the commissioner.

'Listen, Mr Oshevire,' says the commissioner. 'I can understand the way you feel. But try to make things a little easier for you and me. Try to pull yourself together so that you can answer the questions with a clear mind.'

'My mind is perfectly clear,' I tell him. 'I have no illusions whatever about the facts that I am stating here, and God is my witness.'

He sighs, and turns his head to the side.

'Yes, of course, God is your witness. You've been telling us that since your case reopened yesterday. I know God is your witness, but He can also be anybody's witness, and—'

'God can never be witness to a dishonest man,' I remind him, for he seems to have forgotten. 'He can only be witness to truth.'

There is a din of humming from the gallery. I can feel their unspoken approval.

'Will you answer your questions directly, Mr Oshevire,' Major Bello blares at me, half-rising from his seat. 'You must stop wasting our time here with your proverbs and wise-cracks. We haven't come here to listen to all that nonsense.'

'I thank you very much, sir,' is my reply to the mighty soldier. 'It was you who brought me here in the first place. When they told you I was a rebel collaborator, you ordered that I be dragged away from my house and thrown into detention without even giving me the chance to bid my wife and child goodbye.'

'All right,' says the chairman, sternly. 'Enough of that from you. Just answer your questions directly and don't give us any more trouble. I hope you won't force me to do something unpleasant to you. Carry on, Mr Opubor.'

The commissioner clears his throat. He stares briefly at me. But when he sees that my eyes are fixed on him no less resolutely, he looks down at his interlocked hands on the table.

'Now, Mr Oshevire,' he says. 'I am going to ask you one or two more questions. And I think they are simple enough. In the first place, it has been charged that rebel soldiers were in the habit of visiting your house. What do you have to say to that?'

'I do not know about habit,' I reply him. 'And if the charge implies that more than one soldier ever visited my house, then I say that that charge is a shameless lie. Nevertheless, let me tell you all I know and all I feel about this matter.'

'Tell us only all you *know*,' the commissioner emphasises with a raised finger. 'I know what we are going to be running into if you have to tell us what you *feel*, and I don't think we have much time for that. Tell us what you know.'

'All right then,' I say. 'I'll tell you what I know. First of all, let me make it perfectly clear that my house was visited by a Simbian soldier on a few occasions. But there was never more than one soldier. This soldier comes from this state, from my wife's home town, to be precise. They also come from the same street in their town.'

'What town is that?'

'Ukpeke.'

'And what was the rebel soldier's name?'

'Ochonogo—that was all my wife and I knew as his name.'

'Carry on.'

'He knew my wife in their town, and he had seen my wife one day on the streets of Urukpe, and instantly recognised her. Thereafter, he paid us a number of visits.'

'Well, why did you permit him to visit your house ever so often?'

'So what could I have done to him—ordered him to get away from my place, when I knew what that could cost me?'

'But did it not occur to you at the time that the soldier was implicating you by paying all those visits to your house? How do you think the ordinary citizens of your town felt about him visiting your house with so much freedom?'

'The ordinary citizens of my town were not in a position to feel anything. I will tell you how it was with our town when the Simbian army were in occupation there. Perhaps you will then appreciate why I acted the way I did.

'I was at home the day they took over our town. We all suddenly heard that the Simbian army were now in control of the entire state, and everybody was warned to cooperate with them—anyone resisting was to be shot. At first we did not know how to take the new situation. Our position was particularly difficult because there were many Simbas in our town. We share common boundaries with them. Many of our citizens, like myself, had been married to Simba women, and they had borne us children. We therefore found it hard to turn round suddenly one morning and denounce people with whom we had been having a life-long communication. A man does not suddenly reject his brother simply because he has contacted yaws. So we watched for a few days to see what all this meant. But nothing new happened. We were still allowed to go to our farms. Our wives still went to the market. We never heard that anyone was shot. Of course, once in a while one heard that a soldier was involved in a quarrel or a fight with a civilian. But nothing seemed to have changed drastically.

'More than that, the soldiers themselves tried to win the goodwill of people. I am prepared to swear with my life to this. Those of them who knew people or who had relations or friends in Urukpe visited their homes—I do not see that mine was an exception. You could see groups of civilians, who were not even Simbas, walking round the streets of the town with Simbian soldiers—the communion with which I am being charged certainly wasn't confined to me or my household. Besides, some of those soldiers married some of our own girls during that period of Simbian occupation. If anyone should tell me that those girls were forced into marriage by the soldiers, then I would ask why the girls were not simply abducted. For lavish merriment took place in the homes of the girls in some of these cases. I am prepared to mention names here if you should ask me to do so.

'But that was not all. And I wish to mention one incident which perhaps had everything to do with how the people of my town felt in the face of the Simbian occupation.

'The Simbian military authorities had made it clear to us that they were not going to entertain any opposition to their presence. They had assured us that they were in our town to protect us from the hands of a government which did not care for us. They invited us to look upon them as liberators, but warned that they were going to deal ruthlessly with anyone who raised a voice or a finger against them. As I said, when first they took control, we were slightly confused about the whole situation. We didn't know what to do or say. We had never imagined that the war was going to get as far as our town. The road to our town had always been untarred, and very bad. Seldom did we receive any ministers or government officials from Iddu. We didn't think anybody knew we existed—so how could we have become involved in a situation of this kind which we could never have brought upon ourselves directly? If it was true therefore that we were threatened by anyone who did not seek our best interests, it was only natural that we should feel grateful to anyone who came seeking to protect us—we were in no position to consider the issue more deeply, particularly as we hardly knew what it was all about.

'The town council had to take a decision. At the time I was a member of that council, and I here declare that I took part in the deliberation of which I am now going to speak. The *Otota* summoned us all together, and asked us what we were going to do in the face of the new and sudden situation. As I said, we didn't know any better at the time. Besides, you don't argue too much with a man who has a gun. So we decided to invite the commander of the Simbian forces in Urukpe. At that meeting we—the whole council, sitting this time in the *Otota's* house, not the council hall—we assured the commander of our solid cooperation, and promised to hand over to him anyone who tried to cause any trouble. For that was uppermost in our minds then. We did not want any trouble, we did not want anyone to disturb our peaceful existence, and anyone who tried to oppose the military authorities then—whatever his motives might be—was, in our judgment, only a trouble-maker wishing to bring disaster upon our town. That was our attitude to the military occupation.

'The *Otota* sent the town crier round, issuing that warning. We did not want any trouble. People should cooperate with the military authorities. Anybody who tried anything was going to be reported and handed over to them, and God help him. The town complied.

'Of course the commander became our friend. He visited the *Otota* several times, and he visited some of the other councillors. Though he did not visit me, I certainly would have appreciated that gesture from him at the time if he had found the opportunity to do so. Would I therefore try to implicate either the *Otota*, or any of the other councillors, on the ground that the military commander paid them visits, when I know that the entire population of Urukpe welcomed their presence or at least were in no position to put any resistance to it? Why then should I be singled out for persecution because an ordinary soldier, not even an officer, visited my house on a handful of occasions?'

'But, Mr Oshevire, don't you see that you were a rather special case? Your wife is a Simba, and it is only natural that any visits to your household by that rebel soldier would be interpreted as having a much deeper meaning than with other households.'

'But I was not the only one in Urukpe married to a Simba woman?'

'Yes, but why were you the only one of them charged with collaboration then?'

'Well, I don't know. I probably never will,' I tell him, somewhat baffled myself. 'But I am going to say something here. When the federal troops took over the town, all the Simbas ran away, including countless wives long married to citizens of our town who could not by any stretch of thinking be regarded as rebel collaborators. All the wives, I say, ran away—I can't think of any that stayed—and many of them took their children along with them. But my wife stayed. She did not run away. Now, if we were convinced that we had done anything wrong, and we had acted in a way that was not in the best interests of our town, could we have had the courage to remain in the town when we saw hordes of lawless civilians on the rampage in the town, doing violence to people? I say, if my wife did not consider herself Simba enough then to want to run away from the town like all the others—if it did not matter at that time that she was a Simba, why should it matter now just because someone suddenly remembered that one inconsequential little soldier paid us a handful of visits?'

The commissioner sighs, and looks down. You can never suppress the truth.

'There is just one more question, Mr Oshevire,' he says, wiping his face with his handkerchief. 'It was also charged that you helped

a number of rebel soldiers escape from Urukpe at the entry of the
federal soldiers. What is your answer to that?'

'I saved the life of one helpless little boy,' I tell him with all
emphasis. 'And if I had the same opportunity, I'd gladly do it again.'

'All right. You saved the life of a helpless boy. Tell us the circumstances under which you saved the life of this . . . "helpless"
boy.'

'It's nothing to gloat over. But I'll tell you anyway.'

'First of all, what day was that?'

'I couldn't remember such a thing. How could I—did I know
that some day someone was going to call me to account for doing
what anyone with a heart would have done in the circumstances?'

'All right—save your preaching and tell us about it.'

I clear my throat.

'It was just one evening. The federal troops had taken the town.
There was a great deal of turmoil. All over the town crowds of
rampaging civilians chased Simbas about, committing a lot of
violence. I stayed at home all day with my family. But by that
evening things had calmed down considerably and I thought one
could venture safely out again. I had forgotten something in my
rubber plantation—I think it was a key. So I hurried off to get it.
I was scarcely there a few minutes when I heard some noise coming
from the direction of the entrance into the plantation. I looked
back, and saw this young boy running towards me in all panic. He
was running desperately and was almost out of breath. As he ran up
to me I could see that his eyes were swollen and there was some
blood on his forehead. All he had on him was a pair of shorts ripped
to pieces. He fell down on his knees before me, panting and sobbing.

' "I beg you, sir" he prayed, "save me. They are trying to kill me".

'I was touched with pity. A little boy, not more than about
twelve or thirteen years of age! And the way he cried, and made me
feel that if he should die it was all my fault! I just had to do something to save that boy. I had neither the time nor the heart to ask
him what he had done for which he was being pursued—besides, I
knew only too well the horror of the times to wish the same fate for
that little boy who could have been my own son. And the crowd
was hot on his trail.

'There was a hollow, rotting baobab tree that had fallen near my farm-house. I motioned him into it.

' "Quickly, get in there!" I whispered.

'No sooner had he ducked in there than the mob ran towards me, wielding clubs and matchets and howling furiously.

' "Where's the rebel?" they demanded, almost bearing down on me.

' "Rebel?" I responded, startled. "I saw a little boy run desperately into the bush over there".

'They didn't ask any more question. They hurried off into the direction I had pointed, disappearing in the bush in an instant. After they had gone I beckoned to the boy to come out and find his way into another part of the bush. I never saw him again, but I hope to God he was able to make good his escape from that hate-filled rabble that sought his life. My God, every time I think of that incident, I am moved much less with the satisfaction that I saved a life than with wonder as to what has gone wrong with the hearts of men.'

'That's not necessary, Mr Oshevire,' says the commissioner. 'But tell me one thing. Would you say you didn't know that some rebel soldiers were still straggling around the town, and that federal troops were trying to hunt them down?'

'There wasn't a single federal soldier in that mob that was chasing the boy. They were all civilians—at least I didn't see anyone in uniform.'

'Are you sure you looked properly?'

'Well—you couldn't mistake a man in a uniform. And there wasn't a uniform there that struck my eye.'

'How many people would you say were in that crowd?'

'I don't know—they were very many. Maybe twenty or more.'

'And you could tell what every single one of twenty men was wearing?'

'No, I couldn't. But it seems clear that if it was federal troops that were leading that chase, there should have been more soldiers than civilians.'

'All right. But wouldn't you consider it a patriotic thing for a civilian to help federal soldiers track down rebel stragglers?'

'Perhaps. Perhaps it is. But that boy couldn't have been a soldier.'

'What makes you so sure, Mr Oshevire?'

'Why, he didn't have a uniform on. The Simbian soldiers that had been stationed in Urukpe had their uniforms.'

'But you have just told us that he had on a pair of shorts that had been ripped to shreds.'

'Yes'.

'Now how could you have been so sure that that was not what was left of his uniform?'

'Well—I—'

'Besides, Mr Oshevire,' he cuts in, 'are you trying to tell us you didn't know that many rebel soldiers changed to mufti as soon as federal troops captured the town and tried to make their escape in that fashion?'

'Well, I didn't think any Simbian soldiers could have remained in the town after the federal troops got in. As I said, it was evening. The federal forces had now effectively taken Urukpe—and that after a day or two of shelling—and I wouldn't think any Simbian soldiers with any kind of sense could have remained in the town.'

He looks at me sharply, and shakes his head.

'Mr Oshevire,' he says, 'I will forgive you that much ignorance of military strategy—that most pitiful ignorance of the fact that soldiers have many a time lost a captured town simply because they have not taken care to consolidate their victory by "mopping up" the place, clearing it of stragglers and all possible danger. As I said, I will forgive you that ignorance. But tell me one thing, Mr Oshevire. How could you simply shelter a pursued man without knowing what he had done for which he was being pursued? You mean to say that if a thief was being chased and sought for arrest you would take him in and shelter him, just because you saw he was in danger?'

'Would a mere thief be pursued by a mob of twenty or more brandishing clubs and matchets? No, sir. That is unknown in our town. When we pursue a thief we do not carry clubs and matchets— we want to *catch* him and surrender him to the police and see that justice is done.'

'You pursue him unarmed, even if he is armed himself?'

'Well, this little boy wasn't armed, and that made it even less defensible for that mob to be chasing him with such fearful weapons. Besides, I have already said that the times were troubled. I had seen enough of what had happened to several Simba civilians in our town at the hands of lawless people to allow the same fate to over-take that little boy before my very eyes. No, sir, I couldn't bear it.'

The commissioner sighs briefly, and fixes me again with that challenging gaze.

'Mr Oshevire, is it not safe for us to assume that the reason you saved that . . . *boy* had to do with your wife being herself a Simba?'

'I would not question your assumption, but the thought never crossed my mind at the time.'

'How is that?'

'I saw that boy as a human being, and that was my only concern. It still *is* my only concern. I felt deeply moved to see human life in danger. Though that boy's face had been slightly disfigured I could clearly see that he was too young and I could not bear to watch him fall into the hands of a merciless mob that could have taken his life right there before me. I felt concerned then at the total loss of reason among many people in our town—how several helpless people who could not possibly have been soldiers were hunted down and pitilessly brutalised for no just cause. Perhaps you are right that my wife being a Simba had to do with the way I felt. But I should like to think that there are still men around today with reason in their heads and God in their hearts, and that no such people would in any circumstances uphold the kind of terrible lawlessness that was carried on in our town during those unfortunate days. I feel con-cerned that anybody should take me to task just because I took pity on a little twelve-year old boy who faced possible death at the hands of a rabble, whatever was his crime. But I am not ashamed or afraid to have done what I did. I am willing to stand by my action even if I should die for it, because I know I have acted strictly out of the dictates of a pure heart and without any intention whatso-ever to stand in the way of the federal strategy. And God alone is my witness.'

The commissioner sighs, and shakes his head.

'No more questions, your honour,' he turns to tell the chairman, wiping his face at the same time.

All over the gallery there is a low rumble of murmuring. The chairman consults with the panel of commissioners. I do not know what they are saying, but whatever it is I am not afraid. An innocent man has no need of fear, even if he is visited with a judgment that he does not deserve. Stand firm and unshaken. Truth and honesty will always triumph, and a pure heart never loses.

'Ehm,' says the chairman, and the entire hall becomes silent again. 'We have now heard this case through, and I declare it closed. The tribunal now rises for a break, and resumes at two o'clock this afternoon on a fresh case.'

The chairman and his panel rise from their seats. Everybody else—all of us—rise after them. We wait for them to leave, and after them the gallery breaks out again in a loud rumble as everybody makes his way out.

My fellow detainees and I, four of us in all, are led out by the two armed soldiers and one policeman that brought us to the hearings. When we get outside there is already a large crowd waiting to see us. Since this is now a usual happening, I am not perturbed by their presence. I do not think I make a very pretty spectacle anyway, with my bushy face and not-so-clean clothes. But as we walk along towards the Black Maria I notice a young man pushing his way through the crowd towards me—and who should it be but Rukeme himself, to whom it fell to indict me before the tribunal! He comes up and stops beside me. There is a worried look on his face. He is shaking somewhat, and there is a film of tears in his dull eyes. I am uncertain what could be his mission this time, but I greet him with a smile. He doesn't say a word, and I take the initiative.

'What's the matter now, Rukeme? I hope all is well with you?'

He is still shaking and swallowing restlessly, trying hard to subdue his sobs.

'Believe me, Mukoro,' he says, stuttering. 'It wasn't my fault. I was pushed into it. Please—please, believe me.'

'Oh, forget about it,' I reassure him. 'I perfectly understand, and I bear you no grudge. But tell me one thing. How are my wife and child—have you seen them lately?'

'Yes. Yes,' he says, still agitated. 'They are very well. They are all right.'

'Good. Thank you.'

The soldier behind me pushes me forward with the butt of his gun, and orders hoarsely, 'Move on!'

I stumble and almost fall under the thrust of the gun. I look back at him with a calm smile on my face. *Take it easy, friend. Otherwise you won't have much left of me to shoot when the time comes.* We are shoved into the Black Maria.

Toje

It wasn't that I didn't try to keep to the advice of the medicine man. *It would do you a lot of good*, he had said, *to believe that the cure would work.* Of course I tried very hard to believe that it would work. I made all the effort I could within the limits of what time I thought I had left and of the demands I felt the smear made on my personality. But then it all failed. I just couldn't work up within me the tension that I needed to do the job. And the reason was that I found it impossible to disabuse my mind of the conviction that a forbidding odour such as I was wearing on my body was not in the least conducive to an atmosphere of love-making.

But if I felt my impulses hampered by my physical condition, I was—and am even more so now—convinced beyond all endurance that time was running out. *Give it some time*, Emuakpor had advised. But this advice I have found hard to take. I don't know how much time he would have specified, and I am reluctant to go back to the crook and risk being told to keep off women for three months! For who knows what is going to happen now? Oshevire's case has been closed, according to the newspaper this morning, and all we are expecting any moment now is the decision of the military governor. Am I going to wait for him to be released from detention, assuming he is declared innocent by a misguided verdict from Iddu, and so return triumphant to Urukpe while I face a multiple discomfiture?

And now, it appears, I am seeing a more disturbing sign. This time from Oshevire's wife herself. All along I have counted on her un-grudging cooperation and indeed subjugation to my word. I have always felt certain that a woman who owed her life to me would never give me cause to be afraid of failure. But what happened on our last meeting has put the fear in my mind. Not only did I sense some reaction on her part against the stench that I was wearing; it appeared to me, even more painfully, that she had tensed herself against all stimulation from me and just lay passive and unmoved while I fumbled with her.

My God, I cannot afford to fail. . . .

Odibo

Of course I know I don't have a stake in the affair between him and Oshevire's wife. I don't think I have anything to lose if two people elect to lose their heads in reckless orgies. But what I am concerned about is that this affair should provide an occasion for my humiliation. I think it is too much to expect a man to allow someone else to place his foot perpetually on his head. It is definitely too much to expect a man to give up his house for an affair of doubtful virtue and yet be called a fool and an imbecile in the process. All this nonsense has become too much for me to take. Too much!

'Don't tell me,' she says, as I step into the house. 'I know what you've come for.'

I take a good look at her face, for I'm not sure how to take that statement. It certainly sounds encouraging. I can feel the rapport.

'Yes,' I reply. 'But you don't have to go there if you don't want to.'

I put the bundle of yams and the gallon of kerosene down by the door and give her the money that Toje has given me for her.

'Thank you,' she says, looking down blankly at the fresh pound notes that I have put in her hand. 'But what can I do? I have no choice.'

'Odibo,' calls her son, running out from the room, 'I have made a new gun. A big gun. Shall I show it to you?'

'Yes. Show it to me', I reply.

He runs back into the room for the 'gun'.

'Choice?' I ask her. I'm baffled myself for an answer. 'Well . . . I suppose you could tell him you were ill, or something like that.'

'Yes,' she says, holding her head down in her palm, possibly in frustration. 'I know. But how long could I sustain such an excuse?'

'Here is the gun, Odibo,' Oghenovo says, holding out to me a fat long stick with a sharp fore-end.

'Take that stick away from here and stop worrying us,' his mother bawls at him, snatching the stick from him and throwing it back into the room. 'Go into that room and close the door. And don't come out again until I tell you to.'

Subdued, the little boy walks heavily towards the room, clutching an ear of his shirt between his teeth. He bangs the door very loudly on getting into the room.

'Don't be so hard on him,' I plead.

She hisses.

'He's a bothersome gnat.'

A draught of the evening wind penetrates the door and window. It looks as if we are each waiting for the other to make the next suggestion.

'You know within yourself that I don't want to go on seeing him,' she says.

'Then don't!' I reply, with a touch of impatience.

'But what is my alternative?'

'I don't know.' I refuse to look at her now, because my impatience is building up to a point where there is no room for sympathy. 'If you didn't want to see a man I'm sure there are countless excuses that you could give if you really felt the need to justify yourself.'

'But you know how much he means to our survival—mine and my child's. You can't say you don't.'

'No, I don't. But I do know how much he has meant to me. I hardly wake up any morning without looking forward to receiving insults from him when I am only doing him a favour. This whole thing is beginning to—'

High over and above the roof we can hear a prolonged roaring sound. This is followed by a thunderous blast, and that in turn is replied by a ceaseless rattling of gunfire from nearby. No need to be told this is an air raid! Glancing quickly at each other the woman and I dash into the bedroom.

'Quick! Come here!' she shouts, grabbing Oghenovo with one hand.

Together we all dive under her bed and lie face down on the floor. The thundering and clattering noises continue outside. Occasionally, human shouts and wailings, and sounds of falling things. Oshevire's wife has one hand held tightly round my side, and I am doing the same to her. In fact, more by accident than by intent, my hand is lodged caressingly on the softer regions of her backside. And, thus joined with her—albeit in peril—I can feel the conviction grow within me that this is a possession I am inclined neither to part with nor even to share with anyone that wishes me no good.

Okumagba

I just couldn't do it. The situation I was in was much too tense for me to pull myself together and blast the brains out of that god-forsaken whore.

The combined air and guerrilla attack was too swift and sudden. The one followed the other in such quick succession that all I could do was the only sensible thing to do under the circumstances. First came the air raid. The planes this time were a roaring crowd—four planes, much bigger than the small craft that had visited in the previous raid, and dropping bombs enough to sink the whole town under the ground. I was severely shaken and in a state of panic. As soon as the first plane swooped overhead, I put my trigger to action and let my gun rattle off. I don't suppose I hit anything, but at least

I felt satisfied I was doing my duty. By the end of the raid I had exhausted more than half of my magazines.

One of the bombs landed about two poles away from me. It didn't hit any important object—it fell on a clearing—but it dug a ditch huge enough to bury sixty people comfortably, and a mango tree some yards away from the spot was all but uprooted and now tilts dangerously. Several bombs were dropped all over the town— why, the whole town is now in tears!

Scarcely had the planes departed—untouched by all the anti-aircraft fire that we had released at them in an exchange that had lasted about twenty minutes—when all over the town could be heard the *takum-takum* reports from rebel guns engaging our soldiers from the eastern sector of the town. In no time the guerrillas had penetrated to the middle of the town, fighting their way desperately in a suicide bid to capture an already shaken and panic-stricken post, and blasting away at everything in sight. They had fanned them-selves out. I suppose their aim was to throw our troops into general confusion and put us all to flight. But it was a mistake. They had spread their numbers too thinly. You could see a rebel soldier here, another there and two over there. Not too far from here I saw one of them shoot down a goat and drag it to a safe spot. Shortly after, he in turn was cut down by one of our guns.

As soon as I saw him fall, I knew I had to take a strategic position, for offence as well as defence. Quickly I ran into this old council hall and bolted the door securely. All the windows had been shut, and that suited me beautifully. I brought a table round to one of the windows and mounted it. I thrust the barrel of my gun out of the fan-light above the window. From that position I could easily see and engage any rebel soldier that came by without being seen myself. I had scarcely stood there two minutes when two of them slouched by, holding rifles that were not much bigger than toy guns. At once I released a few rounds from my killer and levelled one of them down. The other was thrown into confusion. If the fight were an equal one he could have done me some harm, because he seemed a good marksman. Reacting swiftly, he sent one bullet ripping through the window behind which I stood, missing the right side of my body by only a few inches. But of course he couldn't see me, and I threw him a few seeds from my little darling here. The gun dropped from his hand. He howled only once, like a mad dog, and hit the ground just one step away from where his friend lay.

I could have kissed my gun for a job well done, but there was no time. No more rebels came my way. They must have smelt their fallen companions from afar—I hear rebels have good noses. But for over three hours gun answered gun in a deafening encounter. I had moved my table away to the next window, to avoid making a target of myself through the aperture created by that unlucky rebel. All through the action I stood on quaking feet, fearing every next moment that came. Night had set in before the gun reports died down and the town was drowned once again in an uneasy peace.

It was a very hectic time, and I just couldn't get out of my hiding place to finish off that whoring rebel woman over there. Perhaps if I had felt safe enough at the end of the raid, I could have come out and done the job—all I needed to do was thrust my gun through her window, or blast the door open, and shoot down every damned soul inside that house. There were in it the woman herself, her son and that brooding hulk of a cripple, Odibo. I had seen him go into the house earlier in the evening, and I don't think he had time to come out all through the prolonged raid.

I feel sure now that there must be some dirty business going on among the whole damned lot of them—the cripple had even spent a couple of nights or more in that house. The sight of him going into the place had turned my stomach with anger. I would have been glad of an opportunity to put an end to his hulking life and forever save myself from this most odious detail. Why should I be condemned to watch him go in and have his orgies while I endure every mood of the weather?

But the raid was not the only reason for not venturing near that house. I knew too well what could have happened if I had killed all those people in there. There is no length to which our crazy major would not go to probe their deaths. If a man was crazy enough to put a rebel under protection (and comfortable protection at that), he wouldn't shrink from ordering that the bullet that despatched the rebel be examined thoroughly—just to convince his crazy head that he had done all he could to protect the godforsaken life, and that it was only too unfortunate to have fallen under a gun that did not belong to any of his own men. I was certain the major could have done a thing like that—and then I would only have earned a firing squad for myself.

Well, one day . . . one day. . . . This time I won't have to use a gun—that would be wasting precious bullets on a life that isn't worth a damn. There are too many ways to kill a dog. And this is one dog that I very much wish dead. After that I'll get myself re-deployed for the service I was enlisted for. And woe betide that major if he should put me for a second time on an odious task such as this—nurturing rebels in this town for him when he should be busy securing the town against rebel attacks.

Ali

The toll was too bad, *wallahi!* Too bad. In the air raid, 22 soldiers and 57 civilians. Whole families wiped out and several houses destroyed. The market completely burnt out. Poor old Godin-heaven got his own too—him and his entire family cleaned out. Being near the market his house was engulfed in the blaze that took the market and several houses around. How right he was in what he had said, that the next time the rebels came the story would be different! In the guerrilla attack, 15 civilians and 113 soldiers. Numerous persons, soldiers and civilians alike, badly wounded in both encounters, a large number of them critical cases.

I haven't gone round to see every one of the casualties. Though we have beaten back the attacks, my entire post is in disarray and all I can do now is gather my officers and plan the next course of action, including the exact strength of reinforcements to be requisitioned from Headquarters. Besides, I can't yet face the enormous misery that I am bound to encounter everywhere, should I venture out. And I don't think I have the stomach to listen to people like

Chief Toje lecture me on what I should have done or what I should do. I can gradually feel my prime duty as a soldier coming into harsh focus, and I think I have to face it if I am not to see my whole career terminated in disgrace.

Of course my duty to protect civilian lives and liberties remains, but henceforth I am going to grapple with my military task in more practical terms, rather than devote an unduly large portion of my time to public relations.

Allah! What a disaster. . . .

Toje

So they are trying to blame everything on the air raid and the fighting! They couldn't do what they were supposed to do because of the situation. The situation stopped her from coming to meet me at Odibo's place—yet I was counting every minute that passed, and I had sent off the bastard to call her forty full minutes before the air raid visited. What then could she have been doing? He says too the situation caused him to spend the night at the woman's place. Couldn't he have taken the risk, in the middle of the night, well after the air raid and the fighting were over, and made it quickly back to his own place? Why, I was imprisoned in his hovel—a prisoner more of an anxiety to see him back there than of the fear of the situation.

Well then, if the situation prevented him from coming home, why was it that he got there so late in the morning, long after the first light of day? Add to all this the disdain that the woman has shown lately, and the rather sluggish pace at which that scum has been executing my orders. . . .

The picture is unbearable—*unbearable*! To be thwarted by two people who owe their very existence to me! Unbearable!

I'll lay them a trap. . . .

Odibo

This is heaven! To have a woman sharing my own bed with me—and not only not unwilling to wallow in such lowly circumstances but indeed loving every moment of it and addressing me in language I could have sworn I would never hear! This must be heaven. . . .

'He said he was going to Iddu?' she asks.

'Yes,' I reply, sighing. 'So he said.'

'Did he say when he was going to return?'

'No, but he said it wasn't going to be today.' I cast a glance at her. 'Why, are you worried?'

She stares blankly away for a while.

'No . . . not really. I mean . . . I . . . ,' she hisses. 'I don't know. I really don't know.'

I sigh and turn over on my side, drawing my body and my attention from her.

'Are you angry with me?' she asks.

I maintain my silence, saying not a word.

'Forgive me,' she says, 'I didn't mean to hurt. Please forgive me.'

She draws me over once more to her, then clasps her arm around me, rubbing passionately. Once again our two naked bodies are in warm embrace. I put my arm around her, playing tenderly with the groove of her back. Tickled, she utters a short laugh, low, ecstatic, hungry. I continue working her back, the way she taught me to, until she can stand the feeling no more, and then she shrinks suddenly, laughing again and biting my chest with hesitant teeth and a tongue playing a soothing role. Slowly now, my hand glides down her back, steadily, towards the bristly decline of her groin. Suddenly she shakes herself loose of the move.

'Do you know something?' she says, her eyes staring past my shoulder.

'What?' I ask, somewhat startled by the sudden interjection.

'I don't think we should ever do anything again in my house.'

'I see. But. . . . Why?'

'Well,' she says, 'it doesn't look quite right. The first time we did it was right on my husband's bed, and I didn't like that very much. The last time was on the other bed—but even then it worried my mind afterwards that it wasn't right for us to do any such thing in my husband's house. You—you agree with me, don't you?'

'Well,' I say, sighing, 'I suppose you're right. So, what do you suggest?' I look straight into her eyes.

She doesn't reply at once. She buries her head in my chest.

'I think it is much better here,' she mutters, as though the words are not meant directly for my ears.

'That's all right by me,' I say, somewhat hesitantly. I'm not too sure myself that that is such a perfect alternative.

'Except . . .'

'Except what?'

'Except that—'

She breaks off suddenly. Outside we can hear the sound of a bicycle pulling up against my wall. Instinctively we both sit up, listening intently.

'Isn't that Toje?' she asks.

'I think so.'

'I thought you said he'd gone to Iddu?'

'That's what he told me.'

Quickly, I get out of the bed and throw my wrapper around me.

'Oh my God!' I can hear her whispering in despair.

Toje tries to open the door, but I already have it bolted. Oshevire's wife struggles out of the bed.

'Take it easy,' I tell her calmly. 'The door is locked, and he can't get in yet.'

Toje is still struggling to push the door open.

'What do I do now?' she whispers loud.

'You can dress yourself and hide under the bed.'

'Odibo! Odibo!' Toje blares out, banging hard on the door.

'Who is that?' I reply, feigning a sleepy voice.

'Open the door, you fool!' *That word again.*

'All right, I'm coming.' I look at the woman, who is now dressed after a fashion. 'Quickly,' I whisper to her, and she rushes under the bed. I draw the calico cover down over the visible edge of the bed, to shield her from view.

'Open the door, I say!' Toje howls again.

'I'm coming. I'm just tying my wrapper on.'

I go over to the door and pull the bolt backwards. I greet him with a sleepy yawn and half-shut eyes.

'What are you doing in bed this hot afternoon?' he asks.

'I was feeling rather tired, so I decided to lie down a little. I didn't notice when sleep overcame me.'

He stares straight into my eyes, unbelieving, but careful not to betray his suspicion.

'Are you back from Iddu already?'

'Yes,' he says, pushing me aside and casting a stealthy glance past me to the open door of my room. But I am standing close to him, ready to prevent him should he try to brave his way into my room. This house is mine, no one else's.

'Come on now,' he orders. 'Go over quickly and call Oshevire's wife here.'

'Ehm, she's not at home. I just got back from her place.'

He throws me a challenging look.

'You just got back from her place? Who sent you there?'

'Well . . . I just went to tell her that you had gone to Iddu and wouldn't be back today. I remembered her telling me recently that she never felt safe or happy any time she wasn't sure you were around. All I wanted to do was to reassure her with my presence, so she wouldn't feel completely at a loss.'

He keeps staring at me. I am convinced he doesn't believe me. But I am here to prevent him from doing anything I won't like.

'Are you quite sure about that?' he asks, his eyes glaring with distrustful menace.

'Of course, yes,' I say. 'Is . . . is anything the matter?'

'Suppose I go there and find out you are telling a lie? What do you think I should do to you?'

'Anything you like,' I say. 'But . . . what is the matter, Toje? Has anything gone wrong?'

I tie my cloth more securely round me. I am prepared to go on with this pretence until he pushes me harder than I can endure. But at the moment he is careful not to betray his suspicion and demean himself by any move that may prove to be an error in the end.

'All right,' he says. And casting one more glance into the room he storms outside and grabs hold of his bicycle.

I stand at the door to watch him pedal away to a safe distance. Already I can feel my resentment against the man building up to a point where I think I have to let him understand, in quite unmistakable terms, that I will no longer let him toss my life about with the insolent freedom which he has been using all along. What kind of a man would I call myself if I let him continue to do that?

'Odibo,' the woman whispers, emerging now.

I rejoin her inside. I can see her quaking with fear, and I am irritated by the implication that I am not man enough to stand up to the challenge and defend her.

'Relax,' I tell her. 'What are you so worried about?'

'What do you think is going to happen now?'

'I don't know,' I say, dismissing all care. 'What can happen? Relax, and dress yourself properly. Even if you should be caught, do you want to be caught in this state?'

She looks herself over quickly, and begins to re-arrange her dress.

'He will surely come back, don't you think?' she asks.

'Of course he'll come back. But so what?' I reply, dropping carelessly onto the bed.

'Well,' she says, panting, 'what do you think I will say?'

'What will you *have* to say?'

'Oh, please, Odibo,' she pleads, her face now deeply furrowed and contorted with worry, 'you don't seem to be viewing the situation with the seriousness it deserves.'

'What seriousness? Will he kill you? If he tries any such nonsense the army is there to do him justice.'

Though I am not looking at her, I can feel her eyes on me, burning with frenzied worry.

'Sit down awhile,' I tell her.

'What—and wait for him to come back?'

'Well, what do you want to do then?'

'I think I should be going at once.'

'And if he meets you on the way, are you going to put up any better defence than if you were to remain here?'

'What would I tell him if he met me here?'

'Well . . . we could say you just called in on your way back to check whether he had returned from Iddu.'

From the way we look at each other it is plain that neither of us has very much faith in that sort of defence. But at least the shared dubiety fills the moment where helpless worry could hurt.

'Sit down awhile,' I urge her.

She obeys. Shaking her head and muttering 'Oh my God', she perches herself on the very edge of the bed.

'Or rather,' I say, getting up, 'let's go to the parlour and wait. As soon as we hear him coming we will rise and move towards the door. That way, it would make more sense to say that you had just come in.'

Again she obeys, saying nothing. We both move out into the parlour. She sits down on the bench, while I pace up to the door and back again, bracing myself for the man.

Oshevire

Strange as it seems, what Rukeme told me outside the tribunal hall made up in no small way for all the testimony that he had given against me. In a flash, I felt an access of joy and satisfaction seize my heart. And when that soldier butted me with his gun, I was already in that state of mental relief that could have told him that I didn't care what happened any more because the worst, as far as I was concerned, was over!

It wasn't so much that I was glad that my wife and child were alive and well. That feeling of relief was inspired by the joyful knowledge once again that I had a jewel of a wife. As Rukeme said in the tribunal, there is a strong feeling of resentment against me in Urukpe—and I have little reason to doubt this, considering not only the speed with which I was reported to the military authorities as a 'rebel collaborator', but indeed by the kind of shameless evidence that was levelled against me in the hearings. I should therefore expect that, in the face of all the raids that we hear announced on this radio here in our prison, the same people that handed me over to the authorities would seek to visit their hate on what is left of me. And if my wife has pulled through all this, it cannot be that they have now turned their malice to love. It can only be that, amid all that overwhelming terror, my wife has stood defiant and resolved to uphold the honour of her man rather than undertake a desperate action against herself.

It is with no small joy therefore that my brooding mind has sought constantly to recreate for itself the pride that I once knew in possessing her—remembering how hard she proved to win; and, once won and wedded, what a painful but proud picture she cut on that first night when she made me realise that I was the first to burst open her gate; what an example of womanhood she made of herself by her tireless support of me in my trade; what remarkable courage she demonstrated by sticking with me during the terrors that accompanied the federal liberation of our town, when every single one of her tribe did not hesitate to desert home and family and take to her heels. . . .

A very jewel of a wife. A matchless queen, whose courage and nobility demand only equal demonstration of fortitude from me now as always—particularly now, as I await my verdict knowing full well the odds against me.

Toje

He had better be right. That damned imbecile had just better be right. *She was not at home.* Where could she have gone? A woman who has been confined to her house for so many months, suddenly picking up the courage to stray from that prison so soon after a rebel attack, when she should know that for her this is a most dangerous period. And then he had the nerve to go to her house on his own initiative, without waiting to be sent there by me. I call that the panicky stuttering of a guilty bastard caught unawares. I must know the root of all this. To be so cheaply fooled is the last thing I would bring myself to accept. To be so cheaply fooled and thwarted by two creatures who depend on me for their very lives. . . .

I lean my bicycle against the wall of her house. There is no sign of life on the premises. I knock at the door.

'Aku! Aku!'

Not a voice in reply.

I open the door and go inside. Not a soul here either. I search round the rooms. She couldn't have gone to my house. I have just come from there. Besides, that has never been our arrangement. . . .

'Aku! Aku!'

I pass through the kitchen door and out into the backyard. There I find her son Oghenovo and another little boy whom I vaguely recognise as being Jigere Atagana's son, from just next door. They are cursing and stabbing fingers at each other's chests.

'Your father.'

'Your father.'

'Your father.'

'Your father.'

'Your father.'

'Your father.'

I walk up to them and pull them apart.

'Break it up, you boys,' I say. 'What's the matter?'

'It's his fault,' says one.

'It's his fault,' says the other.

'All right, stop all that now. Run along home, boy,' I tell Atagana's son.

He eyes Oghenovo with menace, then turns round and goes away.

'Where is your mother?' I ask Oghenovo without delay.

'She has gone out,' he says, looking down, a finger between his lips.

'Did she tell you where she was going?'

'She said—she said she was going to Odibo's place, and that she would come back very soon.'

'I see.' *Didn't I know it?* 'Did Odibo come here today?'

He nods yes.

'When did he come?'

'In the morning.'

'Was your mother in then?'

He stares blankly for a while, his finger still in his mouth, then nods yes again.

'And did Odibo go away with your mother, or did she go to his house after he had gone?'

He stares ahead speechless. He doesn't appear to undertsand my question.

'Look,' I say carefully. 'Did your mother follow Odibo to his place, or did Odibo go first and then your mother afterwards?'

He nods.

'Which is it? Odibo went first, and then your mother went afterwards?'

He hesitates, then nods yes.

Need I any further proof?

I leave the boy at once and go for my bicycle. To be fooled and thwarted by creatures who owe their lives to me. . . .

Odibo

The woman keeps whimpering and sobbing, and just won't stop. Occasionally she lifts an ear of her cloth and wipes the tears from her eyes. She is unable to control herself, in spite of my constant plea that she keep her calm.

'God, God,' she sobs, with a deep, pained tremor in her voice, 'what kind of trouble is this, ehn?'

'Well, why do you have to cry about it?'

'I should have gone all this time that—'

'And suppose he meets you as you are just about to step outside the door—is that any better?'

She keeps on whimpering, sobbing and sighing. The whole affair only aggravates me and worsens my mood of resentment and defiance. One more pace up to the door, and there I can see Toje riding up towards my place, the wheels of his bicycle wobbling on the sandy road in the blazing afternoon.

'Well, here he comes,' I tell her. 'So you had better clean your eyes now and put on a cheerful face if you don't want to betray yourself.'

Suddenly she stands up and tries to run into the room.

'Where are you going?' I ask, grabbing her hand.

'Leave me!' she screams softly. 'I can't face him.'

'Look—'

But she tears herself off and runs into the room. She doesn't even have the sense to shut the door.

The whole situation throws me completely off-guard and spoils the procedure I was planning. As I walk back towards the door, Toje has already dismounted and dropped the bicycle on the ground, and now charges in menacingly.

'You brute!' he curses, quaking with passion. 'Where is that woman?'

'She has just—'

'Liar!' he blares, pushing me aside. 'I was told by her own son that she said she was going to your place. Where is she?'

Before I have time to answer, he is already walking into the room. On the edge of the bed the woman is crying vehemently, covering her face with her hands. Toje stops by the door, shocked and unable to believe his eyes. At this point I draw up close behind him, securing the fold of my wrapper more firmly round my waist.

'You slut!' he spits at her. 'You worthless harlot!'

Raising his hand, he is about to storm in and strike her. But I grab him by the hand.

'Toje!' I call threateningly, drawing him back with a vehement jerk.

He whirls round at me with bloodshot eyes and a frothing mouth. But he can see that I am staring back at him with equal menace.

'Leave her alone, Toje!' I warn.

'How dare you, you beast!'

Wresting his hand from me, he slaps me hard across the mouth. I am highly agitated now, but I refrain from responding in the same manner, giving him all the allowance I can until he oversteps his bounds. He tries to rush in again after the woman, who is now weeping wildly. Again I grab him, this time with all vigour on the scruff of his neck. He saunters back under the force of my pull, and a button snaps off from his shirt and drops on the floor. At once he throws his entire rage on me, unleashing both hands one after the other in blinding blows on my face, cursing, spitting, even kicking me with his leg. But I can no longer stand it. With my one hand I sweep his blundering arms away from my face, causing him to stumble aside and fall against the wall. The woman wails aloud and pleads that we stop.

'That's enough from you!' I warn him.

In reply, and panting furiously like a lizard, he swings violently at my face with his hand. The blow sends a sharp pain searing my face. In immediate reaction, I slug him hard across the mouth, and back again across the eyes, and he drops down on the floor at once. He lifts himself up on his knees, and begins to clean the blood trickling from his mouth.

'You asked for it,' I tell him, as he quakes on the floor, unable to recover from the blow or even try to get up.

In my present mood, I am quite prepared to send him to the floor a second time should he try to stand. But he does not attempt to stand yet. Inside the room, the woman wails and weeps and begs. I am now hardened against any further softness or consideration for the fool on the floor. I step aside a bit, keeping a careful eye on him should he try anything silly.

But he doesn't. Slowly, he rises from the floor and stands shakily on his feet. His eyes are much redder now. He spits out a thick lump of bloody rheum onto the floor, and rubs his running nose.

'You'll be sorry for this,' he threatens, breathlessly. 'Mark my words. You'll be sorry for this.'

I refuse to answer him. Without another word, he saunters out of the place. I walk after him to the door, just to make sure. He picks his bicycle up from the ground. He attempts to mount, but lands with a thud. Shaking his head, he rises slowly and pulls himself together. This time he tries to be a bit more careful, and in a moment he is riding his wobbly way towards his house.

When I touch my mouth and look at my hand, I see a paste of blood on it. With an ear of the cloth I clean my mouth, blow my nose, and rejoin the weeping woman.

'Well, stop your crying now, will you?' I throw impatiently at her.

'It's all my fault,' she wails again.

'All right, I've heard you. But stop crying anyway. You are beginning to annoy me with your endless crying.'

Still sobbing hard, she tries without success to get herself under control. I am pacing about aimlessly, as the agitation has scarcely left me. I am confused, but not in the least sorry for anything. After all, he brought it all about. If anyone should blame me for fighting an elderly man, they should also blame him for carrying the fight to my house in the first place.

'Please, Odibo,' pleads the woman, coming out of the room and still very emotional, 'you must let me go now. I don't think I can stand it any more.'

'Go home?' I glower at her. 'Do you know what he is going to do next?'

'Please—'

'Sit down for God's sake! It was you that caused this in the first place.'

She breaks down and starts crying again.

'Well, keep your peace. There's no use in carrying on with your crying.'

'I have to go,' she sobs and pleads, her eyes charged full of tears. 'Please, let me go.'

'Look, I know that man. He is going to prepare himself for a more desperate act. Do you want him to finish you off in your house?'

'But my child—'

'Don't you worry about your child. Let us stay here and wait for him. If it's you he's after he'll either come here or go to your house. He can't go to your house without passing this way. And if he passes this way I'm here to stop him. So sit down and don't give me any more trouble. If he doesn't show up at all, I'll take you to your house afterwards. Look, sit down.'

She obeys without another word. I keep pacing up and down, to the door and back again, waiting to see what happens next. I know things are going to be rough henceforth. But there is a point beyond which a man will refuse to be pushed.

Bastard!

Ali

It doesn't make sense. It just *doesn't* make any sense!

'Madam,' I keep telling the woman, 'stop crying and tell me how it all happened.'

'It's all my fault,' is all she can say, whimpering with disconsolate agitation, dishevelled and frantic and unable even to wipe her tear-soaked face with her loosening cloth. 'It's all my fault.'

I leave her for a while to cool down as best she can. There is a small crowd of soldiers some distance away from my quarters. The civilians have not been allowed beyond the gate, but I can hear them cursing and swearing and demanding that the woman be shot or sent away from the town because she is a 'rebel'. I call the private in.

'Okumagba, tell the soldiers to clear that crowd. I don't want to see any civilians around these premises.'

'Yes, sir!'

'And if the crowd tries to be stubborn, let them fire some shots into the air!'

'Yes, sir!'

I rejoin the woman. Her little son has all along been shaking with fright. But he too begins to cry with his mother, wailing even more loudly and staying as close to her as possible. From the gate the crowd of civilians hoot at the soldiers trying to send them away. To think that not so long ago they were hailing *Ali! Ali! Ali!* with wild enthusiasm!

'Don't cry, boy,' I try to soothe the child, placing my arm on his head and rubbing gently. 'Don't cry.'

The sight of her crying son now seems to cool the woman somewhat. She stops wailing, cleans her eyes, and draws the boy to her lap. But she is whimpering still, coughing and blowing her nose.

'Madam, tell me at least how it happened that they slashed their bodies with cutlasses. Just tell me very briefly what happened.'

She tries to speak, but breaks down again and begins to cry.

'Now stop crying!' I say, in the tone of an order. 'You have to let me know. It's important.'

She tries to get herself under control, and does the same with her weeping boy.

'I—I had just stopped—' and she begins to cry again.

'Now *stop* it, madam!'

'Forgive me,' she says, calming herself and her son. She blows her nose into her wrapper. 'I had just gone over to his nephew Odibo's place. He had been over to my house earlier to greet us and keep us company. I—I hadn't been there l—long,' she sobs again, 'when Toje stormed in, demanding to know where I was. I—I hadn't—' she sobs more vehemently.

'Take it easy,' I say. 'Take it easy.'

'I only went over there to take something. But Toje interpreted my presence there otherwise, calling me a harlot and everything. He tried to hit me, but Odibo held his hand. And—and then Toje got angry and slapped Odibo, striking him vigorously and kicking him down. He tried again to beat me, and again—' she blows her nose and wipes the tears, 'and again Odibo held him. And he turned round once again and started to strike Odibo over and over, many times. Until Odibo himself got angry, and—and they started to fight. I begged and pleaded that they should stop. I was crying very hard. But they didn't listen to me. They fought on and on. And then Toje went home and brought a matchet. Odibo had not allowed me to go. When I pleaded that he should let me go to my house he warned me that Toje might come over there and do me harm. So I stayed. I was still there—' she blows her nose again, 'I was still there when Toje arrived with his matchet. On seeing him, Odibo shut the door at once and bolted it. But Toje hacked the door open with the cutlass. I was c—crying vehemently and begging him—', she breaks down again in sobs, 'b—but he destroyed the lock and kicked the door open. Odibo tried to seize him, but he swished the matchet and slashed Odibo's left shoulder, just above the stump of his crippled arm. Odibo was furious. He ran backwards and grabbed the bench in the parlour and flung it at Toje. This sent Toje to the ground with great force. Odibo tried to fall on him and seize the matchet. But Toje ducked, and Odibo fell down—' She begins to sob more vehemently now.

'Relax. Go on,' I urge.

'When Odibo fell down, Toje came vigorously on him, cutting him twice on the back, and when Odibo turned round weakly Toje cut him a deep one on the chest. With—with a desperate effort Odibo hit Toje hard on the cutting hand with his one arm. The matchet fell from Toje's hand. They struggled for it, and Odibo managed to seize the matchet and unleash it on Toje with all the energy that he had left, cutting him on the face, on the chest, on the shoulder, everywhere he could. Toje groaned and wailed, and fell with his back on the floor. Odibo just managed to cut him severely once more on the waist. After that the cutlass fell from his hand, and he too dropped on the floor. At this point I could no longer stand it— the sight of two groaning and gasping men, and all that pool of blood. So I ran—ran—'

She breaks down again into tears, and this time I let her cry her fill, not even stopping to console her little boy who has now joined her in weeping. I retire into my bedroom to think the whole affair over.

I should have tried to calm the woman and not demanded any explanation from her yet. I should have let her have some rest and tell me all about it afterwards. But something kept bugging my mind and I could not find any peace until I got her to give that little explanation. And now that she has told me what happened, my mind is thrown into an even deeper state of confusion, added to a growing feeling of failure. When Private Okumagba led the weeping woman and child to this place and gave me the news of the matchet fight, a question flashed briefly through my mind: how could she have been involved in all this? The worry lingered in my mind. But by the time I got back from the scene of the fight and confronted the woman, I could not exactly identify what it was that was bothering me.

Now it all seems very clear. The irony of my role has now come into clear focus. Little did I realise that I was all along clearing the ground for such a tragedy. It has all been a terrible mistake—a *terrible* mistake! *Wallahi-tallahi*. How could I have known that by giving the woman freedom and protection I was only exposing her to this sort of exploitation and making her the target of a rotten relationship? How could I have guessed that by trying to reassure the civilian population of this town—by keeping the state of crisis here under control and making the town livable within the limits of the emergency, by respecting the leadership here and making them feel that though there was a war on they should try to carry on their lives as much as was possible under the circumstances— how could I have guessed that a man of Chief Toje's calibre, a man I continued to respect in spite of everything, was going to take advantage of the trust and respect that I had for him? Perhaps I should have known that a woman whose husband had been taken away and who was being looked upon all over the town as a rebel—perhaps I should have known that such a woman had too little chance of living a normal life whatever assurances and protection I tried to give her. I should have known that I was not going to have an easy time stretching the federal will too much in her favour. But if I could have guessed—if I just could have guessed for one moment—if I . . . *Allah!*

Well. . . . It's all over now. Our military doctor has done the best he could and the two men have been taken to the hospital at Okujere, fifteen miles away.

I rejoin the woman and her child in the sitting room. The tears have dried from their eyes. As I enter they look up at me, and I can see in their eyes lingering fear and anxiety.

'Madam, I think you and your child should have some rest, and later your meal. Dombraye.'

'Sir!'

'Take them over to the visitors' room and leave them to have their rest.'

'Yes, sir!'

I slump down into a chair and look out through the window. The crowd of soldiers have gone away now. There is over the premises an atmoshpere of quiet expectancy. Right now I am trying to fight the mood of strained vacuity that is beginning to grow on me. . . .

'Dombraye,' I call as he reappears.

'Sir!'

'Go over and call me the captains. Tell them I want to see them right away.'

'Yes, sir!'

'And,' just before he goes out of sight, 'call Private Okumagba in here first.'

When Okumagba reappears I am still looking blankly out of the window. But I turn to him as he salutes.

'Okumagba.'

'Sir!'

'I'm altering your detail. You are still going to keep watch. But this time you'll be watching Mr Oshevire's house. Is that clear?'

'Yes, sir!'

'Lock up the house and keep the key. You will keep watch over the house, maintaining the same hours as when you were at the Council Hall. After some time, when I am satisfied that there is sufficient peace over this affair, I can then review the detail. All right?'

'Yes, sir!'

I wave him off. He salutes and leaves.

Oghenovo

when the big soldier started to talk to my mother in his big voice and told her to shut up and stop crying, and my mother was crying and crying and crying, and the big soldier was talking more and more in his big voice, and asking my mother to shut up, i began to cry and cry because i was afraid of the big soldier and i thought that he was going to beat my mother if she did not stop crying and that he was going to make her cry more and more. and afterwards my mother stopped crying, and i stopped crying too, and the big soldier told my mother and myself to come in here and sleep, and that other little soldier brought us to this room, and i slept for a long time, and my mother woke me up and told me to eat.

my mother is sleeping now. but before she slept she cried quietly, and i cried too, but she told me to stop crying, and she too stopped crying and wiped her eyes and mine. i don't know when my mother is going to wake up from her sleep so that we can go home to our house. onome said that if i promised not to abuse him again he was going to let me wear his mask and his masquerade dress and do the masquerade dance with him. *when will mother wake up so that we can go home to our house.*

mama, mama, i call her, shaking her body.

mm, mm, what is it, she asks me in halfwaking.

when are we going home, i say.

i don't know, she says, don't worry me.

i want to go home, i say.

you try doing that and they will kill you before you begin, she says.

shall we never go home, i say.

i don't know, she says, stop worrying me. don't touch me again. i want to sleep.

and she closes her eyes and turns her head away from me. i climb the bed and lie beside her and i can feel her body moving up and down in sleep-breathing. *i do not want to sleep i want to go home so that i can do the masquerade with onome.*

outside the window of the room i can hear a soldier shouting. i climb out of bed and go to the window and watch. i can see a soldier standing and shouting orders to two other soldiers. the soldier has a cap on and the two other soldiers don't have any caps on. the two are marching up and down to the order of the first soldier. the soldier shouts, and the two other soldiers stop at once. the soldier shouts again and the two others turn round and march towards him. then he shouts again, and the two soldiers marching without their caps on stop in front of him. then he talks to the two soldiers who stand straight before him and don't move their bodies at all. after some time he shouts again, more gently now, and the two soldiers separate and go away. there are many other soldiers in the compound and some of them are walking with the guns over their shoulders and others have their guns in their hands. *i wish i had my gun here so that i can march like these soldiers and later i will go home and show onome how soldiers march.*

i can see some men now riding on their bicycles from the direction of the gate and coming towards the house. there are three of them and they are old men with their wrappers round their bodies and their hats on their heads. they ride up to the house and come down from their bicycles and leave the bicycles near the house, leaning them on the wall. perhaps they have come to see the big soldier. i run from the window and open the door quietly, so that my mother does not wake up and see me. i go out to the big room in front where the big soldier is. i stand near the door. the big soldier is greeting them and they are greeting the big soldier too and shaking hands with him. then they all sit down and take off their hats. they are not smiling at all and one of them speaks to the big soldier.

our chief has sent us to talk to you about the mother of this boy, he says, pointing at me.

i see, says the big soldier. will you wait a moment please.

and the big soldier walks up to me and puts his hand on my head.

go on and stay with your mother, he says.

so i walk back and he shuts the door and i go to our room where my mother is sleeping. i shake my mother and try to wake her up.

mama, mama, i say. wake up.

what is it, she says, what do you want this time.

there are some men here who have come to take us away, i say.

what, she asks, raising her head and looking into my eyes, her own eyes sleep-tired and red.

there are some men here who have come to take us away, i say.

where are they, she says.

they are sitting out there in the front room with the big soldier, i say. they say they have come to talk about us and to take us away.

my mother rubs her eyes and sits up quickly on the bed and listens.

are we going home with them, i say.

sshh, she says. listen.

so my mother and i listen. but i cannot hear what they are saying because the big soldier has shut the door in the front. *i want to go home and do the masquerade with omone and wear his mask.*

Ali

It says here in the despatch from Headquarters:

The following officers have been assigned to the commands indicated against their names:

  1. *Major Simeon O. Atanda, XXVI Brigade (to relieve Major Philip S. Kalango).*
  2. *Major Isaac N. Okutubo, XV Brigade (to relieve Major Ali S. Idris). The effective dates for handing over will be announced shortly. The officers currently holding the above commands will consequently have to report to Headquarters for re-assignment.*

Re-assignment, so soon after the last rebel hit on my post! *Allah*, I think somebody is trying to tell me something. . . .

Oshevire

I must have slept for over an hour or so. The journey is long, the road bumpy, and the steady rumble of the Landrover's movement must have put some weakness on my body. But I am glad. This is a sleep I have needed for a long time, a peaceful sleep, unburdened by any anxieties. And anxieties I have surely had for some time—for a long time. For one thing, determined though I was to stand up to my problems, I was nonetheless hurt that an innocent man like myself should be visited with an injustice he never deserved. Then there was the concern over the fate of my wife and child, until Rukeme's reassurance took away some of the worry—though, not having set eyes on them, I cannot claim that my mind is completely settled.

And then there was the case of our impatient young man, Agbeyegbe. Poor boy—his anger was too much for him. I happened to be sharing a cell with him and two other fellow detainees. Almost every night he would sit up very late, till the early hours of the morning, reading his books or chanting what he called songs of revolution. And he always had the light on, in spite of our constant pleas to him that the light prevented us from having a good sleep. These spells of protest in him never diminished, because every time he sang he had a new song going.

Two nights ago he over-played his temper. We had all been considerably relieved to find that the light in our cell was off and that our young friend had decided to sleep. Little did we know that all through the night he had been planning to make good his determination to escape. So he spent the night, while the other three of us slept, in tearing his garments and his bedclothes and covers to shreds and tying the pieces together into a very long stretch of cloth.

When he had considered the moment ripe, in the very early hours of yesterday, he sneaked out quietly from our cell in mere underwear and on bare feet, taking his escape tool along with him. The soldiers were asleep by the door, and he had no trouble in walking past them to the huge wall of the prison. The wall is very high, but not insurmountable to anyone who had enough determination in him. At the top of the wall are metal beams sticking up—about an arm-length—out of the concrete and joined together by two or three lines of barbed wire. They provide an excellent hold for anything that gets that far up, and the jagged nature of the wall itself yields convenient foot-holds. These were the advantages that Agbeyegbe tried to use. But he had left just one crucial detail out of his reckoning. One of the police dogs assigned to the prison sighted him and began to bark furiously. The uproar alerted the sleeping guards. They suddenly shook themselves up to action and ran up to Agbeyegbe as he was halfway up the wall. With their guns at the ready, they shouted furiously at him, ordering him to come down or face the consequences. Slowly, Agbeyegbe descended from the wall and jumped down. As soon as he got down, two or three of the soldiers put aside their guns and fell on him. They beat him and beat him and—oh, how they beat that boy!

The police dog and the general uproar had woken us too. The other three of us had got up as soon as we heard the noise. I switched on the light and, when we didn't find our man around, we knew that they had got him. We rushed out to meet the gathering outside, and came in at the point when Agbeyegbe was descending from the wall under the soldiers' orders. As they were beating him we all watched helplessly in uneasy silence—for how could we be sure that intercession would not be interpreted as collaboration? When they were satisfied that they had thoroughly subdued their prisoner, the soldiers dragged Agbeyegbe away to an inner, more secure cell reserved for insubordinate prisoners. We called it 'the box'.

We never saw him again. We were all very sad. For the first time I saw Baba weep. And though some people said the treatment served Agbeyegbe right, it was, more than anything, a sad comment on the undue anger that our young friend had allowed to take control of him. . . .

But now there is a little joy in my heart. It certainly is a relief to know that I am a free man again. And the goodwill that was shown me this morning has much made up for more than three years of undeserved confinement. When it was announced to me that I was free and should go home, and I told them that I had no money to pay the fare to my hometown, one of the guards put a hand in his pocket and gave me a pound note. Another gave me a ten-shilling note. They shook my hand and wished me the best of luck in my new lease of life. I thought that was wonderful, and thanked them profoundly for their goodness. The rigours of our past relationship had vanished completely from my memory, and at that moment they looked more like men! One of the officials who announced my release undertook to find out if there was any military vehicle going my way, and not long afterwards I was put on this Landrover that is on its way to Okhukhu, which is just a mile away from Urukpe.

The two good soldiers in it have promised to drop me at the road junction near our town, from where a road leads off on the left towards Okhukhu. . . . .

I think I am coming to the end of my journey. The landscape here certainly looks familiar. It doesn't seem to have changed at all these past three years and more. The trees are fleeing past the Landrover with the speed of a herd in breakneck flight, but the scene is all too familiar now. Yes, I am home again!

'*Oga*,' says the soldier at the wheel, 'did you say you were going to Urukpe?'

'Yes,' I reply.

'Well, we are there.'

'Yes. Thank you very much.'

'You can get down here and we'll continue on our way,' he says, pulling up by the road-side at the junction.

'Thank you very much,' I say, getting down from the vehicle. 'I am very grateful to you both.'

As soon as I have got down, they move off again.

'Goodbye,' I call after them, waving.

But they are already on their way and do not give me any reply. *God bless you both, good people.*

It is already evening. All I have in my stomach is breakfast. But the joy of return more than makes up for my hunger. I stand for a short while and take a look round the familiar environment, then up at the ashen blue of the evening sky. I can hardly wait to walk to my home, which is not so far away.

The first human being I encounter on the way is the madman Eseoghene. This is strange. He was the last person I saw on that unhappy day over three years ago, as I was being taken to Iddu in a Landrover.

'Ese!' I hail him. 'Are you still around?'

He is huddled near a dying fire under the same huge cherry tree where he has always been. He eyes me darkly and, on recognising me through the overgrown hair on my face, lights up in a faint smile. In his days of sanity he was one of the labourers who cleaned the premises of our chief, and he seems to have retained some of his memory.

'Why shouldn't I be around?' he says, suddenly turning serious again. 'Are you still around yourself? You should be a dead man. You are better dead than alive.'

'Why, Ese?' I ask him. I am slightly shaken. Rukeme might indeed be right about the feeling of resentment against me in this town—so strong that even a madman feels the same way!

'Why should I be dead?' I ask again.

But he turns away his face, then stokes his fire and readjusts the dirty rag around his loins.

'Leave me alone.' he says, very much under his breath. 'My only regret is that I did not get my own share of the spoils, *ha ha ha!*' He breaks out laughing.

I can't understand a word of this. Dead man? Spoils? What spoils? Eseoghene is a madman, but I have been away too long from this place. A lot has surely happened, from what I have heard all this time both from Rukeme's evidence and from the radio in the prison, and I cannot pretend to be in a position to take even Eseoghene's words lightly. Spoils? What spoils?

Still wondering and pondering heavily, I leave him alone and hasten towards my house. The next person that I meet is the tailor Esiri, riding on a bicycle.

'How are you, Esiri?'

He brakes to a halt. He is a little uncertain who I might be. As soon as it is clear to him, he opens his mouth in wonder.

'It's me, Mukoro,' I confirm.

'Mukoro!'

'Yes. How are you? What has happened?'

He shakes his head sadly.

'Too much,' he says. 'Too much has happened. So you are free again?'

'Yes,' I say, quite anxious now. 'What has happened?'

' 'Koro, my brother,' he says, placing a shivering hand on my shoulder. 'Go home and rest yourself, and—'

'Yes, but won't you tell me what has happened?'

In reply he looks round him at the surroundings, following his eyes with a sweeping arm, inviting me to take a look my-self.

'Can you not see for yourself?' he says. 'Can't you see that our town has seen sad times? Take a good look around you.'

Yes—I can see that a lot has happened. I can see two houses shattered beyond recognition and an atmosphere of haunting desolation all over the scene.

'Is that one there not Onokpasa's place?' I ask, faintly recognising the ruined structure.

Esiri nods in agreement. But that has not answered the question that keeps bugging my mind.

'Very sad. But have you seen my wife and child lately?'

He sighs, and shakes his head.

' 'Koro, my brother, please go home and—'

'Why can't you tell me anything?' I press him now, for the agitation is beginning to overtake me. 'What about my family?'

'I . . . I . . . I don't know, Mukoro. I don't know. Please, go home first.'

So saying, he mounts his bicycle and rides off. He neither looks back nor says another word.

This time I can hardly restrain my pace. I begin to run. Has Rukeme then carried his bad faith to the end, telling me that all was well with my wife and child?

I do not stop running until I get to within a few steps of my house. The doors and windows are shut, but otherwise nothing seems to have changed. I stop in front of the door, and am about to put my hand to the handle when I notice a gun lying on the ground right next to the steps of the door. I look around, and I see a soldier urinating at one end of the compound. What can I say? As the soldier turns round and sees me by the door, he immediately runs up to me with a menacing stare on his face.

'Who are you? What do you want?' he asks, quickly picking up his gun from the ground.

'This happens to be my house,' I reply. What can I say?

'O-ho,' he mutters, and his face loosens as he appears to accept my claim. 'Is it you, sir? *Migwo.*'

'*Vren, doh,*' I acknowledge the greeting, though still uncertain what this is all about and who he might be anyway. 'Who are you, son?'

'I am the son of Reuben Okumagba.'

'Oh, I see.' His father is very well known to me. 'I didn't realise you had become a soldier. What is happening here? Where are my wife and child?'

'They are with our commander. I have been asked to keep watch here. Follow me—I'll take you to the army barracks.'

Reluctantly, I walk behind him. He does not say a single word all along the way. I am very much confused. Now I am sure that something has indeed happened. As we go along I can see a lot more damage done to our town by the bombing raids that were announced while I was in detention. There is Bolokor's house, all down to the ground. What disaster! The market too—all burnt down. Oniemorame's house, hardly recognisable. What has—

'Look, my son,' I address my guide, 'can't you tell me at least why my wife and child are with your commander? Are they in any sort of trouble?'

'Don't worry,' he says. 'We are almost at the barracks now. You'll see them.'

I keep quiet, swallowing the urgent saliva. As we approach the edge of the town the military barracks come into view. We walk on until we get to the gate, and one of tke soldies lifts the barrier to let us through. I look at the faces of the soldiers, but they merely return me a blank and unhelpful gaze. It is this lack of communication that convinces me more and more that something wrong must have happened. Okumagba's son and I have moved a fair distance from the soldiers at the gate when I hear them burst into laughter. I turn round quickly, wondering what they might be laughing at. Yes—they are looking at me, so their faces tell me. *What is—*

'We're there now,' says my guide. But my mind is hardly here!

We are about to walk into the house to which the soldier is bringing me when suddenly I hear a woman's voice hailing my name from the direction of a small house attached to the one that we have come to.

'Mukoro!'

I look at the woman, whom I immediately recognise to be my wife Aku.

'Aku!' I call her.

She runs up to me and embraces me with all her strength. At once I can feel the load of worry flee from my heart as I am wrapped once again in the arms I know so well.

'Aku!' I say her name again.

She does not answer me. As I lift up her head, buried passionately in my bosom, I can see that she is weeping with extreme agitation.

'Cheer up, my dear,' I tell her, rubbing her head warmly. 'Cheer up. I'm back now, and I'm all right.'

But she does not stop. She disengages herself from me and settles on the ground to weep even more disconsolately. At this point my feelings begin to dissolve gradually into wonder.

'Well, cheer up,' I say, trying in vain to lift her from the ground. 'It's all over now. There's no point in crying.'

I am beginning to feel embarrassed, for she will not stop her crying. As I lift my eyes from her I can see a little boy trotting towards us from the same direction as my wife came. I do not need to be told that this is my son—I can already see the resemblance, and feel the blood attraction. As he runs up to his weeping mother he stares at me with a kind of resentful wonder in his eyes. I smile at him and hold out a friendly hand. But he shrinks from me and begins to look now at his mother, now at me.

'Aku, stop crying now,' I tell my wife, impatiently. 'Your child is here, and you have to cheer up.'

I raise her from the ground at once. Though she yields to my pull, she is still sobbing, whimpering and swallowing agitatedly. She cleans her eyes with the ear of her cloth and blows her nose.

'This is our son, isn't it?' I ask.

She nods.

'Oghenovo,' I call the boy, who is still staring at me. 'Come,' and I hold out my hand to him again.

He is about to shrink a second time when his mother pulls him closer.

'Come on, go to your father,' my wife says, in a choked voice.

Reluctantly, the boy walks into my arms and allows me to wrap him with a warmth that has built up over a period of more than three years. It is only with manly strength that I check the tears that threaten to overcome my eyes. But my heart is charged with sorrow and with joy—the remembered sorrow of over three years during which my wife and infant child must have languished in helpless solitude, the joy that we all seem to have pulled through our troubles after all. As I clasp my own flesh and blood in my arms and rub my cheek passionately on his own, I can feel the satisfaction now spread over my heart that the worst is over.

When I turn my eyes again, I see an army officer standing at the door of the house, his arms folded across his chest. He must have been watching the scene quietly, and at this point he unfolds his arms and greets my quizzical stare with a smile.

'Good evening, Mr Oshevire,' he says.

'Good evening, sir,' I reply, with wonder in my eyes. *Who might you be?*

'Would you come in here, please?' the officer says, motioning me into the house.

I take my son by the hand as I walk up, but the boy snatches his hand away and goes to his mother. Before my wife can rebuke him again I wave her down.

'Leave him alone,' I say. 'He is only a child, and he doesn't know me yet. Bring him along.'

She leads him by the hand, and we all go into the house.

'Okumagba,' the officer calls.

'Sir!' the soldier replies, smartening up to attention.

'Where is the key to Mr Oshevire's house?'

Okumagba puts a hand into his pocket and hands over the key to the officer.

'Good,' the officer says. 'You are dismissed. You can go back to barracks.'

'Yes, sir!'

Okumagba salutes briskly and walks off.

'Sit down, please,' the officer says, turning to us.

We all sit down. My heart is so much lighter now, but I am still waiting to know why my wife and child came to be placed under military care. The officer clears his throat.

'First of all, Mr Oshevire,' he begins, 'I imagine you must be very hungry now. Would you like to have something to eat first, before we talk?'

'No,' I say, shaking my head. 'I am not hungry at all.'

'Are you sure?'

'Yes, I am sure. I am not at all hungry.'

'Would you like to drink something then? It must have been a long and difficult journey for you.'

'No. Thank you very much.'

'All right. Now, to start with, I am glad that you are a free man again and are back once more to your family. As you probably understand, I am the officer in command of the forces in this town, and it has been my duty, among other things, to defend this town and keep it peaceful. I would therefore like to tell you as briefly as possible what led to my keeping your family under military protection. But, meanwhile—', he turns to my wife, 'madam, would you please excuse us for a while? I want to talk to your husband alone about this. You can go to your quarters and wait for him—I won't keep him here long.'

I motion my wife to leave us for a while. She and my son get up and walk away. The officer waits for them to be safely out of sight before he resumes talking. The anxiety returns to my heart.

Okumagba

Thank God it's all over. Now I'm a soldier again, a proper soldier. It all seems like a dream. All I want to do now is forget the whole rotten business and be a real soldier again.

As I approach my tent, I can't help thinking about the whole mess—at least the way it has ended. But I must confess that, now it's all over, I do not feel as malignant as I did at first. The sight of the man as he came home to his house, so thoroughly ignorant of all that has happened, and expecting to get into his house and reunite with his family, moved me no end. But I remembered I was a soldier, and tried to keep the tenderness under control.

And the reunion—my God, I never wish to see the like of it again.

For when I saw the woman fall down and begin to weep so passion-ately, my bowels were turned far less by anger at her shameless bad faith than by the realisation that the man had been so long a victim of a fate he never deserved. Because, apart from everything else, if he has been set free, it only means that he has been found to be an innocent man. My God, I'm glad to be back to barracks. . . .

'Speedy Okums, Black Devil!' one of my companions hails me as I enter my tent.

'How are you, *bobo*,' I reply, waving at him.

'Speedy Okums!' hails another.

But my heart is still a bit heavy, and I get into my tent at once and slump down into my bunk. No sooner have I lain down than the two soldiers rush into my tent. I welcome them with a stern and not-so-friendly look.

'Welcome back,' one of them, Isa, says. 'Is it all over?'

I nod an affirmative, saying not a word.

Isa sits down beside me, but Oyewole remains standing.

'How has it been, man?' asks Oyewole. 'You look finished.'

'Yes,' I say, 'I *am* finished. It's all over.'

'Tell us all about it,' says Isa.

'About what?'

'About the whole detail.'

'What's there to tell? I did as I was ordered, and now it's all over and I am back.'

I stare pointedly at the questioning Isa. He sighs helplessly.

'It must have been a rough time,' he says, trying to prod a story out of me.

'Yes. Very rough,' I say, looking outside the tent.

'Especially during those raids.'

'Yes.'

I can feel the unspoken questions. But I am in no mood to tell a story and let them gloat over what was certainly not a delightful experience for me.

'We hear the woman's husband is back,' says Oyewole.

'Yes. He's back,' I reply, venturing no further by word or by look.

'I wonder how he will feel to know that while he was away other people were ploughing his furrow. *Hi-hi-hi!* I would like to watch his face as he hears the story.'

I turn my eyes on him, and his face loses its cheerfulness at once.

'Oyewole,' I address him, calmly but sternly, 'if you say that again, you and I are going to be carried out dead.'

'What?'

'If you repeat what you have just said, you and I are going to be borne out dead from this tent.'

All he can do is stare at me with his mouth open. For he knows I am capable of executing my threat.

'Come on, Oye,' Isa says, rising from the ground. 'Let's leave him alone. He doesn't seem to be in a good mood now. He'll tell us all about it some time.'

As they walk away from my tent, the cowardly bastard Oyewole calls back at me:

'Maybe your next detail will be to guard them while they fuck each other!'

One mind tells me to go at him and break his neck. But the other mind advises me to leave the idiot alone and let my present mood burn itself out. . . .

If I ever get married, and I have to go anywhere without my family, I will plug my wife's cunt with a hand grenade.

Oghenovo

my mother is not crying any longer, but the tears are still on her face and her eyes are red and her breathing is that of crying. i want to ask her about the man in that house who she says is my father, but i am afraid to ask her because her face is an unsmiling face and she will not talk to me if i ask her any question. *i want to go home and tell onome that my father has come back from where he travelled to but why was my mother crying when the man came here. i do not like that man because he makes my mother cry.*

mama, i call her.

she doesn't answer me. she only looks at me.

is that man my father, i say.

she doesn't say yes. she just nods her head which means yes. *i don't like that man how can he be my father when he makes my mother cry and now she won't talk to me i will not tell onome about him any more.*

mama, i say. is the big soldier going to beat my father.

no, she says, he is only talking to your father.

what is he telling my father, i say.

i don't know, she says. maybe he is telling him what a good boy you are.

mother says that my father is a good man i will tell onome that my father is a good man and has returned.

mama, i say. when are we going back to our house.

soon, she says, as soon as they finish talking together.

did my father buy anything for me, i say.

no, she says. he is very tired. he is too tired to carry anything.

now i can see the big soldier and my father coming.

they are coming now, mama, i say.

yes, she says.

my mother gets up and cleans her eyes.

go and put on your shoes now, she says. we are about to go.

Ali

All through my talk he just sat there blankly, not even looking at me. I gave him as much of the background as I knew and vouchsafed as much information as either decency or concern for his feelings would allow. But he never said a word, nor did he change the expression on his face one bit. Even now I am not sure that, had I told him any more than I had to or that he needed to know, the expression on his face would have changed at all. He just sat there, listening and looking at the floor.

But I said all I had to. I thought I spelt it all out. Even an infant could have understood perfectly well what the woman had been put through. An infant would have been able to tell that what brought two men to fight with a matchet over a woman was not a decent affair. And an infant would have known that when that woman wept so long and disconsolately on the ground at the feet of her man, it was not so much from joy of reunion as out of a remembered shame. The man himself was embarrassed, and you could tell from the look on his face that he was sure there was more to his wife's weeping than the joy of welcome. I knew from that point that the message of the whole business had begun to get into his head. So when I came to put the whole history before him he was already wise to the shape of things. But he neither said a word nor changed the look on his face—that was when he won my respect. *Kai*, he's a man all right!

However, I spat it all out. I made it clear to him what my responsibility was in these parts. I didn't have to tell him that the concern had cost me my command. But I made it clear that, as long as I was in charge here and until the new major took over from me, I was going to observe that duty and carry out what I knew I was here to do, no matter what happened or who felt hurt. I told him of the delegation from the chief of this town, demanding the repatriation of his wife from the town on the ground that her continued presence was detrimental to the welfare and safety of the community. I said I had told the deputation that it was necessary for the woman to be around until such a time as the trial over the manslaughter case came up in the courts and she would be required as a witness, but that I should be given time to see what I could do about their demand. I told him that, whatever happened, I was still responsible for the safety of himself and his family. I gave him the option of removing voluntarily to a place away from here so long as we knew his whereabouts, or staying on in the town since that at least would provide justification, in the eyes of the chief, for his wife's continued presence. And I assured him that, should he choose to remain, I was prepared to go so far as to give him military protection if he felt the safety of his household jeopardised. Then only did he open his mouth to speak.

'No, thank you, sir,' he said. 'I do not think I would require any protection.'

'Are you quite sure about this, Mr Oshevire?' I asked.

'Yes, I am sure,' he replied.

'That's all right then.'

I let it go at that. But my surveillance is not going to diminish. I am still in command here, and I am going to deal severely with anybody that takes the law into his own hands if that is the last thing I do before I go back to Headquarters. Tomorrow I am going to make this very clear to the *Otota* and his council.

Oshevire

What else can a man do but that which his mind urges him to do and he is genuinely convinced he should do, whatever the consequences are? To do otherwise would be to betray his honest manhood. And I would be the last to allow myself to fall under the pressure of fear.

I have borne the worst that any man could endure. I have survived more than three years of unjust confinement. Although I have earned my release and justice has been done, all through my trial I was fully aware of the dangers that I faced. But I never allowed those dangers to deter me or move me from the path of a sincere and fearless defence of my innocence and integrity. If I have pulled through such a trial, brought upon me by a system I knew was too much for me to understand, why should I tremble when small men here, people whom I know only too well, try to threaten the life of my family, when I know I have a fighting chance and can dare them to carry out their threat?

So they demanded the repatriation of my family from this town? That's all right. Let them come and take us away then. I have not settled down yet to find out who it was that persuaded Rukeme to bring those charges against me—he would no doubt be the same man that reported me in the first place to the military authorities as a 'rebel collaborator'. But if I should put together all that has come to the open so far, I don't think I would be far wrong to say that Toje Onovwakpo had a good hand in all that has been happening to me. In any case, it may never be necessary to find out. The important thing now is that I am back where I belong, and here I am going to remain with my family. We are going to live here like all other citizens of this town who move about with freedom and without any need to be put under special military guard. For that would be no freedom. It would be much less than any man would want for himself and his family. I have done nobody wrong. It is they who have done me wrong. Why then do I need to be protected?

No—that is only the life of a criminal and a coward. . . .

Aku

Dear God, will you not hear my prayer? Will you not save me from this fear? You have been my only guardian for more than three painful years. Will you not help me for just one night?

Oshevire

But . . . there is something else in all this. If there are any honest men left in this town, they should know that the dishonour brought upon my wife—on my household—was totally unjust. But then the stain remains! The smear is there, clear in the air as a hangman's rope, the noose through which the head must pass. And what kind of a life will I be living in this town with my family, when we know that our days are haunted by an indelible shame? What kind of a life is it, to walk about this town every single day of your life knowing that every finger, every sneer, and every mockery is directed at you? I have not got the courage to ask my wife to tell me what happened—the story may be too much for me to bear. I have not yet tried to take a good look at her. But if she has allowed herself to be put to such unworthy use by two men, whatever the predicament that she found herself in, what else is there but a strong likelihood that right now she is bearing within her bosom the seed of such vile communion? And what man would choose to be alive to face every day the ill-conceived fruit of shame?

No . . . No. . . .

Aku

Dear God, will you not listen to my prayer just this one more time? You have seen me through more than three years of the worst trials that a woman could ever face. What I have seen and lived through is, I know, too sad and indeed too shameful to contemplate. But at least you kept me alive and now I am fortunate to have my man back again. Will you not answer my prayer just once more, now that I need your help more than I have ever done? All I am asking is that he should be given the strength to understand and to forgive—is that too much to ask?

If only he would talk to me. If only he would call me and ask me to tell my story. I know well that the details of that story are too sordid and would task the decency and the patience of any man. But at least I will find the strength to tell it all as it happened—every single bit of it, even if it takes me the whole night to do so.

I know, I believe that the good Major has tried to bring what comfort he could. But the Major couldn't have known *everything* that happened. I was the centre of the whole story, and I am in the best position to tell it all, however revolting it would sound. And can you not therefore, dear God, give him the strength to call me and let me explain, whatever he may decide to do to me in the end?

He has neither taken off his clothes nor even touched the food that I cooked for him. It is well past midnight now, and he has been sitting on that chair in the parlour. I dare not talk to him, for how can I tell what that would earn me? He has not said a single word since we left the army barracks earlier in the evening. All he did was sit in that chair. A short while ago he got up and locked all the doors and windows in the house, put the keys into his pocket, and proceeded to empty a full gallon of kerosene on parts of the house. And now he is back on that chair, staring blankly into the dark, and all I can do is lie on this bed, alone and all too painfully awake, and count every moment that passes in fear.

Dear God, if you can only give him the strength to call me and talk to me, ask me to tell my story. . . . If he should then decide to burn me alive, at least I will have had the satisfaction of getting the lingering sorrow off my chest. And if that is the last satisfaction I get before I die at the hands of my man, I think I will be happy.

Oghenovo

. . . *and my father is very angry, and he ties my hands and my feet and lets me hang head-downwards on a rope from the ceiling, and he sharpens a very big cutlass, and heats it in the fire until it is shining red as fire, and he brings the cutlass close to my downward-hanging head and says i am going to cut off your head today with this big fire-reddened cutlass, and i cry and cry and cry, and i beg him to have mercy on me, but he says no i am going to cut off your head today with this fire-reddened cutlass, and i ask him why must you cut off my head, and he says because when i returned you did not smile at me and carry me on your back, and i beg him to forgive me and i say tomorrow i will carry you on my back and laugh till my mouth cracks in my face, and he says no it's too late i must cut off your head now, and then he leaves me crying and goes to my mother, who is also crying, and he ties her hands and her feet, and lets her hang feet-downwards on a rope*

*from the ceiling, and he goes to the fire and heats his right hand in the fire
until it too begins to shine red as the fire, and he comes to my mother and
slaps her hard on the face with his fire-reddened hand, and my mother cries
and cries, and begs him to leave her, and i join my mother in begging him,
but he pays me no attention and continues to slap my mother, and my
mother keeps on crying, and he picks up the fire-reddened cutlass from the
ground and moves towards me, and now he has grown four eyes on his face
and two more legs each as big and as heavy as a tree, and he opens his
mouth very wide, and there is fire blazing at the tip of his tongue, and he
raises the fire-reddened cutlass with his fire-reddened hand and moves
towards me. . . .*

Aku

You have answered my prayer, dear God, but at what price! It is
enough for me that he has called my name and said a few words,
even if all he has done is issue a fearsome order.

'Oghenovo! Oghenovo!'

'Ma.'

'Haven't you put on your jumper yet? Ehn?'

'I am putting it on.'

'If you let me catch you dozing by that wall again I am going to
bury you this night.'

'But where are we going, ma?'

'Shut up there and don't ask me any questions. If you are not
ready by the time we want to leave I am going to drag you naked
with me.'

It is enough that he has talked to me at last, but what grim choice
he is leaving us!

Oghenovo

the big fire is now burning our house. when i turn back to look at the burning house my mother hits me on my head and says come on you foolish child. she is holding me by my hand and making me run to keep up with her walking speed. my father does not wait for us or look at us. *i do not like my father because he will not let me sleep and my mother is crying and my father has set fire to our house.*

mama, i say, i have forgotten my gun. i want to take it before the fire burns it.

shut up, she says, or i'll leave you to burn along with it.

my father does not talk to us, and he is walking very fast and not looking back. *my father is not a good man.* the moon in the sky is very big and round like a very big shining ball. i can see the man in the moon cutting the wood with his axe. my mother once told me that the moonman is cutting the wood because he did not do what god said and he did not go to church on sunday so god punished him by giving him an axe to be cutting the wood forever, and when i asked my mother why is god such a wicked man she said god is neither a man nor is he wicked but he spends every day sitting on a big chair and punishing all bad-doing people and drinking the rain.

we have left our burning house far behind. i try to look back for the last time but my mother pulls me harder and i nearly fall. nearby i can hear a cock crow, and then a dog begins to bark as we move on. we are moving towards the bush and leaving many houses behind. we do not meet a single person on the way, but the moon is shining very bright and i can see everything around us. we are close to the bush now. at the edge of the bush there is a little stream and the moonlight shines on the surface and the surface is like many many shining fishes dancing together and raising their backs. and my father still doesn't talk to us and my mother is pulling me on by my hand

and i am running fast after her. we have now left the town behind. *will i not see onome again i wish onome was coming along with us.*

mama, i say, when are we coming back.

sshh, she says, i don't know. don't talk.

i do not like my father and i don't think he is a good man.

we start walking through the bush now. when i look up i cannot see the moon very well, but it is shining through the bush and i can hear many insects and frogs shouting. my mother once said that the reason they shout is because they are asleep and that is their own way of snoring. the shouting of the insects and the frogs becomes louder and louder now, and my father is walking faster away from us and i am running faster after my mother who is holding my hand, and the moonlight is dancing on the many many little leaves in the bush and the trees are also running past us as we move. suddenly i hear somebody shouting in the forest.

stop! he says. *stop!*

i look round but i do not see the person.

stop! stop! and he shouts other things which i don't understand.

stop!

my mother holds me tighter by the hand and stops. she is shaking and breathing very hard. but my father does not stop. he walks on and on as before, and does not even look back at us as we stop. my mother is still shaking. i hear the sound of someone coming out from the bush towards us. my mother tries to run.

stop! shouts the man, but we cannot see him.

my mother stops again, holding me tight and breathing and shaking very hard. and still my father does not stop.

stop there! shouts another voice, from afar. i think the voice is shouting at my father.

mukoro! my mother screams. *mukoro!* and she is about to run again, towards my father. but the man coming out from the bush shouts *don't move!* i can see him faintly now.

stop! shouts the voice from afar once again.

the man from the bush walks up to us, pointing a gun at my mother and myself. i hold tight to my mother, because i am afraid. suddenly i hear the sound of gunshots from the direction of the other voice. *Kr-r-r-r*, *Kr-r-r-r*, two times. and then the sound of something dropping.

mukoro! my mother screams again. then she lets go of me and drops on her knees and covers her face with her hands and begins to cry.

i look up at the soldier. i am afraid of him. his face is very dark and the leaves have made fearful shadows on it and his two eyes are like those of a black cat. . . .

Ali

Isaac Okutubo is a damn good soldier, the tough no-nonsense kind. I respect him. No doubt that he'll hold this post well. As I hand over my command now, I have just this wish for him: that he has sense enough to tell there's more to a soldier than his gun, and better luck than I've had. But—if I had the same chance, if I was to hold this bloody post again, *Allah*, I'd make the same mistakes all over!

The Victims

Isidore Okpewho

A man with two wives is not always to be envied. Obanua's first wife, Nwabunor, angry and humiliated, convinces herself that her rival is out to oust not only her but her only child. The new wife, Ogugua, casual, uncaring, goes her own way. Between them Obanua is driven to drink; behind them tragedy looms.

Isidore Okpewho's first novel presents a powerful study of the tensions in a polygamous household under economic and psychological stress.

'A kind of bush-village *L'Assomoir* complete with chorus of hags, rewarding proverbs, and strong social protest against superstition and exploitation, it should not be missed.'

The Guardian

Drumbeat 14
ISBN 0 582 64266 3

Violence

Festus Iyayi

Idemudia's unremitting struggle for survival in a city offering cruel contrasts between direst poverty and ostentatious wealth almost destroys him, his health and his marriage. The bond between him and his wife Adisa is stretched, strained, battered and betrayed, yet from their sufferings miraculously emerge a deeper insight and a closer unity.

Festus Iyayi's first novel was written from his own observations of conditions existing in his native Nigeria.

'It is a consciously political and radical book, though the politics are transmuted into the art of fiction; the characters are real, the scenes dramatically described and the emotions movingly portrayed.'

West Africa

'An ambitious attempt to represent the inequalities of wealth and opportunities in a post-colonial society and the accompanying corruption and violence. His achievement is that he has succeeded in avoiding the pitfalls of crude pamphleteering and ideological sermonising to which more experienced writers have succumbed in tackling this worrying theme.'

Time Out

Drumbeat 1
ISBN 0 582 64247 7

Flowers and Shadows

Ben Okri

The sins of the father are visited on the son . . . and when the father has become as consumed with reckless ambition as Jonan and the son is as sensitive as Jeffia, the Okwe family is on a collision course to ruin.

Told from Jeffia's point of view, the story, set in Lagos, covers youthful dreams and disillusionment, love and friendship, tragedy and despair – and resilience and the rebirth of hope too. The author, Ben Okri, was still in his teens when he wrote this novel, his first.

'Lagos, overcrowded as it is with contradiction, leaps to life in this most readable first novel. . . . Such is its acute obser-vation of everyday life that anyone seeking to understand the popular basis for the resentment expressed by the "bottom of the heap" against the arrogance of soldier-rulers, or the corruption in high places which so debilitates society, could do far worse than read this book.'

West Africa

Drumbeat 20
ISBN 0 582 64301 5